CW00821664

TAMING THE CEO BEAST

IONA ROSE

SOME BOOKS LTD

Publisher: Some Books

978-1-913990-45-9

AUTHOR'S NOTE

Hey there!

Thank you for choosing my book. I sure hope that you love it. I'd hate to part ways once you're done though. So how about we stay in touch?

My newsletter is a great way to discover more about me and my books. Where you'll find frequent exclusive give-aways, sneak previews of new releases and be first to see new cover reveals.

And as a HUGE thank you for joining, you'll receive a FREE book on me!

With love,

Iona

Get Your FREE Book Here:
https://dl.bookfunnel.com/v9yit8b3f7

PROLOGUE – AXEL

My eyes felt grainy as I pulled into the rest stop. A quick check of the time showed I had been driving for thirteen hours nonstop. And had it not been for the fact my body felt as though it was going to give up the ghost, I probably wouldn't have stopped. But it wouldn't do for me to end up in a ditch somewhere, or under an eighteen-wheeler and have my family plan a double funeral. How ironic it would be! I could see the headlines: *Son killed in accident on his way to father's funeral. More news at ten.*

I sighed and rubbed my hands over my head and face as I sat in the parking lot for a few minutes. I was less than two hours from home. It still felt surreal. My thoughts went back to the morning last week when my sergeant told me I had a phone call. The last thing I had expected to hear was Axel Vance Sr. had left the land of the living.

I tried to remember the last conversation I'd had with my father a month ago. It had not been anything outside of the norm. The company wasn't doing as well as he wanted. His personal investments were doing extremely well. He'd be off to the Mediterranean with a group of friends from his college days the next week. Then he had an expedition in Africa. I remember I had ruefully thought if he put ten percent of the energy from his expeditions into the company it wouldn't be struggling the way it is now.

The company. It was mine now.

I sighed. I hadn't expected to take over Vance Security Solutions so soon. I had an assignment overseas in a few weeks and would be away for a few months. Hopefully I could talk the vice president into running the operations until I returned.

I got out of the truck and stretched, feeling every muscle in my six foot plus frame cry out. I was tough. But I was human. I checked to ensure that my weapon was concealed beneath my uniform before I entered the diner. I found an empty table in a corner where I had a view of the dining room and my back was against the wall. I scanned the menu just as the waiter approached.

"Evening, soldier. What'll it be?"

"Coffee. Is your BLT any good?"

The lanky man grinned. "Folks come just for the BLT."

"In that case, make it two. One to go. Can I get the coffee now?"

"Sure thing."

A minute later, I held a steaming mug in my hand. As I sipped, I looked around the room. There was a couple who had eyes for no one but each other. From this distance, I could see the exaggerated flash of her hand, her engagement ring catching the light with each movement. Then there was an older couple sitting with their little girl a few tables away from me. I almost frowned at the irresponsibility of parents having their child out on a school night. But then I remembered it was summer.

"And grandpa took me to the jewelry museum. Mom, did you know that the Cullinan diamond is the largest in the world? When I grow up, I'm going to own a diamond mine and make you the most beautiful necklace."

I smiled as the blonde tween girl looked up at her mother. I saw the flash of her dimples as she smiled. Her mother smoothed her flaxen ponytail as she patted her on the head. Her father bent to whisper something in her ear and she burst out laughing. I wondered what private joke they were sharing as I continued my observation.

An older couple paid their bill and stood to leave. I could see strands of gray at both their temples. The woman walked with a slight limp and the man held a steadying hand beneath her elbow. I watched as he assisted her through the door. The three couples could have easily repre-sented the stages in relationships. But where did I, a twenty-two-year-old soldier, fall in the picture? Perhaps if there had been a single woman sitting in a corner somewhere, we could both represent the stage of being single strangers. What a story it would be to tell our children and grandchil-dren about meeting in a diner off the highway.

My eyes went back to the couple with the child. The little girl laughed and chatted incessantly. From the snippets I could hear, she had been spending a few weeks with her grandparents and her parents had picked her up a few hours ago. I remembered a time when I was like her. Excited about being with my grandparents, or even my parents for that matter.

I took another sip of coffee as I watched the young girl. She was so innocent, as all children are. I wondered when she would be thrust into the harsh realities of the world. How long could her parents shield her from the atrocities? It made me remember one of the reasons I had chosen the military. In a roundabout sort of way, I felt as though that choice could help me to save the world. If I had my way, no one would ever know pain, sickness, or hurt. Little girls like her would be untouched. They would find their sweetheart and fall in love. They would get married and live happily ever after. In a perfect world, that could happen. But all I could do now is hope that her parents protected her for as long as they could.

My sandwich came and my stomach rumbled as I dug into it. The waiter was right. It was good. But then again, cardboard would have tasted like heaven now. I hadn't eaten for close to twenty-four hours as I had done double duty for a few days in order to have these few days off for the funeral.

My thoughts turned to my father again.

Of all the things to take him out, a common cold. A cold which quickly progressed to pneumonia. And it was over before anyone could process what was happening. The few times I had spoken with my mother since, she had sounded as though she was still in a fog. And understandably so.

My parents had been the anomaly of arranged rich marriages: they had actually loved each other.

She had been twenty-two and fresh out of college and my father had been twenty-five and already running the family business when they got married. They were the children of business partners and their alliance had been arranged from birth. But they were also childhood sweethearts.

When I had come along three years later, they had been devastated to learn that I was to be an only child as another pregnancy was risky for my mother. I had the love of ten children poured on me.

It had been my father's suggestion for me to enter the

military to learn more about security that had pushed me to enter the service. And I grew to love it.

My eyes clouded briefly as I realized in a few hours, I would face the task of putting him into a hole in the ground forever. I had insisted that my mother take a trip afterwards, and I had seen to it that her ticket was booked for a cruise. The only thing I wished was that I could go with her. But I promised myself when my tour ended, she and I would take a vacation together.

I got a refill on my coffee and sat waiting for my to-go order and the bill, when I felt the hair on the back of my neck stand up. I glanced around cautiously. Then I saw her. The young girl was staring at me, a small smile on her lips. When my eyes met hers, she raised her hand to her temple and saluted. I chuckled and touched my temple briefly with my fingers. Her smile grew wider.

I looked beyond her as the waiter approached my table. Then I felt a cold hand grip me as I looked at the door.

A dirty, disheveled man pushed his way inside. The instant I saw him dip into his waist, I knew what was happening. I shrank back into the wall, knowing that my uniform made me stick out like a sore thumb.

"Nobody move! You move, I shoot your fucking heads off!"

He grabbed the waiter by the collar and hauled him to the register.

"Gimme all the money! Now!"

I could hear the shrieks as the other workers ducked for cover. I could see the waiter was shaking as he emptied the contents of the register into the bag the robber was carrying. I sat quietly, calculating how long it would take me to cross the floor and disarm him. But the way he was looking around wildly told me he was probably high. And being high with a weapon equaled unstable. Besides, just my uniform was a target.

He grabbed the bag with the money and I waited for him to leave. But instead, he began to look around the dining room. The instant he saw me, I knew I would have to discharge my weapon. The only problem was the couple with the girl was between us.

Everything seemed to happen in slow motion. My hand was on my weapon as he raised the gun and pointed it at me. I heard screams as the mother covered her daughter's face. The scream seemed to break his concentration and I saw him turn to look at the couple. I was halfway out of my seat when he grabbed the girl. The mother pounced on him before the father could and I heard a single shot ring out. The woman slid to the ground, blood already beginning to pool underneath her.

I heard the girl scream once more.

"If you call the cops, I'll kill her too!"

He dragged the kicking screaming girl to the door, brandishing the gun the whole time. The second he was outside, chaos erupted in the diner. I watched as the man knelt over his unconscious and bleeding wife, distress etched on his face. I could hear the workers calling the paramedics. I was already out of my seat and heading out the door into the warm summer night. My training kicked in as I covered the few feet in record speed. They had not gotten far, and the little hostage was not going quietly.

I could see he had her by the hair as she continued to fight. As he raised his hand to hit her, I tackled him. The girl fell one way and he fell another. He had been so focused on the girl he had not heard my approach and I caught him off guard. By the time he raised the gun, I already had his wrist between my fingers. I pressed his pulse point and he cried out as the gun fell from his hand.

I moved quickly and with a few punches, had him in a daze. I looked up at approaching footsteps and found some of the workers.

"I need rope!"

"Got some!"

One of the waiters helped me to tie the robber's hands behind him. I turned to the girl who was shaking like a leaf. I knelt by her and put my hands on her head to feel her scalp. She winced, probably from where he had tugged her hair. I smoothed her hair away from her face. In the light of the lamp post in the parking lot, her clear hazel eyes looked back at me. The warmth and innocence I had seen in the diner just a few minutes ago, were now replaced by fear.

I felt her face. Her skin was clammy. She was going into shock. I rubbed my hands along her cheeks and her arms.

"What's your name, sweetheart?"

"L-Lisa."

"You're safe now, Lisa."

I stood and bent to swing her into my arms. Her little hands clung to my shoulders as I strode across the parking lot. Before I could step inside, a frantic waitress burst outside.

"Don't bring her in here!"

"I want my mom and dad!"

Her bottom lip trembled as her eyes filled with tears. I looked at the waitress. She was looking at the girl with a pitiful expression. Then she looked at me. And I knew.

"Don't bring her in here," the waitress whispered, tears clogging her throat.

I felt a dead weight in my arms and looked down. Lisa had fainted. A crowd had begun to gather outside and we could hear the wail of the ambulance in the distance. I looked down at the girl in my arms, wishing with all my heart that I could have protected her a little longer from the harsh realities of this cruel world. In a split second, life as she knew it had changed forever.

I sat on the tail of my truck as I looked at the scene unfolding before me. The paramedics had arrived a few minutes ago. I had handed Lisa to them. They had immediately placed her into the vehicle and closed the door. I watched as the police taped off the scene and began processing the robber. He was now conscious and sitting in the back of a police car. I had already given my statement but for some reason I could not move.

My gut tightened into a knot as the stretcher came out, a sheet covering the form of the woman. I swallowed hard as bitterness rose within me. For a few dollars, a woman's life had been taken. A husband was without his wife. A daughter without her mother. I stared at the stretcher as it rolled along to a second vehicle. Life was so unfair.

"Vance?"

I looked up at the police officer who spoke.

"Thanks for being here and what you did. The situation could have been far worse and we would have a double homicide on our hands."

I shrugged and shook his hand.

As the parking lot emptied, I got into my truck and pulled out onto the highway. I was way behind the time I had told my mother I would get home, and I had not called. But then, neither had she. I could only surmise that she was too busy with the final touches for tomorrow that she hadn't even noticed my absence. But I would rather be late than wake up in the morning and read the news of a mother dead and a daughter kidnapped and later killed. I was in the right place at the right time. And it was not as though my father was going anywhere anyway.

I shook my head at my cynicism as I continued my journey home.

1

LISA

T en Years later

"LISA? HONEY?"

"Coming, dad!"

I attached one more bead in the series so that I would not lose track of my work when I came back. I hurried into my father's room. He was half standing, half leaning against the four-poster bed. His cane was a few feet away out of his reach.

"Dad! Why didn't you call me sooner?"

"I thought I could get to it."

I shook my head at him and pursed my lips in mock severity.

"Are you trying to get me fired from my job as cane-getter and general caretaker?"

He laughed and swayed unsteadily. I picked up the cane and placed it in his hand. I masked my concern with a smile as his fingers trembled with the effort to hold the cane steadily.

"Do you have it?" I asked gently, my hand on his back.

He nodded silently. But I could see his jawline was tight as he gritted his teeth with the effort it took for him to take even a few steps. It seemed as though every week he became frailer and frailer. He had another doctor's appointment tomorrow. But I could almost hear the conversation already.

We will need to run some more tests... he is a healthy man... all his vitals are reading well... it's a mystery. Why is a forty-eight year old healthy man declining so rapidly?... we will need to run some more tests... we need to keep him overnight for observation...

Usually by the last suggestion my father would put his foot down. He was adamantly against any sort of hospitalization. He had likened it to having one foot in the grave and had declared that the day he set foot in a hospital was the day he had decided to join my mother.

The first time he had said it a few years ago after his first doctor's visit, I had gone as white as a sheet. It had been shortly after my eighteenth birthday, but six years had still not dulled the heartache of what had happened that night in the diner.

I remember waking up in the ambulance while the paramedic was checking me over. Gone was the bright blue gaze of the soldier with a crescent scar at the corner of his left eye. In its place was a dark-haired woman with equally dark eyes, prodding and poking me. Through the back window I had seen blue lights flashing. Then suddenly, the back door opened.

"Keep her here," a gruff voice had announced before slamming the door shut once more.

I remember the tender gaze of the paramedic as she

smiled at me. It had not quite reached her eyes, eyes that had been filled with pity as she looked at me. It had been a day later that it had all made sense. My mother's body had been loaded into a separate vehicle, my father by her side.

"I'm sorry, Lisa. I shouldn't have said that," he apologized afterwards.

I looked around now to find my father standing at my elbow, his back bent slightly and his weight on the cane. I could only hope that tomorrow's appointment yielded something substantial. I didn't want him to be among the statistics as a rare condition that had been diagnosed when it was too late.

I placed my hand under his elbow as he took a few steps across the room. We stopped in the doorway to allow him to rest. Today seemed to be worse than yesterday. He needed the cane more these past days.

He smiled at me and his face lit up. He was still a very handsome man despite the physical challenges he was having. As a matter of fact, there was nothing wrong with his mind and heart. It was just his legs and hands that were the problem.

I helped him into the living room with some effort, and he took a seat in his favorite armchair by the window. Though it was summer, I placed a light blanket across his knees and handed him one of his magazines. I bent down to place the water bottle within reach and kissed his cheek gently.

"If you need me, I'll be right over there."

I pointed exaggeratedly at the table where all my beads were spread out.

I resumed my task of making a set of waist beads for a bridal party. The client would be picking them up this evening. But I was through before midday and had them all packaged and ready to go.

This was the pattern of my days and had been for the past two years when my father became sick.

At first, he had ignored the weakness in his limbs and attributed it to fatigue. But one morning when he had fallen in the shower and couldn't get up, I had gotten the neighbor to assist me. I had taken the day off from my new job as a secretary. By the end of the month, I had been released as I had either been taking more days off or coming in late while tending to my father. After the fall, he had taken a disability leave. Thus began the series of doctor visits, hospital tests, various diagnoses, and the depletion of any emergency savings we may have had.

After a year, my father's job had given him the option of taking early retirement for medical reasons with a portion of his pension. And I had become his main caregiver. Many twenty-two year olds would have stuck their parent in a home and moved on with their lives. But all we had was each other. And that was how it had been for the past ten years.

He had rearranged his life for me, ensuring I lacked no time or attention as I went through my awkward teenage years. The period of life when a girl needed her mother most, he was there, filling the gap the best way he knew how. So now the tables had turned and it was my time to be there for him.

It had taken strategic management and systematic saving to keep our heads above water financially. My mother had a few investments which we had refused to touch unless absolutely necessary. I had skipped college and had done a one-year certificate secretarial course as I had not wanted to go to college at the time. I was thankful I didn't have a student loan hanging over my head at a time like this. With his illness, I worked either part-time or from home. I had signed up with an employment agency and got a few temporary jobs through them. I had also picked up a hobby of jewelry making and found that I was not half bad. I had a few clients and advertised by word of mouth. The bridal set was through a friend of a friend. Every penny counted, no matter how small.

That evening after the order had been collected and paid for, I sat at the dining table. I had seen to it that dad was comfortable in bed, the remote control and tablet close at hand. I pulled out my laptop and opened the excel file with the data for the monthly expenses. One by one, I added up every cent I had earned from jewelry and the few days I had gotten a transcription job. Then I added my father's pension and the monthly allowances he received from his insurance policy. Then I began deducting the bills: rent, utilities, medication, food. I looked at the figures and breathed a sigh of relief. The bead job had allowed us to break even this month and I didn't have to dip into our savings. Dad's medication was still partially covered by insurance. Had it not been for that insurance coverage, we would have been in the poorhouse a long time ago.

I closed the laptop and got ready for bed. The last thing I did before I showered was check the windows and door. One could never tell with a ground floor apartment. After my shower, I checked on my father. The room was dark as he had turned off the television. But I could see his face in the light of the tablet.

"Hey, Dad."

He looked up at me and smiled.

"Hey."

"I'm heading to bed now. Rest well, okay?"

"You too, sweetheart."

"I love you."

"I love you too."

I looked at him a little longer before I moved away from the door. I stood in the shadows where he couldn't see me. I heard him sigh deeply.

"Irene, you would be so proud of her. She's got a heart of gold. We raised her well. I miss you so much, baby. Rest well in heaven."

I felt as if a fist was squeezing my heart. Irene. My mother.

Quietly I slipped away from the door and went to my room. I lay staring into the darkness for a long time before sleep came.

Over the next few weeks, our pattern continued. More tests. More possible diagnoses. More experimental treatment. And we were both weary of it all. And to make matters worse, I could feel as though my father's fighting spirit was growing weak. I could feel him giving up the war for his health. And if that happened, he was as good as dead. And I knew why he was giving up. In a few days, we would relive that awful night. This year would make it ten. We both missed my mother terribly, but I knew he missed her more. It was my fear that if whatever he had did not kill him, a broken heart would.

The day before the anniversary of mom's death, I went grocery shopping. I deliberately chose that day and uncharacteristically went to get the groceries rather than have them delivered as usual. The neighbor from upstairs was watching Dad while I went out. She was a sweet woman and former nurse, so I was confident he was in good hands.

I stopped at a flower stand on the corner and made a quick purchase before I hopped on a bus. The ride was a short one. But it could have lasted for eternity for all I cared. It was a ride I never wanted to take each year, but forced myself to take for my father's sake. Tomorrow he will take the ride with me. I had budgeted for a cab as he would not be able to handle the walk to and from the bus stop. My stop came up too quickly and I disembarked.

I stared up at the wrought iron sign, my eyes clouding with tears. I clutched the bouquet as I walked quickly among the headstones. I found the spot, shaded by a tall oak tree. I brushed away the leaves that had covered the ground and pulled the weeds that had grown up since the gardeners had last weeded. I traced her name on the headstone. Irene Evadne Mulligan.

I sat at the foot of the grave and looked at the headstone.

"Hi, Mom. It's me. Lisa. Well, it has to be me, right? I'm the only child you had. Unless you've gotten others that I don't know about in heaven. Am I a big sister to some little angels?'"

I laughed at my own joke. Then my throat clogged with tears.

"Dad isn't doing well, Mom. He misses you terribly. We both do. But I know he misses you more. There isn't a day that goes by that he doesn't talk about coming to be with you. He tries to joke about it, but I know he's serious. He blames himself for that night you know. He keeps saying it should have been him and not you who tried to rescue me. He keeps saying I should have been sitting beside him. He keeps saying that you should have lived and he be the one taken. Oh, Mom! I blame myself too! I just had to stop and use the restroom. And then I just had to get something to eat. Why did I make us stop? You would be here right now if it wasn't for me!"

Sobs ripped through me as I poured out my heart to my

mother. When the worst of the storm had passed and the gulping sobs became soft whimpers, I stood and wiped my face. I looked at the headstone for a few minutes more. I kissed the bouquet and placed it in the center.

"I love you, Mom. Dad and I will come tomorrow. But I had to see you first. I will continue to be brave. And I will continue to fight for him. I will continue to be strong."

I knelt once more and touched the headstone. Then without a backward glance, I walked out of the cemetery.

I got the shopping done before stopping in at the craft store. I usually had my orders delivered, but took advantage of browsing in person as only so many things were in the online shopping portal. I bought a few items, using my discount card and the sales discounts for a further discount.

By the time I got home that afternoon, my spirits were lighter. Dad was sleeping. I slipped a ten into the neighbor's hand as she left. I got started on a simple dinner of mashed potatoes and beans that could be kept warm until we were ready to eat. Then I buried my nose in the bead tray. I had no orders, but I liked to keep busy. Sometimes I posted pictures of my work on social media and had an instant sale.

I was halfway through the necklace when Dad woke up. I went to assist him to the bathroom then to the living room. Apart from his afternoon naps and bedtime, I tried to keep him out of bed. I did not want him to become an invalid and bedridden.

He sat at the table as I dished up the meal.

"What do you want to wear tomorrow?"

I watched as he swallowed silently.

"What I always wear. My suit."

I smiled and nodded. "I expected that answer."

We ate in silence. While he watched television, I tidied the kitchen. I could tell his thoughts were nowhere near the comedy on the screen. We both were miles away. But we'd get through tomorrow. We always did.

That night after I put him to bed, I went through my nightly routine of locking up and showering. I stopped to say goodnight and was surprised to find that he was already asleep. That night as I lay staring at the ceiling, I wondered how he would hold up tomorrow. Not only that, I wondered if I would have him by my side next year, or if he would get his wish and be by my mother's side instead. Only time would tell.

2

AXEL

I strode through the airport, feeling eyes on me as I did. My sunglasses hid my eyes as I perused in turn. I knew the image I presented. Who would not look twice at a tall, well-built man with a buzz cut and a thick black beard? Especially if you were a woman. There was power in every step. I exude masculinity and knew it. I also knew my confidence rolled off me in waves. And people just felt safer with me nearby. That was the intention. I was a walking brand. It also helped that the polo shirt I wore bore the name and logo of Vance Security Solutions. I'd lost count of the number of casual conversations I had struck up in the terminals I had been in and out of on this trip, and the number of business cards I had handed out with our company information.

Nine years ago, when I had come back home to take the reins of the company my father had left behind, it had felt like I was trying to climb a never-ending mountain. It had taken me months to wade through the mess he had left behind. I had to fire some and hire others. There had been times when it seemed as though we were going to sink. I'd had to rebuild our brand and reputation from the ground up. And now VSS was synonymous with safety and confidence in the products we offered. And if things continued on this trajectory, it could become a global brand. I was certainly working towards that end.

I found my gate for my last connecting flight and waited for boarding. As I watched the planes come and go, I used the rare moment of idle time to reflect on the last decade.

Losing my father had been a blow. Somehow children never expect their parents to die. Worse if they were in the prime of their life and the death was rather sudden. The overseas duties right after his funeral had come at a good time as well. I had needed the space to deal with myself. I knew my mother loved me and meant well, but the last thing I needed then was her hovering over me. Our separation after the funeral had done us both a world of good. When I had returned, we had both begun our healing process. I couldn't say we were entirely okay even after ten years as grief never ends. But we were much better with the passing of time.

I watched as my plane taxied up to the boarding gate. I had my boarding pass in hand and my backpack. I had been out of the country for a month, refreshing my combat skills as well as renewing my international licenses as a security service provider. In all the years of traveling I had done, there was never any greater feeling than that of returning home. It had only been in the last year or two, though, that I had felt confident in being away from the company for longer than a few days. I had a good staff for the most part. I knew I was a hard taskmaster. Those who could deal with it, stayed. Those who couldn't, left. For the past year, I had noticed a trend of those leaving, though. After my father's assistant, who I had inherited, retired last year, I couldn't seem to keep an assistant. I didn't know what it was. But they didn't last more than a few weeks.

Before I had gone on my trip, I had dismissed Nadine. She had been, what, number ten? Admittedly she had lasted the longest – an entire month. But just when I thought I would finally have someone who I could depend on, she had left without a backward glance. I hated to think it had anything to do with my exacting instructions regarding the way I wanted the suits in my closet to be arranged. And so, what if I had gotten into a shouting match with her regarding a document she had misfiled, only to find it where she had said it would be? And so what if that shouting match had been in the middle of the entire office and I had continued to yell at her, despite the file being found? She had called me every name under the sun and I had told her if she hated working with an asshole of a pig such as I was (her words, not mine), she could leave. She had taken my advice and done just that. The last thing I had done before leaving for my trip was to contact the temp agency and put in my request for an assistant. Each time I called them, I always waited for them to tell me they were unable to fulfill my request. But they never did. And so, Monday morning I met Geraldine. She lasted a week.

A few months after my return, I raced through assistants once more. It was beginning to wear on my nerves and I was beginning to lose count. This last one seemed set to break Nadine's record, though. But that was more on my part of not wanting to admit defeat in not keeping an assistant than on her being efficient. As a matter of fact, she was one of the most inefficient ones yet. And I was reaching my boiling point. Her dismissal was inevitable. Yet still, I would give her enough rope with which she could hang herself. As I waited in my office one Friday evening, I felt as though her hanging day had come.

I was furious. I could feel the blood coursing through my veins, growing hotter with each passing second. Where the hell was that dimwit of an assistant?

I turned smartly on my heels as I made another circuit of my office. I knew that everyone was on edge as they watched me through the open blinds. Good. I wanted them to be on edge. That was the only way to run a tight ship in this operation.

I checked my watch once more. Only Elizabeth Vance could think of throwing a party at this time of the evening, peak hour and a Friday at that, and expect every guest to be in attendance. Her excuse was that her bedtime was eleven and she would be damned if she would inconvenience herself for the sake of those who could not make it at her five pm start time. If ever I wanted to know where I got my sense of entitlement in having things done my way or else from, I didn't have to look further than my mother. But being her only child didn't exempt me from her wrath. I was supposed to be at my mother's half an hour ago. A whole fucking thirty minutes late already, not counting getting dressed and the one hour drive it would take for me to get there in rush hour traffic. Something had told me some shit like this was going to go down when I saw time passing and no sign of Deidre, my nincompoop of an assistant. The transportation contingency, the helicopter, was waiting on the roof even as I paced. The journey would be ten minutes at most.

I looked up as I heard a buzz of conversation. I saw a flash of red curls. Deidre.

"Out of my way! I'm late! He's going to kill me for sure!"

"Just let us know where you want to be buried."

She stopped, one hand on her hip, the other holding a suit bag over her shoulder.

"Now is not the time for your stiff jokes, Candace."

Candace, one of the marketing agents, stared her down.

"Now is not the time to be arguing with me about my jokes. You're the one that's in hot water." She pointed her chin at my office and I watched as Deidre turned to look at me staring at her.

"Oh shit!"

She moved as though she was on fire and in a few seconds, she was in my office.

"I'm so sorry Mr. Vance, sir. But I have your suit."

With a flourish, she presented the suit bag. She even had the audacity to smile and curtsey. I looked at her coldly.

"Do you have any idea what time it is?" I spoke softly, deadliness coating every word.

"I know you're a little late-"

"A *little* late? Try almost an hour, not counting travel time."

"I'm sorry sir, it's just that-"

I cut her off as I opened the bag and examined the suit. I felt as though my blood pressure was going to go through the roof.

"What is this?" I held the suit out to her.

She moved from one foot to the other uneasily.

"Well, you see-"

"No. I don't see. What – is – *this?*"

"I know I was supposed to pick it up yesterday. But by the time I got to the cleaners they were closed. And they're not open today."

I looked up at the ceiling and closed my eyes. I took a deep breath before I looked at her.

"Would you care to explain to me why a suit that I

personally left at the cleaners last week just so that I would not be in a rush to have it cleaned, was not picked up during the full eight hours of their daily operation any time before they closed yesterday? Why?"

"Ummm. I-I forgot."

I blinked a few times. "You *what*!?"

"Forgot. I forgot," she barely whispered.

"Didn't you write it down in your diary?"

"I did."

"And?"

"I left my diary at the office."

"What is the point in having a diary if you're not going to read it?"

"But I got you another suit! I went to your house and picked the best one you have in the closet."

"You picked a gray suit for a black and white event."

"I didn't know!" she began to wail.

"There's a lot you don't know."

"I'm trying my best, sir!"

"You're not trying hard enough."

"I'm going to do better. I promise!"

"See that you do."

I started to take off my shirt and heard her gasp. Right now, I could care less about offending her sensibilities whether to my scars or my muscles. I ripped the shirt off and was in the process of putting on the shirt she had brought when my cell phone rang. I swore softly as I saw my mother's number. I was in deep shit. I put the phone on speaker.

"Yes, Mother?"

"Um, sir. May I go now?"

"Not yet."

"Axel Lionel Vance! I don't believe you! How could you treat your own mother this way?"

"I was unavoidably delayed at the office, Mother. I'm getting dressed as we speak. I'm taking the helicopter. I'll be there before you know it."

"I'm not talking about your tardiness. That's another discussion. But do you have any idea how humiliated I feel right *now*?"

"I'm sorry, Mother. But-"

"And your assistant of all people!"

I stopped in the middle of buttoning my shirt. I stared at Deidre who was staring at the phone as though it was a loaded gun pointed at her.

"What about my assistant?"

"Donna called me *this morning*-"

"Deidre. Her name is Deidre."

"Donna, Deidre, Diane. Her name could be Dumbo the flying elephant for all I care. She called me this morning in the middle of my spa treatment. I had the phone on speaker Axel! Now the whole city knows that Elizabeth Vance's son does not give two hoots about her."

I continued to stare at Deidre. She had gone as white as a sheet and was wringing her hands while doing that hop from one foot to the other which I absolutely hated.

I tried to speak as calmly as possible.

"Mother, you know I love you."

"If you loved me, why didn't you buy my birthday gift before today?"

"Your birthday gift?"

"Your assistant called me in the middle of my spa treatment to ask me what I wanted for my birthday. At first, I thought it was a joke someone was playing on me. But then she said she was *your* assistant and you had told her to get my gift. You couldn't even do it yourself, Axel? I am so *embarrassed*! And even now at the party I can tell that people are whispering about it. 'Didn't you hear? Her own son didn't get her a gift. He's not even here. He had one of his little workers get her something at the last minute. How absolutely *awful* for her!' I know what they're saying behind my back while they smile in my face."

"Mother, those were not my instructions to Deidre. Your gift was already bought. She was supposed to pick it up." My eyes narrowed on Deidre who looked as though she was praying for the floor to open up and swallow her up, saving her from my wrath. "Unless she forgot to do that too."

"I beg your pardon?"

"Nothing. Don't you dare leave now."

"What!?"

"Not you, Mother. I have something to deal with here at the office. There are necks to be squeezed."

Deidre yelped. And before I could bar the door, she ran out. I watched as she scurried to her desk. The office was nearly empty by now. I watched as she grabbed the appointment book from her messy desk and scampered out. I would deal with her next week. For now, I had to do damage control.

"So, Mother. Is this event strictly black tie, or can I wear the gray suit I'm wearing now?"

I took the phone off the speaker, confident that I could hear her shrill screams nonetheless. I was right.

3

LISA

"That's great, Dad! Come on! Take one more. I know you can."

I watched my father the way a mother watches her child as they accomplish a milestone towards independence. My father was attempting to feed himself some of the soup I had made for dinner. I forced a bright smile as his trembling hand lifted the spoon to his lips once more. It was disheartening to watch. But what else could I do?

Summer had given way to autumn. We were awaiting the results of another round of tests. Finally, we were making some progress with information and heading towards a formal diagnosis. The initial reports showed that there was a disconnection taking place between the nerves responsible for motor skills and his brain. As a result, his muscle memory was also being affected. A round of treatment had been prescribed. The result was that for the first time in months, my father could hold a spoon and lift it to his mouth without spilling the contents too much.

I saw the bead of sweat on his brow as he concentrated on the task. He gave a wan smile as he sipped the soup and lowered the spoon.

"I'm full now."

"You did great, Dad. Before you know it, you'll be back to your old self. This medication seems to be helping a lot."

"It is. If only it didn't have all these side effects."

"That's the least. We're seeing progress. And hopefully, when we know what is really wrong, we can have the most appropriate medicine prescribed."

"I hope so too, dear. I'm a bit tired, though. I think I'll have an early evening if that's okay with you."

"No problem, Dad."

I helped him through his bedtime routine. I took the time to stretch and rub his muscles which were becoming flabbier through limited use. I also noticed a new rash on his back. But the doctor had said that this was one of the possible side effects of the new medication. I applied the anti-itch cream which had also been prescribed for it.

When I finally had him dressed and in bed, I gave him his final dose of medicine and handed him the remote control and tablet as usual.

"Love you, Dad. Sleep well." I leaned down and brushed my lips against his cheek.

"Love you too, sweetheart. Get some rest yourself."

I smiled and ran my hand through his still thick head of wheat blonde hair. I had inherited his looks in every way. Only my mother's striking hazel eyes with hints of green bore any evidence to her having given birth to me.

I turned off the light and looked at him as he watched the television. The past few weeks whenever I checked on him before I went to bed, I had to turn off the television and remove the tablet. I knew it was because he was getting more tired more often, and sometimes the effort was too much for his hands.

I went back to the living room and began to tidy the space. I moved to the kitchen and had the dishes washed up in no time. I went through my routine of locking up before I went to shower. Tonight was my wash night and so it took a little longer as I shampooed and conditioned my thick hair. It fell in waves down my back, almost to my thighs by the time I had it dried and brushed. I braided it into two pigtails, securing the ends with rubber bands before I moisturized my skin and slipped into my pajamas. I checked on my father, turning off the television and removing the tablet as he had fallen asleep. As I crawled into my bed, I took the newspaper and a highlighter with me. I perched my glasses on my nose as I began to scour the want ads.

I didn't want to worry my father, but money was becoming even tighter. For the past few months, I had to dip into the savings a little more than usual. The insurance company was also becoming more difficult with honoring their percentage of his medication. I had a meeting with them next week regarding his health policy and the reports I needed to submit regarding his condition. His doctors promised to have the formal report done for me to take to the meeting. But if push came to shove, the worst-case scenario could find us having to fork out more cash out of pocket for his treatment.

I scanned the pages of advertisements, circling a few that seemed to have some potential for my being able to work from home. I would make some calls tomorrow and hope that some of them would pan out. Then there was the temp agency. Each time I called to ask if there were any remote jobs available, the answer was no. There were many short stints available, but I didn't want to leave my father unsupervised. I could have asked Nora, the neighbor above us. But even the small tip could go a long way for us financially when it was added up. Nope. We didn't have a cent to spare on anything other than necessities.

Over the next two weeks, I managed to find a transcription job. The client sent me the recording via email and I would send the finished document back. But that didn't last. Then there was one that wanted a voice actor, and they liked the sound of my voice for the project. The only catch was that I had to record in person. The day they chose was an appointment day for my dad. So that fell through.

And thus went our lives.

One evening as he sat at the dining table, I could tell that his thoughts were far away. And whenever he got that faraway look, I knew he was thinking of my mother. Another milestone, their wedding anniversary, was approaching. December would make twenty-five years that they would have been married. I put on a bright smile as I reached across to pat his hand gently.

"A penny for them?"

He looked at me, blankly at first. My heart wrenched at the emptiness in his eyes. And for some inexplicable reason, I felt a coldness sweep over me. He swallowed convulsively and I saw his eyes mist over.

"I can't do this anymore, Lisa." His voice was thick with unshed tears and I felt my eyes prick in turn.

"Dad-"

He shook his head and held a trembling finger up.

"I can't. It's more than missing Irene."

"I miss her too, Dad," I whispered as I fought back the tears.

"Please understand that it's not about her, Lisa. It's this

thing, whatever it is, that's tearing my body apart. I hate what it's doing to me. And I hate what it's doing to you."

"But Dad-"

"No, Lisa. I know you don't mind. But I do. I'm nothing but a burden to you."

"Don't say that Dad! You're not!"

"I am! Do you know how it feels not to be even fifty and feeling like a hundred? I'm in the prime of my life depending on my daughter to wash my ass."

"Dad!"

He shook his head as the tears coursed down his cheeks.

"I love you to life, Lisa. But I can't put you through this anymore. I can't. You have done so much for me these past two years. You deserve to move on with your life. You deserve to be out with your friends instead of taking care of me. You deserve to be out with a nice young man on a Saturday night instead of cooped up taking care of an old man. You deserve a life. I've lived my life and it's time for me to move on and let you live your own."

"But Dad! You just said it yourself, you're still young and in your prime."

"I want you to admit me, Lisa. The next time the doctor wants to admit me to the hospital for observation, let them. If they want to put me into a care facility, let them. At least you can be sure that I'm being supervised. And when my time comes to go, you will be well taken care of financially. My death insurance will cover my funeral. Make it a modest one as I won't know and appreciate anything fancy anyway. Keep it minimal. There will be enough money left over to take care of you."

"Dad! Please stop talking like this! You're not dying!"

"But I am, Lisa!" his voice choked on a sob. "I am! Look

at me. I can't walk without help. Most days all I want to do is stay in bed. I'm getting weaker. My muscles are weakening. I can't stand. You heard what the doctor said at the last visit, right? I'll soon need a wheelchair. But I'm not going to let it get to that. I want you to admit me. Okay?"

"No! I won't do it. And I won't let you do it either. I won't let you give up!"

I went to kneel beside him as he put his head into his shaking hand, sobbing. The tears I had been fighting to hold back broke free.

"I won't let you give up." I held his hand and squeezed it. "We will get through this. We will. You'll see. Next year, you will be strong again. And the following year you will be working again. But I'm not giving up. And neither are you!"

I hugged him and felt his trembling hand clutch at my shoulder. I don't know how long we remained in that embrace. But when at last our tears subsided, I helped him through his bedtime routine. This time he refused the remote and tablet and fell asleep almost immediately.

After I had my shower, I felt restless. I stepped outside to the little stoop at the front of the building. The night was cold, but I needed the bracing chill. I looked up at the sky, something I realized I hadn't done in ages. Somehow as I looked up tonight, my thoughts went back to another time in my life when I had been looking up at the night sky. Then it had been partially obscured by the shape of a bald head. I remembered the kind blue eyes which had looked down at me.

"Where are you!?" I cried into the night sky. "You rescued me then. Where are you to rescue me now? You couldn't save my mother. But please! Save my father! Please!"

I sat on the front stoop and buried my face in my hands. I didn't care who saw me. I pulled my jacket around me even closer as I rocked back and forth. Suddenly, I jumped almost out of my skin as I felt an arm around my shoulders. I looked around to find Nora beside me.

"Lisa! Is everything okay with Gerald? What on earth are you doing out here? You're going to catch pneumonia. Come. Let's get you inside."

I allowed her to lead me back into the building. I followed her like a child as she took me to her apartment. I watched as she bustled around the kitchen and I soon had a steaming mug of cocoa in my hands.

"Now, talk. Is everything okay with Gerald?"

I shook my head and the tears came again. It was not until that moment I realized I had never had an outlet. And so, I talked. I poured my heart out to Nora. I told her about the night my mother had been murdered and how I had almost been kidnapped. I told her how hard it had been at first with just my dad and me. But somehow, we had gotten over my teen angst and shuffled through those years.

Dad and I had moved to this building when I was eighteen and Nora had been the first one to greet us. Back then, she had been a nurse and recently widowed. Now she worked from home in medical administration and taught nursing courses online.

She had been the one who had helped me with Dad after his first fall. As I spoke about how his health had been deteriorating and how he felt, she reached over and patted my hand comfortingly. The tears continued to roll down my cheeks.

"I love my father, Nora. I don't want him to die. I wish I could fight for him. I wish I could get him to fight for himself."

She sighed heavily. "And that is the truth Lisa. He has to be willing to fight for himself. That is more than half the battle. I can't tell you how many patients I've seen decline rapidly the moment they gave up. You are right. He has to be willing to fight for himself. But by the sounds of it, he's throwing in the towel. And he thinks he's doing it for you. He wants you to move on with your life and removing himself from the equation will do that."

"But I don't want him to die!"

"I know you don't, dear. None of us ever want our loved ones to go."

"But what am I going to do?"

"Keep fighting. That is all you can do. Keep fighting. Keep hoping. Keep praying. Keep believing in a cure or at the very least, a miracle."

I took a few deep breaths as I looked at Nora. I smiled.

"Thank you, Nora. I needed this so much."

"No problem, dear. And if you ever need me, don't hesitate to call me. Listen, I know money is tight. You don't even have to pay me. All I need is my laptop. If you ever need me to watch him, just let me know. No charge."

"But-"

"No charge. Besides, I would be using your internet and electricity. I would say I need to pay you for that. So, we would be even. If you need me-"

"I'll call. Thank you, Nora. I really appreciate this."

"Anytime dear."

I hugged her and hurried back to my apartment. I checked on dad again. He was still fast asleep. I changed my clothes and crept into bed. As I lay looking at the stars in the sky, I felt a lightness in my spirit. I couldn't help but feel as though a weight was off my shoulders just by talking with Nora. It helped to know that if push came to shove, I could indeed ask her to watch Dad. This would give me a little more freedom to get a better job at least.

Tomorrow was Friday. Tomorrow I would call the agency. Hopefully, they'll have something for me. If they did, I would take Nora up on her offer.

4

AXEL

I raced through the parking lot, the cold December breeze ripping through my jacket. I glanced at my watch and swore loudly. If I could pull my ass out of this shithouse of a bind, I was going to wring Fiona's neck when I got back to the office.

I ignored the elevator and took the stairs two at a time. I could only hope that I would not be too late.

"Why me!? What the fuck have I done to deserve this? Can't I have one, just ONE fucking competent assistant? Am I such a horrible person that I have been cursed like this?"

I stopped to catch my breath on the landing before climbing the last flight of stairs. This huffing and puffing didn't work. I needed to get to the gym as I was feeling a bit out of shape. But who could get to the gym when I was always stuck in the office or in one meeting or another. I knew I was losing my edge and I needed to make some time to keep my body in shape. That was going to be one of my new year's resolutions for sure. I was still a young man. And had I still been in the service, I would have needed to have much more stamina. I was getting soft physically, and that would not be tolerated. Nope. January first would find me in the gym.

I huffed and puffed up the last three steps and rounded the corner. I watched in dismay as a familiar figure stepped into the elevator.

"Mr. Christie! Wait!"

I darted into the corridor and caught the elevator door just before it closed. I looked into the annoyed face of the client I was supposed to meet almost an hour ago instead of in a few minutes, all thanks to the bungled scheduling done by yet another incompetent assistant.

"Vance." He frowned and pursed his lips. "You're late and I'm a busy man."

"I know, Mr. Christie. But could I have a word please? If you'd just step out of the elevator, we can talk this over." I didn't want to have this conversation with an audience.

I waited with bated breath as Mr. Christie seemed to weigh whether or not he would honor my request. I exhaled with relief when he stepped out of the elevator. I moved my hand and allowed it to continue its journey with the remaining occupants.

"Make it fast, Vance. You've already wasted enough of my time."

"About that, Mr. Christie. My assistant made an error with the time she gave you. My reservation is actually for noon. But I didn't realize she had told you our meeting was at eleven until she admitted just now that she had mixed up the times with the clients. I do apologize for the mix-up and hope that we can still have our meeting?"

He looked over his glasses at me and I couldn't help but feel as though I was groveling. Me. Axel Vance. Groveling. If I didn't have Fiona's head for this, my name would be changed from Axel to Wuss. My resolution to be more accommodating with incompetent assistants had gone out the door after I dismissed Deidre. I couldn't afford for their incompetence to cost me my business reputation.

Slowly, Mr. Christie checked his watch.

"I can give you half an hour. Forty minutes tops."

"Great. Shall we?"

I gestured to the restaurant entrance and we were soon seated. The meal was a quick one. And true to his word, he did give me no more than forty minutes. But I had what I came for: a contract for providing security services for his hotel chain nationwide. I would be kept busy with this one for sure and it would seal the expansion of VSS, a project I'd been working on for over a year. As the world became more technology oriented, I had to move with the times. This was but a toe in the market. But in true Axel Vance fashion, I would soon kick the door in with my big foot. VSS was going to become a company known among the elite as the best security providers worldwide. If only my father could see me now. I tapped the business card against the palm of my hand as I paid the lunch bill. This was a big contract and would look good on the books for December.

As we shook hands in the parking lot and made arrangements to have our attorneys draw up the relevant documents, I shuddered to think of what would have happened if I had been a few minutes later. Yes. I was definitely going to have a few words with Miss Fiona when I got back to the office. And now that the damage had been controlled, I allowed my rage at what could have happened had I missed the meeting, to return.

I hopped into my car and wound my way through the Friday lunch hour traffic. I was back at the office by two. My anger had not dissipated and I knew everyone felt it the minute I entered the office. As I approached my office, I spotted Fiona at her desk, her back was turned to me and she was on her phone. Her bare feet were propped up on the open bottom drawer. I wrinkled my nose at the smell of nail polish as she painted her fingers. I went to stand in front of her, pleased to hear her gasp.

"Sandra. I'll call you back."

She hurried to disconnect the call and cover the bottle of polish with which she had been applying a bright red color to her nails.

"Mr. Vance. I didn't expect you back so soon, sir."

"My office! Now!" I roared. I could hear a pin drop in the office. And I was sure I heard a snicker. It was no secret to me that someone was about to win some sort of pool for guessing how long this assistant would have lasted.

The door crashed against the wall as I all but kicked it open. I was pleased to see her go pale as she realized she was in a heap of trouble. I didn't even bother to close the door behind her as she scurried past me.

"Do you know you almost cost me over a million dollars?"

"I beg your pardon, sir?"

"Christie was almost gone by the time I got to the restaurant. What could have possessed you to tell him I was meeting him at eleven, when I specifically told you to book the restaurant for twelve? Where the fuck is your head!?"

"I-I'm sorry. It won't happen again."

"That's the fifth time I'm hearing that this week. It comes so fucking easily off your tongue and I've had it with your incompetence, your sloppiness, your tardiness, I've had it! And-"

I was interrupted by my cell phone as it rang. I took it out of my pocket and saw that it was a client calling. I pointed at the still open door.

"Get out! We'll finish this conversation later. Good afternoon Mr. Gregory." I turned my back as Fiona left the office, closing the door behind her.

"Vance! You're a hard man to get on the phone."

"Well, you know the end of the year is a bit busy. What can I do for you?"

"I need a few of your men for an event I'm having. I'm expecting a few celebs and want to provide them with extra bodyguards."

I pulled out a notepad and soon had three pages filled with information and the specifications of the job.

"Got it. I'll get on it and send my best."

"No, you won't." I heard the cynicism in his voice.

I laughed softly. "Why would you say that, Mr. Gregory?" I knew what was coming.

"You're not sending yourself are you. Therefore, you're not sending your best."

I let out a deep belly laugh. "You have a point. I'll send the best that were trained by the best."

"I guess I don't have a choice."

"No. You don't. Great doing business with you as usual, sir."

"The feeling is mutual."

"I'll have the contract drawn up and sent over by the latest Monday morning."

"Great."

I ended the call and made a few more scribbles on the notepad in front of me. I ripped off the sheets and went to the outer office. Fiona's desk was a hot mess and she was nowhere to be found. I frowned.

"Where the hell is she?" I said to no one in particular.

"She stepped out a few minutes ago, sir." Lola, one of the other secretaries responded.

"Did she say where she was going or when she would be back?"

"I don't think she's gone very far, sir. Her purse is still there."

"Hmph! Tell her to see me as soon as she gets back."

Just as I was about to turn to go back to my office, Fiona came through the door. I watched as she approached, her ear glued to her phone. She was laughing and talking as she walked to her desk. Her steps faltered as she looked up and saw me. She tried to retreat but it was already too late.

"Ummm. Sandra. I'll have to call you back later."

She disconnected the call and took a step back. But it was no use. My nostrils were assailed with the overpoweringly sweet perfume which rolled off her in waves. But the perfume, as heavy as it was, could not completely hide the smell of smoke. I narrowed my eyes on her.

"Where have you been?" I spoke slowly and carefully, not daring to think that she would be so barefaced and stupid. But the tickling of my nostrils told me otherwise. I pinned my eyes on hers, tuning in to every expression. The way her eyes darted away from mine told me something was amiss.

"I just stepped out for a minute, sir."

"To have a smoke." I stated rather than asked.

"I wasn't smoking, sir." Her eyes widened with mock innocence.

"We have a strict prohibition policy of which I am sure you are very much aware, Fiona."

"But sir! I wasn't smoking! I swear! I just stepped out for some air. Th-There were some men from another office smoking where I was standing. Maybe that's what you're smelling." She licked her dry lips as the lies rolled off her tongue.

Without hesitation, I lunged for her hand. She shrieked. I pulled her fingers to my nose and recoiled at the stench of nicotine. I dropped her hand and looked at her in disgust.

"And I suppose you were just holding a cigarette for one of them as well."

She nodded energetically. "I actually was! He needed his hands for a few moments and-"

"Shut the fuck up! You know the company policy! And you're lying on top of it!"

My fist hit her desk. The force made a stack of papers slide to the floor. I pointed at her.

"Get this mess cleaned up! NOW!!!"

I turned to Lola and thrust the note papers at her.

"Get these ready for Monday morning."

"Yes, sir."

I turned back to see Fiona scrambling around her desk and fumbling with papers.

"As for you. See me before you leave." My tone had a deadly finality to it. Anyone within earshot knew what was coming. And if Fiona had a shred of common sense left, so did she.

I stormed back to my office and slammed the door behind me. I buried myself in work for the next hour, waiting for Fiona to come to my office. When I saw it was after five and the office had started to empty as it usually did on a Friday and there was still no sign of Fiona, I stepped outside. Her empty desk met me. In the middle of the desk was the appointment book. I checked the drawers and saw all the papers which had been on the desk had simply been stuffed into them, still unorganized. I closed my eyes and started to count backwards from one hundred. When I got to seven, I turned on my heel and went back into my office.

I dialed a now familiar number and leaned back in my chair.

"Good evening, Mr. Vance. It's Shirley. I was just about to call you, sir."

"Hey, Shirley." For the director herself to call me and to be so official in addressing me, I knew that one, she had company in the office and two, Fiona had already reported to the agency.

"We have already started the paperwork for her exit from your company. Would you care to tell us what happened this time?"

"She almost cost me a big client that could make or break my company, and on top of it, she's a liar. Shirley, I can't keep going through assistants like this."

"Perhaps if you were a little more easygoing-"

"I put up with her foolishness for two damn weeks. Her tardiness, her inefficiency, her smoking, and her lying."

"Smoking? She didn't say anything about that."

"You know we have a strict policy and I trust you to find persons who can adhere to my policies. Please ensure that the next one you send has at least an average brain and some skills, and if she is going to lie, at least she can be convincing with it."

"We are sorry that it has come to this, sir. We will send someone over on Monday morning."

"See that you do. Maybe number twenty will do the trick."

"Twenty-seven." I heard the humor in her tone and could picture her with pursed lips concealing her smile.

"Pardon?"

"This will be the twenty-seventh assistant we're sending to you, Mr. Vance."

I whistled softly. "That has got to be some sort of record."

She chuckled. "It certainly is. But you are a hard man to please and we are running out of options. We may have to start recycling from the beginning of the list. I wonder if Lorraine-"

"Hell no. Not Lorraine. She didn't last three days! And I can think of a few others I don't wish to encounter ever again, whether in this life or the next. Find me someone good, once and for all. Make sure number twenty-seven is the one."

"I'm about to speak with her. I'm sure she will be the right fit. Young. Bright. Efficient. Doesn't smoke or drink either."

"She sounds like an angel, Shirley."

"You would make the most angelic trade in their halos for horns, Axel."

I burst out laughing at that. "I look forward to meeting this angel on Monday morning, bright and early."

"I look forward to sending her to you. And I have a good feeling about her."

"I hope your good feeling is the right feeling."

"We'll just have to wait and see, won't we. We'll talk."

I disconnected the call and sighed. I thought about when my woes with finding an assistant had begun. Why on earth Beatrice had decided after twenty years with the company and working with me for eight of them, that she had to up and retire and move to an entirely different country was beyond me. She was like a second mother to me and had been one of the people who had enough backbone to work with me. When she told me of her retirement plans, I had thought she was joking at first. But when the agency sent her replacement and she was training her, it hit home.

But it was not until Beatrice had left that I realized just how efficient she was. The first girl had lasted for three weeks before I got a call from Shirley saying that Stacey, I think that was her name, had reached out to them for mediation. Now here I was, twenty-five girls after her and looking to meet number twenty-seven in the next forty-eight hours.

As I packed up my desk and headed to the parking lot, I prayed that she would at least last through Christmas.

5

LISA

I tried not to eavesdrop as I sat waiting for the agency director, Shirley Adams, to finish her phone call.

When I had woken up this morning with the intention of calling the agency to ask them if there were any openings, I had been shocked to hear that they had been about to call me as the director needed to speak with me. They had said any time between five and six was good. It didn't sound good to me. Why would they be having meetings after working hours? Nevertheless, I took Nora up on her promise and left her playing a game of scrabble with my father an hour ago. When I got to the agency office, it became apparent why this meeting would be after hours. There were ten of us waiting to be seen. I was number seven. I watched as the first three went in and one by one they came out, their faces long and an envelope in hand. They were ushered away from the rest of us who were waiting. I couldn't shake the feeling that something was wrong. When number six came out and I saw traces of tears in her eyes, I knew I needed to leave. But somehow my ass was glued to the chair and my feet were numb.

"Lisa Mulligan?"

The secretary had looked over her glasses at me and I had nodded. My legs wobbled as I followed her down the corridor and into the corner office where Ms. Adams sat waiting. The last time I had seen her was at our orientation almost two years ago. I took the seat she offered.

"Thank you for making the time to come in, Lisa. I'll get right to the point. We have been conducting a review of our personnel and we realized that you haven't taken any jobs for a few months now."

"My father is still quite ill and I'm not able to leave him. But, I'm in-"

"Hold on." She had held up her finger as her phone rang.

"Good evening, Mr. Vance. It's Shirley. I was just about to call you, sir."

My heart raced and my stomach did somersaults at the ominous tone with which Shirley had started the conversation. I remembered the six girls who had entered ahead of me. I glanced at her desk as she continued to talk on the phone. My name was clearly marked on the envelope in front of her. I gulped. I pressed my hands together and closed my eyes tightly, praying that it was not what I thought it was. I looked up as she chuckled.

"It certainly is. But you are a hard man to please and we are running out of options. We may have to start recycling from the beginning of the list. I wonder if Lorraine-"

She laughed loudly, clearly amused by whatever the person on the other end was saying. Her eyes fixed on me and she smiled gently.

"I'm about to speak with her. I'm sure she will be the right fit. Young. Bright. Efficient. Doesn't smoke or drink either."

She threw her head back and laughed once again.

"You would make the most angelic trade in their halos for horns, Axel."

I could hear a man laughing on the other end of the line. Shirley kept smiling at me.

"I look forward to sending her to you. And I have a good feeling about her."

She twirled her pen as the person responded.

"We'll just have to wait and see, won't we. We'll talk." She hung up the phone and looked at me.

"Tell me something, Lisa. Have we ever sent you to VSS?"

I shook my head slowly. "I usually work from home."

"From home?" She scanned some documents in a folder. "Oh! You're *that* Lisa. How is your father?"

"As I was saying earlier, he's still not well, but I do have some help with him now and can be more available for jobs. I called this morning to ask if there were any vacancies and was told to come in for a meeting with you instead."

"Oh! I see. It's good to hear that you will have some help with your dad, because I do have a vacancy that has just come up actually."

She pushed her chair away from the desk and walked over to a filing cabinet in the corner. She withdrew a file and came back to her seat.

"It helps that you've never worked with VSS either."

"I beg your pardon, but what is VSS?"

"Oh. Vance Security Solutions. They're one of our biggest clients. That was the CEO just now. He needs a personal assistant. The one we sent a few weeks ago was dismissed."

I swallowed. "Dismissed?"

"She violated company policy. By the way, you don't smoke or drink, do you?"

I shook my head. "No. I don't."

"Excellent. What about time management? Do you have a tardiness problem?"

I thought about the many times I had shown up with my father for his appointments at least half an hour early. And even for this meeting, I had been waiting since four thirty. I shook my head. "I'm always on time."

"Wonderful. Your skills are secretarial. Have you ever been someone's personal assistant before?"

"If you count my father-"

"Great. You have experience. How would you rate your efficiency?"

"My efficiency?"

"How well do you get things done?"

"I-I'm not sure I would be the best judge of that."

"Don't you have to set appointments for your father, pick up medication, keep track of his vitals etcetera?"

"Yes. But-"

"You're efficient. Can you start Monday morning?"

"For how long? You said the last assistant was two weeks?"

"This is actually an open vacancy which we have been trying to fill for almost a year."

I gawked. "Is something wrong?"

She smirked. "Let's just say that Axel is not the easiest person to work with sometimes."

I sensed a red flag if ever there was one. She seemed to sense my hesitation and barreled on with the conversation.

"Before you say no, I want you to think about a few things first. You do know that this was an exit interview right? Let's face it, Lisa. You haven't been taking any jobs.

When you don't take jobs, we don't earn a commission. We were going to let you go. But as you have indicated, your time is more available now. We need you to take this job."

"And if I choose to pass on it and wait for another vacancy?"

Silently she pushed the envelope across the desk towards me. It looked like a knife being thrust into my heart.

"It's December. There are no vacancies. Everyone wants to make a few extra dollars for the holidays."

I gulped. I bowed my head silently. "And if I choose to take the job?"

She pulled out a notepad and scribbled something on it. She pushed it across to me and I looked down. My mouth dropped open. I looked at her with wide eyes.

"Is that for real? That's what I would earn for a month?"

"No dear. That's what you would earn for two weeks. So do the math-"

"Shit! I mean – I'm sorry. I didn't mean to – but that's a lot of money!"

"Like I said. They are one of our best clients. And it *is* a clear vacancy."

"But can they pay that much!? There has to be a catch somewhere."

"No catch. That is a legitimate salary."

"You said the CEO is not the easiest person to work with. What's wrong with him?"

"I'm not going to beat around the bush. He is a bit of a tyrant. He's ex-military so quite exacting in how he likes things to be done. Not everyone has been able to live up to his standards."

"What's the longest anyone has ever stayed with him?"

"A month."

"A *month*!?"

"But a month on that salary is like three months. What is the worst that can happen? You last for a month and walk away with money as though you worked for three months. And I'm sure you need that money, dear. Your father's medical bills must be high."

I sat silent, looking at the figure on the paper. I was already calculating the dent just a month's salary could make in our bills. Imagine if I lasted longer. But the eerie feeling of working with an unpleasant person made me think it would not be an easy feat.

"So?"

I looked up at Shirley. "So?"

"Are you going to take the envelope on the left or the notepad on the right."

I looked down. On the one hand, I would be in a worse financial position than I was in currently. On the other hand, I could make a dent in the mounting expenses. I just had to last a month. It could not be that bad.

"I'll take the job."

"Excellent!" She reached out and pressed the intercom on her desk.

"Amanda, please prepare a VSS contract for Lisa. I'm sending her out now." She released the button and stood. I took it as my cue to stand also.

"Thanks again for taking this job. It's saving me a lot of time that I don't have right now to find a replacement. The last one left just this evening."

I smiled ruefully. "I hope I won't be in a similar position in two weeks."

"And even if you are, I'll have a little more wiggle room to find a replacement."

I blanched at her lack of confidence in me.

"Amanda will give you the details."

As I walked out, I looked back to see her move my envelope to the bottom of the pile. I didn't even look at the next girl who walked in after me.

I followed Amanda into a room beside Shirley's office. She looked me up and down over her glasses as she told me to take a seat.

"You're a brave one."

"I beg your pardon?"

"Did Shirley tell you about VSS?"

"She did."

"But did she tell you about the CEO? Axel Vance? The meanest boss ever?"

"She-she hinted at it a bit. Is he truly that awful? She said that he has a problem with his assistants."

"That's sugar-coating it. He's a downright beast! Did she tell you how many assistants he's been through?"

"No."

"Twenty-six. In less than a year. You're number twenty-seven."

"Twenty-six? But if the longest anyone has ever stayed is a month, it means some of them lasted for a week?"

"I think the current record for the shortest stay is three days."

"No wonder the salary is high. He's trying to bribe them to stay."

"I wouldn't call it a bribe. The task is genuinely worth the money, even outside of the CEO being a tyrant. And it does come with perks that are not included in the salary."

"Perks like?"

"Well, if he has to travel overseas, his assistant goes with him, all expenses paid. If he has an important meeting at some swanky restaurant, his assistant goes with him to take notes. She eats free of course. She has access to his home, his car, his credit card. No one has been able to last more than a few weeks to truly experience some of those perks, though. But Beatrice was living the life."

"Beatrice?"

"His previous assistant who he inherited with the company. She retired a little over a year ago. She had to give us a job description along with a thorough list of expected duties. It's a fantastic position. If only someone can manage to hold on to it long enough to reap the benefits. Let's hope twenty-seven is your lucky number. Here's the job information as well as a document explaining the company's policy on a number of things. Fiona, that's the one who left today, came in here reeking of cigarette smoke. That is strictly prohibited, among other things. Take the weekend to look through everything. In the meantime, sign here please."

She handed me a printed sheet. I quickly scanned the contract formally documenting the terms of my employment to Vance Security Services in an open vacancy. I noted that the salary discussed with Shirley was the salary in the contract for the stipulated two weeks. At the end of a three-month probation period, there would be an increase.

I signed on the dotted line and handed the paper back to her. She signed and stamped it, then photocopied it. She handed the original to me and filed the copy. She took out a manila envelope and handed it to me. I placed the documents into it then slipped it into my purse.

"Let me just drive a few points home. Be on time. Be early if possible. But one of his biggest pet peeves is tardiness. Be neat in your appearance. There is no dress code but be professional in your attire and appearance. You already know smoking is a no-no. Be proactive. Think ahead of him and figure out what he will need before he asks. Stay organized. Keep his appointments in order and keep on top of them. Try not to get on his wrong side or it will be all down-hill from there. We're counting on you bringing this one home for us, number twenty-seven."

"Sounds like a tall order."

"At least try and last long enough to collect for the first two weeks and give us time to find number twenty-eight. Just remember: be on time."

I blanched for the second time that evening at some-one's apparent lack of confidence in my capabilities of keeping this job.

I allowed her to show me out and was shocked to see that it was already dark. How long had I been in there?

As I trudged to the bus stop, I reflected on the turn the meeting had taken. The envelope in my purse was evidence that I had not dreamed it all.

As I waited for my bus, I checked the map app on my phone for the exact location of VSS in relation to my house. I was forty-five minutes away. Be on time. The words kept echoing in my head. I needed to use the weekend to figure out the best bus and route to take on Monday morning to ensure I would be on time.

6

AXEL

I checked my backpack once more before locking up the house and arming the alarm. The trip was an impromptu one, but I just felt the need to unwind. I climbed into my truck and took the route that would lead me to the mountains. It was cold but I had the window slightly cracked. I didn't mind the bracing chill in the air. As a matter of fact, I needed it.

The three-hour drive went by and it was a little after eleven when I pulled up to the gateway. I found the control panel and punched in the code. The gate slid open and I drove through. I waited for it to close behind me before I continued my journey. A mile up the driveway brought me to a dead end. Or so it seemed. I pressed a button on the dashboard and the 'trees' slid apart, revealing the continuation of the driveway. I drove through and again waited for the entrance to be concealed once more. I rounded a corner and the cabin lay in front of me. The front was awash with lights from the solar light posts.

I turned off the engine and sat for a while, allowing the silence to sweep over me. I stepped out and pulled my jacket around me as the freezing mountain air ripped through me. I grabbed my backpack and headed inside. The first order of business was to get a fire going which I did in short order. The cabin heated up quickly. I opened the doors of the rooms to allow the heat to spread throughout the space.

Next, I had a shower to wash away the grime of the day. As I allowed the hot water to beat down on my body, I sighed pleasurably. There was something to be said about bathing with water heated by the sun. It was the same feeling I got sitting in front of a wood fire versus an electric heat source. There was something about the naturalness of it all that just seeped into the bones.

I reveled in the shower for a few minutes before reluctantly switching off the water. I reached for a clean towel and wrapped it around my waist. I ran my fingers through the stubble of a beard as I examined my reflection. I was contemplating letting my hair grow out, but the military man in me couldn't wrap my mind around anything but a neatly groomed head. The beard was an experiment which seemed to be working. After I had gotten past the first few itchy days of stubble, it had started to grow in nicely. I might just keep this for a while.

I pulled on sweatpants and a hoodie before heading to the kitchen. The last time I was here had been summer and I always left a stash of non-perishable goods behind. The supply was running low, though. I made a mental note to replenish the cupboards the next time I came. The freezer still had some of the fish I had caught the last time I was here. This was one of the beautiful things about having solar energy: everything kept running for free. I took out a packet to thaw for breakfast before opening a can of soup on the stove top.

I took the bowl over to the window along with one of the

packets of crackers I had brought with me. The simple meal was filling. As I sipped and munched, I looked out over the dark backyard and into the night sky. The stars filled the sky. I felt as though I could reach out and touch them, they were so bright.

My mind was blank. I didn't want to think about anything tonight. I simply wanted to breathe. I closed my eyes and did just that for a few moments. I felt the stress of the past week and months begin to dissipate. I needed to get away more often.

I washed the bowl and checked the windows and doors. The fire was crackling away. I added a few more pieces of wood before heading to the main bedroom. The electric blanket I had turned on before my shower made the bed nice and toasty. I found clean sheets in the closet and made the bed. As I lay back and closed my eyes, my relaxation felt complete. A huge yawn escaped me and my eyes began to burn with the need for sleep. I rolled over and did just that.

When I woke up the next morning, the sun was shining brightly into the room. But as bright as the sun seemed to be, I knew it was cold outside. I stretched and did some floor exercises before heading to the kitchen. The fish was thawed. I rustled up some biscuits and slid them into the oven. I got some hot chocolate going while I fried up the fish with some powdered seasoning. I enjoyed the hearty breakfast and packed some of the leftovers for lunch. I took a moment to check my fishing gear before loading up my stuff.

I zipped my jacket before stepping out onto the back porch. The cold mountain air greeted me. I walked past the in-ground swimming pool which was covered and headed towards a trail entrance at the bottom of the yard. Three years ago, my realtor had told me about this steal of a property that had come into his hands. He hadn't wanted to advertise it until he had shown it to me. The second I'd set eyes on the river and the waterfall, I was sold.

It had taken me just a year to build the three-bedroom ranch style cabin along with the swimming pool on one acre of the property. I'd built it a few miles in from the main road as well as implemented all the security features. Anyone who came here, often thought the property was an idyllic getaway with spectacular views of the mountains. But the surrounding fifteen acres were an untouched paradise. And I chose to keep it this way. The hiking trails often came as a shock when anyone ventured beyond the swimming pool. And it was one of these trails I now took to get to my favorite fishing spot. The bracing air kept me moving as I hiked along the trail. Soon the sound of water reached my ears. I couldn't help the excitement I felt as I rounded the bend and found the river running beneath me. I was transported back to the first time I ever went fishing with my father one summer.

I found my usual spot on a rock and soon had my line cast.

It had to have been close to twenty-five or so years ago that my father had taken me on a father-son fishing trip. My excitement had been endless as we had sailed out to sea on his yacht. I'd landed my first fish within an hour, and I was hooked.

Over the years, that was one of the things I could always count on with him. No matter how busy he was with his globe-trotting, he always made time for me and our fishing trips in the summer. It was on these trips I got to see a different side of my father. This man was a far-removed version of the billionaire he was in his other life. This man could lift a finger for himself. This man could wear ragged clothes. And though I liked the wealthy Axel Vance, Senior, I loved the simple Dad.

I sighed as I thought about how much I missed him now. Gone were the little talks we always had on these trips. It was on one of these trips that I told him I had done 'it' for the first time with a girl at school. He had laughed and asked me how I felt about it and told me to check the back of his sock drawer for some 'insurance'.

It had been on a fishing trip that I had told him of my desire to enter the military, not only because I loved it, but also because I wanted to hone my skills in the security field to enter the family business with him. He had looked at me puzzled and asked me why I would want a failing business. I'd told him it didn't matter, as long as I got to work with him.

That wish had not come to pass, though.

I thought about how quickly everything had happened after the funeral and the reading of the will. As I had expected, I inherited the company and enough money to live for a hundred years without working if I chose. Everyone had expected me to sell the company. Instead, I had appointed a family friend as CEO while I went on my duties overseas. Brian Chambers was the son of my father's personal friend and business contemporary. They were all in the security business and so I thought it was the best move to have someone who knew the business at the helm while I was gone. What a mistake that had been.

When I had gotten back from overseas, I had jumped in with both feet. It had been touch and go for a few years as I'd struggled to deal with employee issues. I also had to rebuild the clientele and their trust in our brand. I refused to believe that my father was such a poor businessman. But after years of wading through the mess, I realized his heart had simply not been in the business. He was an investment guru, not a security professional. But that was where I came into the picture.

I had rebuilt the brand almost from the ground up. I paid off debts to suppliers, reviewed staff and cut and hired accordingly, and changed the location of the business office. I also had the logo and uniform redesigned. Then, with a team of expert marketers, I put the VSS name out there.

The response had been slow at first. But then we started to pick up traction. And growth had begun.

As I looked back over the last ten years, from the moment I knew the business was mine until now, I felt a deep sense of gratitude for whatever favor the universe had chosen to bestow on me. How many thirty-two, almost thirty-three-year-old people could boast of a military career and a successful business? From the outside looking in, anyone would think I had it all. But wealth and success were not the only ingredients for a happy life.

I screwed my face up as I thought about my mother's not so subtle hints about my settling down. And I knew why. Bethany Chambers, the daughter of that family friend, was still single and waiting for me according to my mother.

Bethany and I had practically grown up together in a sense. She had spent most of her school life in boarding schools overseas but holidays were always a blast when she was home. I had never viewed her as anything more than a sister, so it came as a shock when my mother presented her as a potential wife. I had balked at the thought and still did. Bethany simply was not the type of woman I wanted as a wife.

There was nothing wrong with her per se. She was a stunning woman: jet black hair and green eyes with curves in all the right places. She was a good conversationalist and knew as much about the security business as I did. But there was no chemistry. Despite my mother's pleas to give her a chance, I refused. In one of our heated debates on the matter, I had point blank asked her why she should marry for love and then turn around and expect me to marry for business. It had shut her up for a while. But now and then, she still tried to slip Bethany into the equation.

I felt a tug on the line and snapped into action. The fish was a fighter but I held on, determined to land it. It flopped onto the river bank and I ran to it, quickly dispatching it and placing it in my cooler. I baited the line and cast it once more. I looked up at the cold blue sky.

I thought about the email I had seen just before I left the office yesterday evening. Guardsman group was making yet another offer to buy VSS. This would be their third offer this year. And they were not the only ones looking to bring VSS underneath their wings. The moment VSS had made a turnaround for the better, the offers had started rolling in with all kinds of incentives. I had felt flattered by the offers and also encouraged. It meant I was doing something right. Chambers had been the first offer, using the angle as a friend of the family to form an alliance between the companies. I felt it was on this premise that Bethany was being pushed at me as well. But my mother forgot I had inherited her backbone on all counts.

It wasn't that I didn't want to settle down one day. But right now, I was hyper-focused on the business. I had some exciting ideas for the new year to take VSS to the next level. I would give it a few years to solidify as a business model. Maybe then I could turn my attention to settling down.

I sighed at the thought of a relationship. I'd been serious when I told my mother I would marry only for love. I had watched her and my father's love for each other over the years. And I had also watched some of their contemporaries whose relationships were rotten. They remained together simply because of the financial benefits. But I was determined no amount of money could coerce me to be miserable for the rest of my life. I would find the right woman at the right time. And when I did, I would not let her go. I would make her mine. We would have a child or children and go on family trips or vacations together. There would be no doubt that I was married and a father. And I would dote on my family, no matter where we were and what we were doing. I would have a daughter and we would have a special bond and our little inside jokes that only we knew.

Instantly, my thoughts flashed back to the night I had been on my way home for my father's funeral and I had stopped at the diner.

The father and daughter had that sort of bond. I remembered how the two blonde heads had met across the table, followed by whispers and laughter. That was the kind of bond I wanted with my child. I wondered what had happened to them after that fateful night when their wife and mother's life had been snuffed out so senselessly. Were they still close? How had they weathered that period of their lives? Had the little girl grown into a beautiful woman? Was she still a daddy's girl?

I thought about how glad I had been to be there at the right time to snatch her from danger. If I could have, I would have held her all night to protect her from what was happening inside the diner. None of my missions overseas had impacted me as much as those few minutes when I had run out of the diner in pursuit of the murderer and would-be kidnapper. If and when I had a daughter, I would hold her forever and keep her from the ills of this world. I could only hope that the father and daughter had found peace and had moved on with their lives.

Another bite on the line tugged my thoughts back to the present. This fish was not as big as the first but would still do nicely for either dinner or for taking it back with me to the city.

The rest of the morning passed in peace and quiet. I polished off the remaining fish and biscuit I had made for breakfast. The day had warmed up a bit but it was still quite cold. I called it quits after three more fish and headed back to the cabin. I expertly cleaned the fish before separating the ones to take back from the ones to eat and leave behind.

I took a nap which was not something I usually had the time to do. But I considered this a mini vacation and so anything could be done. My only regret was that the temperature was not conducive to a swim in either the pool or the river. I made a mental note to look into getting the pool heated in the coming year.

After dinner, I took out my laptop and tethered it to my phone to access the internet. I found an old movie and indulged with a few beers as I watched. It had felt like ages since I had done anything like this. It seemed as though all I did these days was work. But it was with a goal in mind. If everything came together as I had envisioned, VSS would be moving to the next level in the security industry. I would need to be twice as efficient as before and my staff would need to be running at the same pace. There would be no room for stragglers.

I sighed in frustration as I thought about my need to be efficient. The year had not been kind to me as it pertained to personal assistants. Twenty-six. In less than a year. This had to be some kind of losing streak record or something. But come Monday morning, I would meet number twenty-seven. I made up my mind to work with whoever it was. I had to break this streak somehow. At the very least, I hoped she would last beyond Christmas which was less than three weeks away.

On Sunday afternoon, I cleaned and locked up the cabin once more, checking to ensure that no trace of food was left unattended. I re-armed the security cameras along the driveways as I left. The drive back to the city felt a bit depressing. As always, after some time away, I was loath to return. The only reason I didn't move to the cabin was the fact I needed to be in the office daily. But who knew? Maybe one day I would move to working from home and make the commute only once a week. Maybe the house in the city would become the overnight spot. Who knew what the future held? One thing I did know was I was going to try my best to make it through the rest of the month and pray to the heavens and every part of the universe that the assistant would make it as well.

7

LISA

"Dad? Are you sure you'll be okay with me gone? If you don't want me to go, I'll call and turn it down right now."

"I'll be fine, my dear."

"But you need me."

"You said that you had made arrangements with Nora, right?"

"Yes, but-"

My father reached a trembling hand across the dining table and covered my hand with his.

"Lisa. It's a good salary. We need the money. I know you said this boss is some sort of tyrant. But you're not a coward. So, what's the real reason you're hesitating now?"

I took a deep breath and sighed. When I had come home on Friday evening and told Dad and Nora the good news about the job with the unbelievable salary, I'd been on cloud nine. But now, Sunday evening, the clouds cleared and I had plummeted to reality. Could I admit that it wasn't the job that scared me? Could I admit that I didn't want to leave my father? It was not a case of not trusting

Nora. I did. But there was still a part of me that felt as though I was deserting him in his time of need.

"Lisa?" he stroked my hand softly and I looked up to find him staring at me. "What is it, dear?"

I chewed my bottom lip.

"I just feel as though I'm abandoning you."

"Far from it, my dear. It's not as though you're leaving me on my own for the day. Nora will be here. I promise to behave." He chuckled and winked, and I couldn't help but smile. He rubbed my hand once more before withdrawing it and picking up his spoon. He took a sip of the soup I had prepared for him.

"We do need the money. If the salary is what it is, it will go a long way into putting a dent into these bills."

I looked at him sharply and he smiled sadly.

"Just because you don't tell me, doesn't mean I don't know, Lisa. And it's okay, dear. This job may just be the start of something good. And maybe this last round of treatments will do the job as well. Go to work. I'll be fine with Nora."

I looked at him for a few moments before nodding.

"Okay."

That night after I had put him to bed, I went through my closet once more. The pickings were slim. But Friday I had pulled out a few outfits and had enough to mix and match to get me through a work week. I spent some time ironing the skirts, slacks, blouses and the one dress I had found. I then went about finding tights and other undergarment layers for the week. I pulled out my one pair of formal boots and gave it a good polish and shine. I put away all the outfits except the one I would be wearing in the morning.

Afterwards, I sat in front of the vanity and practiced a few hairstyles until I settled on a high bun. I could wrap my ponytail and secure it with pins in less than five minutes in the morning. I gave my eyebrows a quick pluck as well. I was not a make-up person apart from Chapstick. But now that I was a working girl, I might have to invest in some makeup.

I went to the kitchen and checked the refrigerator. I wasn't sure how lunch would go so I would need to make a sandwich in the morning as well. The last thing I did before going to bed was to set my alarm and put my phone to charge.

I was up a full ten minutes before the alarm went off the next morning. I rushed to shower before starting breakfast. I needed to be at work by eight-thirty and planned to leave home by seven-thirty. Nora would be there by that time as well. The journey was forty-five minutes but this would give me a full fifteen minutes to spare.

"Dad? Are you awake yet? Are you ready to shower?"

"Yes, dear."

We went through his morning routine. I kept my eye on the clock. I had more than enough time to spare.

I got him dressed and seated with his breakfast while I went to do my hair and get dressed for work. By the time I went back to the kitchen, it was seven twenty-five. I was in the middle of swallowing toast while making a sandwich when I heard a crash behind me. I spun around to find my father's cereal bowl on the floor as he leaned against the table. There was leftover cereal all over and the bottom of his track suit was soaked.

"Dad!"

"I'm sorry, dear. I was just trying to help by taking the bowl to the sink."

I stepped over the mess and took him by the arm.

"It's okay, Dad. Let's get you changed."

"No! You'll be late."

"I have enough time. Come on."

I helped him back to his room and soon had a fresh pair of pants on him. I then helped him back to the living room before going to the kitchen. I was in the middle of wiping the floor when Nora came into the apartment.

"What are you still doing here, Lisa? You're going to be late! Give me that! Go!"

She grabbed the mop from me and I grabbed my purse. It was not until I was halfway to the bus stop that I remembered the half-made sandwich on the counter. I would just have to grin and bear the hunger today. It was nearly seven forty-five by the time I got on the bus. I felt relieved to know that I would still make it on time. But that relief was short-lived when I saw the bumper-to-bumper traffic. With every stoplight and screeching of the brakes, I felt my heart sink. The last thing I had been told was to be on time. And now here I was, fifteen minutes away at eight twenty-five. I felt bitter disappointment rise within me. And if I were not this close already, I would have gone back home. But I was not a coward. The least that I could do was show up, though late. Maybe I could explain why I was late and make amends by being on time forever.

I scrambled off the bus and all but ran around the corner to the building where VSS sat on the seventh floor. I took a deep breath as I entered the reception area. The receptionist looked at me over her glasses.

"Good morning. Can I help you?"

"I'm the new personal assistant for the CEO of VSS."

"You do know you're late, right?"

"I was stuck in traffic."

"Try telling that to Vance. Seventh floor. Use the third elevator from the left and the code two-seven-PA. By the end of the day, you'll have your access code. If you last the day."

I felt my cheeks burn as I thanked her and ran to the

elevator. It slid open immediately and I was whisked to the seventh floor. What kind of clout did VSS have to have an elevator all of their own? The doors slid open and a few steps brought me to a security panel. I punched in the code and the door buzzed open. I found myself facing a desk in an outer office. A bored looking woman looked at me.

"The new PA I assume?"

"Yes."

"You're late."

"I know. I had-"

"The new PA's here."

I shut my mouth as I was cut off abruptly by the receptionist speaking into the intercom.

"She's late," another woman replied. "He seems a bit mellow this morning. Let me tell him she's here."

"Have a seat dear. Did you take a bus or a cab?"

"The bus."

"How much was your fare?"

"I beg your pardon?"

"The least we can do is give you fare to get back home."

"But, I don't understand."

"You're almost twenty minutes late, dear. You have no idea who Axel Vance is, do you?"

I shook my head helplessly, my heart dropping. "I don't."

"How much is your fare?"

The intercom interrupted before I could speak.

"He says to send her in, Rosie."

The woman named Rosie raised her eyebrows as she looked at me.

"Okay."

The intercom went silent and Rosie pointed at the double doors.

"Straight through those doors."

She went back to what she was doing and I approached the doors, wondering what I would find beyond. I took a deep breath and pushed them open. I wasn't expecting to find a huge space filled with cubicles. I looked around in a daze. A few people looked at me curiously as I looked around. How the hell was I supposed to find my new boss?

"Are you the new PA?" A deep voice boomed across the space and I looked ahead to see a tall man standing at the only enclosed office in the space.

I nodded.

"This way."

It felt as though I could hear a pin drop as I walked through the office towards the man. With every step, my knees shook. But if I thought I was nervous before, when I got to within a few feet of him and took a good look at him, I felt as though I had fallen down a rabbit hole. I was twelve years old again and looking into the blue eyes of the soldier with the crescent scar against his left eye. It was him! My mouth fell open. Then I caught hold of myself.

"Good morning, Mr. Vance, sir. I'm very sorry to be late. I'm a very punctual person but I had a slight mishap this morning. It won't happen again."

He stared at me and I felt dozens of eyes piercing my back as the office seemed to take a collective breath. He nodded and stepped aside, inviting me into the office. I heard a few gasps as the door closed behind me. My heart raced as I looked at the man I had thought about just a few days ago. Had my desperate cry for his help somehow screamed through the universe and resulted in an unusual chain of events leading up to this very moment?

I kept staring at him. Maybe I was wrong. But what were the odds of another man with a military background having the same deep blue eyes and a crescent scar?

"Have a seat, Ms.?"

I took the seat he offered. "Mulligan. It's Lisa Mulligan." I looked at him closely as I told him my name. That night I had told him my name as well. Did he recognize me? His blank expression told me he didn't.

He pushed a diary across the desk towards me.

"That has a list of all my appointments to be made this week. You need to call and confirm times and dates and keep me informed of any changes. That is just for starters. Get through that by the end of the day. That will be all. Your desk is the first one on the right outside this office."

He turned his attention to the computer screen in front of him and I felt dismissed. Without a word, I left the office. I stood at the door for a little while looking around the office space. I saw the empty desk and took a seat. I looked up to find a woman at the desk across from me. She was staring at me blankly.

"You're staying?" she asked, surprise lacing every word.

"He gave me this book and told me to make appointments by the end of the day."

Her eyebrows shot up, disappearing beneath her curly bangs.

"Well!"

Without a word, she bent her head over her desk and got back to her tasks. I looked around and saw a few people staring at me. I smiled and waved slightly, receiving a few shocked stares in return. Without another word, I got busy.

The diary was a mess. And so were the drawers. I hunted through the mass of papers until I found a somewhat clean notepad. I made a list of all the appointments and the contact numbers and went about making the calls one by one. By ten-thirty, I had them all set. I made the notations on post-its and stapled them into the relevant pages of the diary.

Next, I turned my attention to the drawers. I went through each piece of paper, and quickly identified a system for organizing them. I was elbows deep in the middle drawer when I smelled something divine. I looked up to find the woman from the desk across from me holding out a cup of coffee.

"I'm Lola."

I smiled. "Lisa. Thanks."

"Rosie takes our lunch orders."

"Rosie?"

Lola pointed her thumb at the main door. "You met her this morning."

"Oh!"

"We get lunch from a few places around here."

I felt my cheeks color. "I had planned to bring a sandwich with me this morning but forgot it. I don't have enough cash. But this coffee will hold me until I get home. Thanks."

"Oh. Lunch is paid for by management."

I blinked in shock. "What?"

"VSS foots our lunch bill, within a certain price range of course, but he doesn't skimp. Transportation is also covered as well as overtime."

"Are you serious?"

She smiled. "Get your order to Rosie. Nice having you on board, Lisa. I've been watching you. I think you'll make it."

"Thanks for the vote of confidence."

I went to give Rosie my lunch order and found an array of menus from which to choose. I went for Chinese and headed back to my desk. At about one, I followed Lola to the break room which was a floor above us. I was taken aback at the expansive space which was divided into two areas. Lola and I took a seat by the window in the space set up with tables and chairs for eating.

"We get forty-five minutes for lunch and ten minutes in the afternoon for coffee again."

"Thanks for letting me know all of this, Lola."

"Okay. Check with Rodney in HR before you leave so he can give you your access code."

"HR?"

"The row of cubicles in the corner by the water cooler. Rodney is the third cubicle on the right."

"Okay. Thanks."

We talked a little while longer and she gave me a crash course on VSS. Before we knew it, lunch break was over. I visited the restroom before heading over to find Rodney. He had me complete a few forms and information sheets before issuing me with a code to access the office.

"Welcome aboard, Lisa. We can tell that you're different and we really do hope that you last."

I put on a brave smile but inside I was a nervous wreck. I hadn't seen my boss since he'd dismissed me. Could it be that hard to work for him?

I went back to my desk and completed the paperwork I had started. With Lola's help, I found stationery and soon had the papers filed and labeled. She showed me where a laptop was kept in the cabinet that I could use to do any typing that was needed. Finally, she went through the process of preparing contracts for clients which would be my only typing task.

At about five, I realized the office started to empty. I had finished all my tasks long ago but was conscious of the fact that I had been late that morning. I kept staring at the closed door. What should I do now? Did I knock and tell him I was leaving? Did I wait for him to come to me?

I looked at the clock as it crept closer to five-thirty. I had just gotten up the nerve to knock and stood at the door with my hand raised when it swung open. I swallowed nervously, clutching the diary between my hands.

"I-I made all the appointments."

"Took you long enough to make a few calls."

I frowned at his abrupt tone and squared my shoulders.

"I was finished before midday."

"Let's see it."

I held out the diary to him and watched as he flipped through. He frowned as he flicked at the post-its.

"What's this?"

"The pages are a bit messy and unkempt. There's no way to figure anything out among all those other scribbles."

He looked at me and it took everything in me not to tremble.

"I-I also found some papers in the drawers and organized them. Lola showed me where to find everything I needed. I've also been to HR and completed my employment forms."

"I see." He flicked his wrist and checked his watch. "Everyone is almost gone. It's past the end of the work day."

"Well, sir, I was late this morning. I won't rob you of your time."

He stared at me once more and I couldn't help but feel like an insect under a microscope.

"I see." He closed the diary and handed it back to me. Without a word, he went back into his office.

I waited until five-thirty before I picked up my purse and headed out of the office. As I waited for my bus, I received a surprise phone call from Shirley. When she asked how the first day had gone and I told her that he had allowed me to stay though I had been late, her response had been that it was a good thing I had a pretty face. Even after the call ended, I mused on what she had said. What had she meant by that? Was I to assume that I had been pardoned because I was pretty? Whatever the reason was, I had been pardoned. And I was glad. I was glad I had a job when I needed it most. And I was going to do everything to keep it for as long as I could. At the very least, I could only hope not to get on my boss' wrong side. But so far so good.

My thoughts turned to more critical matters as I sat by a window seat, watching traffic go by in the streets. Was Axel Vance my soldier savior from that night so long ago? Only time could answer that question.

8

AXEL

I sat staring at the papers in front of me without really seeing them. Instead, my thoughts were on the new PA.

This morning when I had seen eight-thirty and she was nowhere to be seen, I had decided to simply upgrade Lola's responsibility. She had been with the company for three years. She knew the requirements. It would have been easier to replace her as a secretary. But imagine my shock when Lola told me the new girl had arrived and they needed to know if they should send her away. My staff knew me well. But I had further shocked myself when, without hesitation, I had told them to send her into the office. It wouldn't do having the staff become too familiar with my ways. I knew this had thrown them for a loop all day. And it amused me.

As I had stood at the door watching the little slip of a girl walk through the office, I had begun processing the advertisement for the position of secretary I would be posting in the papers. I had been brusque and cold in my conversation. But she had flipped the script on me.

All day I had waited for her to knock on the door. But

she had remained silent. From time to time I checked the office cameras and saw her working away at the desk. By that afternoon, I had forgotten all about her as I fielded call after call from clients and other potential clients who were seeking to renew contracts or enter contracts.

Just now, I'd stepped out of the office with the intention of putting all the tasks into a file for Lola tomorrow. And Lisa Mulligan had shocked me.

I looked at the stack of papers in front of me. So she had completed her tasks quickly today, huh. Tomorrow I would have much more in store.

Without a second thought, I went to her desk and stopped short. The usually bare space now had a filing tray marked with 'in' and 'out'. I couldn't remember ever seeing that tray since Beatrice left. I placed the papers in the 'in' section and went back to my office. Let's see what she would do with those tomorrow.

The next morning, I walked into the office at seven-thirty. I made it a point of duty to be the first one there and the last one to leave. I didn't require it of my employees. But it was only fair to display the behavior I wished for them to emulate.

I pulled up the office camera as I sipped my coffee and bit into my breakfast sandwich. I watched as one by one employees came into the office. Most of them relaxed for a while before work started. This was their norm. But I wasn't at all interested in them this morning. Nope. I was looking for a little blonde head.

At approximately eight-fifteen, she entered. She seemed to have brought the sunshine in with her and bathed the office in her warm smile. I watched as she greeted those she passed on her way to her desk. She took off her jacket and hung it on the back of her chair before putting her purse in the bottom drawer. I saw her look at the tray. She picked up the papers and rifled through them. Her fingers moved quickly as she rearranged the documents. She stood and went to the filing cabinet where stationery was kept. Lola must have shown her around. She retrieved a laptop and file jacket and went back to her desk. Then, to my utter amazement, she got to work. I sat back in shock. I checked my watch. It was eight-twenty-three. My PA was at her desk and working a full seven minutes before work began. She was too good to be true. That was it. She was going to take those seven minutes back at one of the breaks or the end of the day. But it never happened.

I was surly as she came to my office to have me sign the contracts she had typed and printed. But I couldn't afford to let her see how her efficiency had thrown me for a loop. I had psyched myself up to grin and bear the new PA until the new year. But she was actually *good*. I didn't know what to do with her. And I dared not relax my guard either.

But by day four, I realized I was robbing myself of peace of mind in worrying about Lisa. When clients called to actually commend me on getting someone so efficient and polite, I had to give credit where it was due. And so, I did the unthinkable. I began to trust Lisa was up to the challenge of being my PA. Thus far, I had given her basic tasks that kept her in the office. Now I was going to turn up the heat and see how she would respond under pressure.

I waited until Friday after she returned from lunch. The instant she was at her desk I stepped outside.

"In here. Now." I spoke quietly but it felt as if it echoed throughout the office.

I saw Lola's eyes go wide as she looked at Lisa, a look of despair on her face. Lisa looked at me and stood immediately. She took the diary with her along with a pen. Usually,

I would have to remind the PA to take their tools whenever I summoned them. Why the hell did she not stop doing this efficiency thing?

I waited for her to slip by me before closing the door. She took a seat while I went to sit on the edge of my desk. I looked down at her, startled by the sincerity in her clear hazel eyes as she looked up at me. For a moment, I almost forgot why I had summoned her. I felt as if I were coming under the spell she seemed to have cast over the office. I watched how people watched her. I watched how they interacted with her. She was a charmer, that much was certain. How else could she have gotten sour Rosie to laugh? I cleared my throat.

"Christmas is coming."

"And the geese are getting fat." Her lips bowed up into a smile and I had to fight back a smile of my own.

"Excuse me?"

"You know the song? 'Christmas is a-coming and the geese are getting fat. Please put a penny-"

I cut her off abruptly. "I usually get the staff gifts. That's your job to get those gifts in time for the office party on the twenty-third."

Her eyebrows went up. "That's eleven days away."

"And?"

She shook her head. "Nothing. What do you usually do?"

"*I* do nothing. You do everything." I reached into my wallet and handed her a card. "This has more than enough funds on it to get gifts for everyone. Do you have a driver's license?"

"I do." She plucked the card from my hand and examined it carefully.

"My car is in the parking garage should you need to move around in the process. That's all."

I slid off the desk and went to my seat, effectively dismissing her. I busied myself with the computer monitor, watching out of the corner of my eyes as she slipped out of my office. Immediately I pulled up the office camera and watched as she placed the card in her purse. I followed her as she went over to HR and slipped into Rodney's cubicle. A few minutes later, she was back at her desk and went on the laptop. For the next few minutes, she typed rapidly then went to collect some papers from the printer. The next thing I knew, she started walking around the office and distributing these papers. Each department she went to left people smiling in her wake. She popped outside to Rosie and I switched cameras just in time to see Rosie's face light up as Lisa gave her a sheet of paper. Now my curiosity was peaked. What on earth was she up to now?

Any further thoughts on Lisa were cut short by a phone call. By the time I got off the call all thoughts had turned to the new request I had gotten. I fielded several other calls that afternoon and it was not until close to six that I packed up my desk. Being a Friday, most people were already gone. As I passed Lisa's desk, I glanced curiously at a sheet of paper sticking out from the tray. I pulled it out and skimmed the information. It was a form of sorts that was titled 'pixie gift list'. What the hell was a pixie gift list? There was a space for the department name then the names of the staff in that department. Each person had up to three slots to fill in a gift item.

I placed the paper back in the tray and left the office.

On Monday morning when I walked into the office, I did a double take. I stepped back outside and checked to make sure I was on the right floor. I was. There, in the corner of the reception area across from Rosie's desk, was a Christmas tree, strung with lights. There was a wreath on the door. Slowly I opened it and found the office strung with several garlands along the cubicles. I looked around, there was no-one there. Then I heard it. Humming.

Quietly I placed my backpack on the floor and followed the sound. I rounded a corner of the cubicles and found a pair of feet sticking out from beneath a desk. The person stopped humming long enough to pull themselves from beneath a desk holding an extension cord. Lisa.

"What the hell are you doing?"

She spun around, her eyes going wide.

"Good morning, Mr. Vance. I thought the office could use a little sprucing up for the holiday. I'm so very glad you're here too. I need your height. It will save me getting a ladder."

Without hesitation, she took me by the elbow and led me over to a corner where a huge wreath was leaning against the wall. She plugged a cord into the extension and the wreath lit up.

"Could you hang that for me please?"

She reached for a hammer and nail and I took them from her wordlessly. With a few taps I had the nail in place and hung the wreath as instructed. She stepped back, her finger on her chin as she examined it.

"Shift it a little to the left please. Turn it just a smidgen counter clockwise."

I did as she instructed and was graced with one of her bright smiles.

"Perfect. Thank you."

I checked my watch. "What are you doing here so early?"

She waved her hands around. "I had to get this done."

"Why?"

"It's Christmas!" she laughed and clapped her hands. "Trust me. The staff will love it."

I gave her a long, thoughtful look before stepping past her to retrieve my backpack. As soon as I got into my office, I switched on the camera feed. At the same time, I called the lobby to find out what time Lisa had arrived this morning. I put down the phone, stunned. Six o'clock. She had arrived by taxi at six and made several trips to and from the lobby with several packages.

I rewound the cameras and watched as she single-handedly assembled and decorated the Christmas tree in the reception area. Then she had moved to the cubicles. I came back to real time and watched as the staff entered the office, their faces wreathed in smiles. Some wore Santa hats and others wore reindeer horns. It was then I noticed that there was a box at the door with a sign. As each person passed they took out either a hat or a pair of horns.

Lisa sat at her desk, her smile a mile wide. I swallowed hard. If she kept going like this, I might actually keep her.

The week went by and I soon found out what the pixie list was all about. The gift list had been generated and would be posted. Each member of staff would draw a name and choose a gift for that person from the list given. The draw was to take place at lunchtime on Friday. The gifts would be presented at the office party on Tuesday. I watched and waited for the draw. But nothing happened. It was not until the mid-afternoon break that I saw any sign of activity from Lisa. She seemed to be making some sort of general announcement in the office. I could see disappointment on their faces and several people came over to console her with a pat on the shoulder. I was curious but wouldn't allow my curiosity to get the better of me. But I needed to know. Then I had an idea. I stepped out of the office.

"Ms. Mulligan. A word please."

She looked up from what she was doing and calmly took up her diary and pen. She slipped by me and took a seat. I got straight to the point.

"The office party is Tuesday. What is this thing you have called a pixie list?"

"It's a list where people give a range of gifts they want. I had thought of saving you some money by having the staff buy their own gifts with this pixie activity."

I felt anger surge out of nowhere. "Those were not my instructions."

"I know, sir. But I've lost the list and it's too late to redo it in time for people to shop." she seemed to be fighting back a smile and I became even angrier.

"Do you think incompetence is funny?"

"No, sir. I don't."

"So, are you telling me that you have no gifts for my staff?"

She held up her hands helplessly. "Perhaps if we give each person a hundred-dollar gift card they can buy their own gift."

I looked at her with disbelief. The phone rang and I waved my hand at her.

"We'll finish this conversation later."

Being the Friday before Christmas, I was swamped with work. By the time I was done, the office was empty. I passed by Lisa's desk and saw it was tidy as usual. I remembered what had happened earlier and smiled smugly. I knew she had been too good to be true and would mess up eventually. I would be generous, though and allow her to finish the year.

The following Monday I was out of office as I did a series of site visits for new clients in order to put their security packages together. Today was the last possible day for any such visit as the office would be closed after today. We reopened on the twenty-seventh.

The following day, I spent signing bonus checks and slipping them into gold envelopes. These usually accompanied a gift and I was again furious at Lisa for her ineptitude. I dressed carefully in a suit and red tie with a green pocket piece. I chose the SUV for tonight's drive and was soon at the Pegasus Hotel for our staff party. As usual, I got there early. But as early as I was, there was one person who seemed to have beaten me to it. One look at the blonde bun had me gritting my teeth. Lisa. I stood in the shadows at the doorway and watched as she moved among the tables. She seemed to be checking a list in her hand and retrieving brightly wrapped packages from a huge box in the middle of the floor. There were two waitresses assisting her and following her directions as she pointed from the box to various tables.

I felt my pants become soaked. A waiter had spilled water down my leg. "Excuse me! I didn't see you standing there! I'm so sorry!"

Lisa and the waitresses looked up and she came over immediately. Without a word she took my hand and grabbed a napkin from a nearby table. Then she did the most surprising thing. She knelt down and began gently pressing it on my pant leg.

"Take off your shoe."

Wordlessly, I lifted my foot and allowed her to undo and slip off my shoe. She felt my sock.

"It didn't get far. If you stand by the heater for a while, you'll be dry in no time."

She slipped my shoe back on and she placed her hand beneath my elbow. As I stood by the heater as instructed, I

watched as she completed her task. As she had said, my
pants were soon dry. I walked over to the head table where
she was working and flicked a finger at one of the parcels.

"What's this?"

"A gift."

"A gift?"

"A gift. You told me to get gifts for the staff, didn't you?"

"What about the gift cards?"

She had the audacity to laugh outright in my face.

"Did you really think I was going to give the staff gift
cards?"

"But you lost the pixie list."

"I lied." She shrugged. "The pixie list was a lie too. I just
needed a way to find out what people preferred so that I
didn't buy gifts no-one wanted or would want to exchange
right afterwards."

"So, you bought the gifts after all?"

She looked at me as though I was slow or something.
And I had to admit, whenever I was around her, I felt off
balance and out of control. As I looked at the gifts on the
tables, I felt as though the wind had been taken out of my
sails. The only fault I had found had been justified and she
had redeemed herself. Lisa – all the points. Axel – negative a
hundred. Silently I pulled the wad of envelopes out of my
jacket and handed them to her. She looked at me curiously
before taking them. I headed to the bar and had a drink as I
watched her place each envelope underneath the ribbon of
the respective gift. When the first member of staff arrived,
she slipped outside. I watched as the room filled up and
people's faces lit up when they saw their gifts. The room was
soon filled and I went to my table. Lisa was nowhere in
sight. I looked at her empty seat and saw only an envelope
with my handwriting scrawled across it. I felt something hit

me in my gut. She had not gotten herself a gift. There was a twisting in my chest that I couldn't understand. It was the strangest sensation.

Then, out of nowhere, I felt my eyes drawn to the doorway. It was as though I was being pulled by an invisible magnet. I looked across the room and everything seemed to fade.

I watched as Lisa wended her way among the tables. She was wearing a red dress with strategically placed sequins and green stilettos. Her hair was caught back by a red and green bow and flowed behind her. I swallowed hard as I fought the urge to look to see how long her hair was. She smiled and greeted everyone she passed.

"Wow!" I heard Rodney give a long, low whistle. "You got a good one this time, Vance. Try not to scare her off. We actually like this one this time."

He dug his elbow into my rib and chuckled. I looked at him then looked at Lisa as she approached. Automatically, all the men stood as she got to the table. I felt a smug satisfaction at being the first to pull out her chair. As she slid into the seat, I saw her move her hair aside to avoid sitting on it. Damn!

The rest of the night seemed to go by in a blur. The highlight of the night was the opening of the gifts. People squealed excitedly and some even came over to congratulate Lisa on pulling the wool over their eyes. She simply smiled and took it all in stride.

I was hesitant about opening my gift. She hadn't come to me for the pixie list so I had no idea what this could be.

I toyed with the bow before finally opening it. I felt her eyes on me as she leaned across to take the paper as I unwrapped it.

"I do hope you like it."

I shrugged casually.

I pulled a pair of fingerless leather gloves out of a box.

"Gloves? You got me gloves?"

She smiled. "Not just any gloves. Look in the envelope."

I picked up the envelope nestled beneath and opened it. Inside was a single receipt. It was for a full year's gym membership at one of the most exclusive gyms in the city. I looked at her and she smiled. I spoke before I could stop myself.

"How did you know?"

She shrugged and smiled mysteriously. "I have my ways. Excuse me."

I watched as she slipped out of her seat and walked over to another table to chat with a few people.

That night after I got home, I looked at the gloves and the membership receipt. How did she know?

Christmas came and went in a flash. Then we were on to the new year. On the last day of work of the old year, I asked Lisa to leave the diary behind so that I could review some items. That evening, I took both the old diary and the new one I had given her the day before and began to go through some tasks.

As I went through, I picked up Lisa's notations on several items, including my quarterly resolutions to get back to the gym. So that was how she had known! I also saw notations for my mother's birthday as well as other important dates. I couldn't say that I was surprised to see she had already transferred some pertinent information to the new diary as well. I closed both books and placed them on her desk.

As I packed up to leave the office, I couldn't help but think about Lisa. Where on earth had she come from and why was it only now that our paths had crossed? But even as I thought about our paths crossing, I couldn't help feeling that I knew her. She was far too young to be a classmate. But there was something familiar about her. I pushed the thoughts aside.

I drove home, happy that I had come to the end of another year. I also knew that a part of my happiness could be attributed to Lisa. Rodney was right. She was a gem of an assistant. But I also felt strange feelings that popped up at odd times when I would catch her staring at me. I began to notice more about her hair and shape. She was a tiny little thing but curvy. The first day back in the office after the Christmas party, her hair had been back in a bun. I had to curb the thought of going out to her and asking her to let down her hair. There was no doubt in my mind that not only did she intrigue me as an efficient assistant, I was also attracted to her as a woman. And that was where I came to a grinding halt.

I had a strict 'no relationship' clause for staff. And I was not going to break my own rules. So attractive though she was and attracted though I might be to her, Lisa Mulligan was off limits. But if she gave me any reason to fire her, she would no longer be in my employ. Then the rules wouldn't apply. But I had to choose. Did I want a good assistant or a girlfriend? I couldn't have both in one package. I sighed. It was a case of damned if I do and damned if I don't. Only the new year would tell which side of the coin I would have.

9

LISA

"See you on Monday, Lola. Give Timothy my birthday greetings, please."

I looked up from my desk and smiled at Lola as she left the office. It was the first Friday of the new year and I was deliriously happy. I had reached the one-month mark at VSS. No other PA had passed one month, Shirley had said. Each week when she called to check on me, I couldn't help but feel as though she was waiting to hear me say I had thrown in the towel. But my reports were sincere. I had no problems with Axel Vance nor the job requirements. The beast which everyone feared had not manifested once since I'd been there. There had been times when I felt his displeasure, but more often than not, it was someone else's error, not mine. I'd had a close call when I'd been deceptive about the pixie list. But I had redeemed myself there as well. I had beat the odds at work. And things were improving at home as well.

It had been so small that it wasn't discernible at first. But looking back at my father's progress over the last few weeks, I saw marked improvements when compared to where he had been in November. He was smiling and more relaxed. I also saw signs that his appetite was improving and I had teased about his love handles gaining momentum as he began to put on some weight. There were still mobility issues that required him using a cane, but his steps were much stronger now. Most evenings when I got home, dinner was ready and he was bathed. Nora had not faltered once in her promise to be there to help me.

Nora had all but moved in and I was grateful for her presence, especially during Christmas when I had needed to get the decorations to the office early that morning. She had also helped me shop online for most of the staff Christmas gifts, and had slept over when I stayed up to wrap them all.

I watched her with my father and noticed a twinkle in his eyes whenever she was around. I was torn between being happy about his happiness and loyalty to the memory of my mother. But I pushed my feelings aside. He deserved to be happy. And if Nora made him happy, I would not stand in the way of that.

"Enjoy your weekend, Lisa!"

"Thanks, Jeff. Same to you."

"Oh! I almost forgot!"

I watched as the accounting clerk came over to my desk. He perched on the end.

"I noticed Charlotte's beads and she said you made them?"

"I did."

"My girlfriend is into that sort of look. Can I talk to you on Monday about getting some stuff made for her?"

I smiled. "No problem!"

"Great! Take care. Don't let him turn you into a slave."

He jerked his thumb in the direction of Axel's closed office door and I laughed.

"Far from it."

"Good. We want to keep you."

I smiled at that last remark as he walked out of the office. We want to keep you.

Ever since the Christmas party, various members of staff had complimented me on the gifts they had received. And most of them expressed the same sentiments of wanting me to stick around. It was just this week that I had been having lunch with Lola as usual and she had pointed out this was my fourth week. She had confessed that she had been sure I would have copped a record for the shortest stay, mere minutes, that first morning when I had arrived so late. She told me she had expressly asked Axel if I should be given bus fare or taxi fare to return home. He had shocked not only her, but the entire office by having me remain.

"And we're all the better for it now. You're the best assistant he's had all year, you know."

I had confessed to her I had been just as shocked at his asking me to stay. I told her about how the agency had warned me to be on time and I was sure I had committed some sort of cardinal sin that morning.

"Axel is a bit of a stickler for order. I guess it comes with the territory of being in the military. You do know he's military, right?"

"Present or ex?"

She shrugged. "I think he still has some partial activity for special assignments or something. But he's dedicated to the company. I think he would've been further in the system if his father hadn't died when he did and he had to take over VSS. This is my fourth year here. But from what I've heard, when he got the company ten or eleven years ago, it was a mess! I can't understand how a family as rich as the Vances are could have run such a sloppy operation. As bad as it sounds, a lot of the staff that worked under his father share the sentiments that Axel Junior is doing a way better job than his father ever did. The company is completely turned around and then some. He's doing an excellent job. And now that he has such an awesome assistant, he'll get that burr out of his briefs that has everyone on edge."

I'd reflected on that conversation all week and had caught myself smiling. It was a good feeling to know I was having such a positive impact on Axel and the company. And it didn't hurt to see the money hitting my account. This morning I had received the notification of my second two weeks salary being deposited to my account. Those two payments, coupled with the hefty bonus I'd received at Christmas, had put a huge dent in the bills. And I had even splurged a little on last minute Christmas gifts for my father and Nora.

I finished the contract in front of me and placed it in the out tray. I had fallen into the habit of leaving things in the out tray in the evenings. I found them signed and on my desk first thing in the mornings. So, I had no doubt when I came in on Monday, I would be able to send these to the clients.

I put away the laptop and checked to make sure the cabinet was locked before I left the office.

I was still ecstatic about making it to the end of my first month and decided to treat myself to some ice cream. I hurried home with my package and walked in to shrieks of laughter from my father and Nora.

"What's so funny, you two?" I smiled as my lips twitched to join in their contagious mirth.

"Lisa! You got here just in time, dear. You be the judge." Nora beckoned me into the living room.

I hurried to place the cold treat into the freezer before going to the living room.

"The judge of what?"

"Look at this. Tell me what it is."

I looked at a scrawled drawing of what seemed to be some sort of animal. I could make out the four legs and a tail.

"Is it a dog or a cat?"

"You see! I told you, Gerald! My point!"

"Lisa! How could you throw me under the bus like that? You can clearly see that it's a koala bear!"

My eyebrows went up as I looked from the picture to my dad then back at the picture.

"A koala bear!? Ummm. Nope."

"I knew I could depend on you to be impartial, love." Nora smiled at me as she reached for a fresh sheet of paper. "My turn. Do you want to join us, Lisa?"

"Nope. Us Mulligans aren't known for our drawing skills, clearly."

"Ugh!" My father clutched his chest dramatically. "My own daughter!"

I shrugged and grinned. "Sometimes it's the ones closest to us that can do the most damage."

I left them laughing and drawing while I went to shower. Nora had asked me to pick up a game of Pictionary the week before. She said it would help him regain strength in his hands.

By the time I showered and got out, Nora had set the table for dinner. We shared about our day as we ate. I was surprised to hear dad had helped her figure out a technical issue with her laptop and had even written her a program to prevent any further software issues. It almost brought tears to my eyes to see him like this. He was getting back to his old self mentally. He hadn't brought up the suggestion of admitting him again. There were still some challenges and the issue of mobility and weakness in his legs. But I was thankful for small mercies. Who knew? If he continued to have mental improvement, it would soon cross over to physical manifestation as well.

After Nora left, I got dad ready for bed. These days, he has been sitting upright in bed watching the television. And it was rare that I had to turn it off after he had fallen asleep.

I turned on my tablet and started to browse. My thoughts drifted back to Axel. Out of curiosity, I typed in his name. I was surprised at what I saw.

There were several articles which spoke about the current CEO of VSS. Allusions to his military background were made and I soon found myself staring at younger pictures of Axel. As I pulled up image after image, I was even more convinced that Axel had been my rescuer. One of these days I was going to ask him outright.

I turned off the tablet and lay in bed looking at the ceiling. Suffice it to say, Axel was an enigma.

I did believe all that had been said about his being a hard taskmaster. And I suspect had I not been able to stay a few steps ahead of him, I would've been on the receiving end of his wrath many times. But it was he who was always in for a shock.

His face at the Christmas dinner had said it all when he had looked at the receipt for the gym membership. Not only that, this week, I'd made it a point of duty to ask him if he'd been to the gym as yet. With a sheepish grin, he had shaken his head. I had playfully chided him and warned him not to let his money go to waste. The next afternoon, he had left the office at four. He'd made it a point to stop at my desk to let me know he was out of the office and could be reached at the gym. He had gone twice this week. I was going to see to it that he remained consistent and didn't bury himself in work all the time.

As the month wore on, I settled into my job more comfortably and began to spread my wings a little further. There were little things I had done that I knew he noticed. Refilling his office refrigerator with healthy juice options and water had been one thing. I had also had the cleaners change the drapes in his office to blinds. I noticed his armchair was a bit ragged and had had a replacement brought in one afternoon. He had been speechless as the movers had made the switch in the middle of a conversation with a client. That evening after he had left for the gym, I had brought in a new executive chair. The following morning as I had sat at my desk working on beads before work started, I had watched as he walked into the office. Out of the corner of my eye, I saw him look at me then look back at the chair. Without a word, he had walked into the office and closed the door.

Thus passed another two weeks at VSS.

He had never taken back the credit card he'd given me to use for the Christmas gifts. And after I had cleared things with accounts, I'd made purchases where necessary, like the juices and furniture. It came as no surprise, therefore, when he called me into his office and sent me on a mission.

"I have an important client coming from out of state. I need you to get a few things done today."

I held my pen poised over my notepad, scribbling quickly as he rattled off a list of grocery items.

"I made a booking with the cleaning service to do a deep cleaning today. Check to ensure that they've done it please.

Also, I'm going to be tied up here all day. You'll need to pick him up at the airport this evening."

He dug into his pocket and handed me his car keys. My fingers closed over the fob, still warm from his body. As his hand brushed mine, I felt as if electricity ran through my body. I struggled to keep my expression neutral.

It was something I had noticed lately. I was very aware of Axel as a man. And it bothered me. I felt conflicted by my emotions as I wasn't sure if I was attracted to him because he was an attractive man, or if I was attracted to him out of gratitude for what he had done for me. Whichever one it was, it always threw me for a loop. It was also a feeling I tried to keep under control. The worst thing I could do was think about falling in love with the likes of Axel Vance.

I had been a mere child when we had first met. Surely, if he knew who I was, he would see nothing more than a child. He was ten years older than I was for heaven's sake. Also, there was a strict no fraternizing policy for staff, so any possibilities with Axel were out of the question. Then finally, and the most cringey of them all was the fact that he was my boss. How cliché would it be to have the PA fall in love with her boss?

So armed with all of these reasons, I kept my feelings in check.

"Here's the address."

I looked at the small post-it on which he had scratched some information.

"The code for the gate is built into the dashboard switch. Press it twice to open and once to close. The code for the doors is on the back."

"What time is the flight and who am I picking up?"

"Four fifteen. Adam Brinkley. Tall guy with shocking red hair. You can't miss him. Get to the airport early and make allowances for traffic. Take him straight to the house then bring the car back here."

"Okay." I checked my watch and saw that it was nearly lunch time. "I'll head out after lunch if that's okay with you."

"As long as you get the job done."

He turned to his computer which was always a sign of my being dismissed. I held the keys and notepad tightly as I went back to my desk. Around one I packed up quickly and Lola looked up, surprise on her face. I hurried to reassure her with a smile.

"I'm not fired. Just being sent on a mission out of the office."

She pressed her hand to her chest and breathed an exaggerated sigh of relief.

"Don't scare me like that again. I've had to watch twenty-six girls before you pack up that desk. Remember?"

I laughed. "You sound traumatized."

"I am! And to make matters worse, you're the only one I've ever liked."

I laughed again as I stood and shouldered my purse.

"I won't be back for the rest of the day so I'll see you in the morning."

I left the office quickly and went to the parking garage. With a click of the button on the key fob, I found his car. It was a sleek, black SUV which screamed money. I almost went to return the key and take a taxi instead. But it was a step in the right direction. First, he had entrusted me with his card. Now he was giving me his car to drive.

Slowly I climbed up into the driver's seat. I adjusted the seat so that I could reach the pedals. Then I adjusted the mirrors.

My first stop was the supermarket. I picked up everything on the list and even included some freshly cut flowers for a bouquet. I got everything loaded into the car just as the first few drops of rain started. I checked the address once more and plugged the information into my phone's GPS. Half an hour later, I had left the sudden showers behind and pulled up to the gates of a house in a very wealthy neighborhood. Norbrook Heights was the kind of place where celebrities had a 'cottage' to chill in, separate from their mansions in other parts of the country. I pressed the button on the dashboard as I had been instructed and the gates swung open. I waited for it to close before proceeding up the driveway.

I took in the home which was a modest two-story. There was a cleaning company van being loaded as I approached. I rolled down the window and smiled.

"Hi! All done? Mr. Vance asked me to check."

"All done."

"Thank you!"

I waited for them to leave before I unloaded the groceries. I tried my best to leave as little a trace of any smudges on the freshly cleaned floors as possible. After loading the fridge I hunted for a vase. I found one and filled it with water. As I was arranging the flowers in it, I glanced outside. There, in the backyard, was a flower garden. The clock in the kitchen read three-fifteen. I had a few minutes to grab a few stems and add them to the arrangement before heading to the airport which was a forty-five minute drive from here. I grabbed a pair of scissors and stepped outside. The in-ground pool gleamed and reflected the sky. It must be nice to hang out here in the evenings.

I got the flowers and headed back inside. But then, the unthinkable happened.

I was not sure if it was a wet spot, or if I was simply walking too close to the edge. But one moment I was walking and the next my feet were gone from underneath me. The flowers went flying from my hands as I shrieked. And with a plop, I fell into the pool.

The shock of the cold water stunned me for a few seconds. Then the enormity of what had happened hit me. I had fallen into the pool. Fully clothed.

I stroked my way to the shallow end and scrambled out. I looked down at myself. I was dripping wet from head to toe. Without a word, I started to strip.

I wrung my dress and tights out as much as I could. I had to get them into the dryer. I looked in dismay at my dead phone which had been in my pocket. There was no resurrecting that right now. First things first. I needed to get my clothes into the dryer. I also needed to do something about my hair.

I found the laundry room easily and stuffed my clothes into it. I stripped out of my bra and panties as well. It felt awkward being naked in my boss' house but there was nothing else I could do right now. I would mess up his car if I got into it in wet clothes. I didn't even want to think about the time right now. I would have to cross that bridge when I got to it. I could only hope there would be some flight delay so that Brinkley would not tell Axel I had been late picking him up from the airport.

I unwound my wet hair and began to think about options for a new phone while I waited for my clothes to dry.

10

AXEL

"Vance." I answered the phone without a second thought.

"Hey! Axel! It's Adam!"

I checked the clock. It was three-thirty. Lisa should be on her way by now.

"My PA should be on her way to the airport by now."

"That's what I was calling to tell you. I have a two-hour delay on my end. Flight's not coming in until after six."

"Oh! Okay then. No problem. I'll see you then."

As soon as the call disconnected, I dialed Lisa's number. With the extra time before the flight landed, she could bring the car back and I would go get Adam myself after work. I frowned as it immediately went to voicemail. I tried three more times and got the same result each time.

I turned on the car finder app on my phone. It said that my car was at my house. I tried calling Lisa three more times. There was still no response. And the car had not moved. Instantly I had a flashback to another sour experience with PA's. I didn't remember her name or face. But I did remember a similar scenario of sending her on an errand to my house in the middle of the day. And when I had been unable to reach her and had gone to get the item myself, I had caught her in the pool with her boyfriend doing anything but swimming. I saw red as I thought of Lisa and another man in my house.

I called a cab and was downstairs in less than ten minutes.

I tipped the driver extra for taking every short cut and breaking every speed limit to get me to my house in twenty minutes. I stormed up the driveway, my anger building with every step. There was the car still in the driveway. I walked around the back to the pool. I saw flowers scattered on the surface of the water. What the hell! I made my way inside through the open back door, raging. I heard humming, the same kind of humming I had heard a few weeks ago when I had walked into the office before Christmas.

My heart pounded as I turned the corner. The sight that greeted me made my blood explode. But this explosion shot downward, pooling in my groin. Within mere seconds my cock was engorged.

A waterfall of blonde hair cascading down a very naked body greeted me. I watched as she bent over and the hair parted, giving me a perfect view of her firm ass. She lifted one dainty foot to step into her panties and I saw her pink labia wink at me.

A stifled grunt escaped me and she spun around.

"Ahhhh!!!" she covered her chest with her hands as her panties hung off one leg. "What are you doing here?"

"It's my house! What the fuck are *you* doing here *naked* in *my* house!? And where is he!?"

"Where is who? Have the decency to turn your back!"

"The man you're here fucking!"

"What the hell are you talking about!?"

I turned obediently, watching out of the corner of my eyes as she scrambled into her clothing. She did not bother to put on her tights and hastily pulled her dress on, zipping it in a rush.

"He left already then?"

"Mr. Vance, sir? I have no idea what man you're talking about."

"Why haven't you answered your phone?"

"It's dead. It got wet when I fell in the pool."

"What were you doing outside by the pool?" I felt my anger slipping as I watched her braid her hair. I held my backpack in front of me to shield the outline of my cock which I was sure would be visible by now.

"I was getting flowers from your garden for a bouquet for your guest. Oh shit! What time is it? I should be on my way to the airport!"

I snapped back as I remembered why I was there in the first place. But I was sorely distracted by the images of her naked body which were now seared on my brain. I had to do something before I did something I would regret. I turned around abruptly and walked out of the laundry room. I said the first thing that came to my mind.

"Forget about it. You're fired."

"*WHAT!!!???*" I heard her steps behind me and turned in the archway leading to the kitchen.

"You heard me. Fired."

"You can't do that!" her eyes flashed as she looked up at me, crossing her arms over her heaving bosom.

"I can and I have." I continued into the kitchen, and dropped my backpack on the floor as I rummaged through the refrigerator for a beer

"You have no grounds."

"Does your contract not stipulate that I must be able to reach you at any time between eight-thirty and five?"

"Yes."

I popped a beer and took a swig before looking down at her. I leaned against the counter and sat, discreetly adjusting myself as best as I could. If she didn't stop looking at me like that, I was going to take her into my arms and kiss the daylights out of her. Where the fuck had that thought come from!? I cleared my throat.

"I wasn't able to reach you just now. You're fired. I'll see to it that you get your severance pay." Somehow Lisa had gotten under my skin in the worst possible way. This was one sure way I could remain in control and get her out of my space at the same time.

"You'll do no such thing. You have no grounds on which to do this! I'm going to sue you for wrongful termination!"

"Go ahead and try number twenty-seven."

I saw her cheeks go red at my words. She knew exactly what I was talking about and I felt like a heel for doing it. But I could not afford to lose my edge. She was dangerous to my peace of mind.

I continued to watch her as she stormed into the living room, her braid twitching behind her. My finger itched to undo it as I held her close to me. I could imagine my hands on her waist as I bent her over the way she had bent over in the laundry room. My cock lurched at the thought and I tightened my hand around the beer can instead.

"You'll be hearing from my lawyer Axel Vance!" she came back to the kitchen and walked right up to me, poking me in the chest. "You have no right to do this! I'm the best PA you've ever had and you know it!"

I looked down at her and the tears simmering just below the surface of her eyes. I felt an inexplicable need to apologize and swing her into my arms and take her upstairs. I muscled up the last shred of resistance I had.

"I look forward to it."

"You're going to regret this!"

She spun on her heels once more. My eyes followed her as she stormed back to the living room. I followed and stood in the archway, watching as she slipped on her shoes which were by the door. She slung her purse over her shoulder and I saw her rub her hand across her face.

Damn! I had made her cry. And for what? Because my pride would not allow me to admit that I was attracted to her and that she could lead me around with her pinky finger? I was hard pressed to figure out at what point I had crossed over from admiring her efficiency to admiring her as a person.

She took out her phone and shook it a few times. I watched as she walked out the door and headed down the driveway, still trying to turn on her phone. I felt like a beast. But I would not be weakened by a slip of a woman like her.

My eyes were glued to the sway of her ass as she disappeared in the distance. I walked into the control room beside the coat closet and watched through the cameras as she approached the gate. I palmed my cock through my slacks, squeezing it and feeling the surge of desire. I pressed the buzzer to open the gate and I saw her look back at the house. My eyes glazed over slightly as I watched her slip through the opening. I pressed the button again and it swung shut. By this time, I had my zipper down and my cock in hand.

I leaned back against the wall and closed my eyes as the images of her body flitted through my thoughts. I stroked my cock, tugging on it as I wondered what it would feel like to have her hand on me. With a groan, I left the room and headed upstairs to the shower. I stripped and stepped under the cool stream of water. But nothing helped. With a cry of helpless desperation, I turned off the shower and gave in to the need. I took myself in hand, tugging and pulling expertly as I allowed my imagination to run wild.

In my imagination, I hadn't caught Lisa naked accidentally. Instead, she had been waiting for me to find her when I came home from work. And the moment she'd heard me in the house, she had bent over, ready and waiting for me. I would have dropped my backpack and walked up behind her, dropping my pants. I would have nudged her knees apart and knelt down to lick her sweet pussy from behind. She would have trembled in my arms. Then I would have stood and held her by the waist, putting just the tip of my cock inside her. She would have looked at me over her shoulder, pushing back against me.

As I stroked my cock in time to the imaginary sex I was having with Lisa, I felt sweat break out on my forehead. I just knew she would be tight, gripping me like a vice. I had a flash of the full globes of her round breasts, pretty pink nipples upturned. I imagined titty-fucking her, looking down into those hazel pools as her tongue crept out to glaze the tip of my cock with each upward thrust.

My hand became a blur as I imagined her mouth on me, those pretty pink lips circling the head, her tongue dragging along my length. I would lie back on the floor and allow her to have her way with me before finally pulling her on top of me. I would spank her tight little ass as she rode me, her pussy wet and hot.

I threw my head back as my legs began to tremble.

"Ahhhhhh! Fuck!"

I groaned and grunted as ropes of semen shot from the head of my cock, splashing against the tiles. I leaned one hand against the wall as I bent my head, stroking every drop out of my twitching cock. My groin was tight and numb all at the same time. My vision felt blurred and my breathing was ragged. With a trembling hand, I found the shower knob and turned the water on, watching in a daze as the creamy liquid began to wash down the drain. I adjusted the spray so that it fell from the showerhead like rain. I stayed there until I felt some sense of normalcy returning.

I reached for a washrag and soaped my body twice before rinsing off the suds. I grabbed a towel and wrapped it around my hips. A quick check of the clock on the wall showed that it was nearly five. I had just enough time to grab a snack before heading to the airport.

I was in the kitchen fixing a snack when my eyes caught a vase with flowers. Lisa came up before me once more. And now I felt utterly miserable about what I had done. I had acted irrationally and I knew it. There was no justification for firing her. But my pride would not allow me to reach out and apologize.

I belatedly wondered how she had gotten back to the city. Had her phone started working? Where was my sense of decency in allowing an unaccompanied woman to walk through a strange neighborhood? Had I become so depraved and desperate to get my rocks off that I had lost all sense of moral conscience?

She had been gone for almost an hour already. That would be too late to catch her and offer her a ride back. At this point, I could only hope that she was okay.

I grabbed my keys and headed to the airport. As I drove, I kept a lookout for Lisa. But when I got to the main road, she was nowhere to be seen. As I turned towards the airport I reflected on what had happened in the shower.

I tried to think about the last time I had been with a

woman. That would have been last year when Leslie was still around. She hadn't been like a girlfriend or anything. We had mutual needs and had come to a mutual agreement to meet those needs. But when she had moved to Europe, she had taken her pussy with her. My hand had been taking on the duties ever since. But there was nothing quite like the warmth of a woman's body in my bed. But Lisa was not just a woman.

I feared that there was something about her that would tip me over the edge, sending me into a zone of vulnerability that a man only feels for a woman he-

I drew a halt to my thoughts right there. I was not going to go down that road. Instead, I began to process the journey ahead in my quest for a new assistant once again. I was not going to even call Shirley. I would follow through on my original plan of promoting Lola and finding another secretary instead for her spot. Tomorrow morning, first thing, I would deactivate Lisa's access code. Then I would have accounts write her severance check and call it a day. Yes, as of tomorrow, I would begin to work Lisa Mulligan out from under my skin. She was dangerous, not only to my body and mind, but potentially to my soul.

11

LISA

I allowed my anger to fuel my steps as I followed the road. My tears blinded my eyes to the beauty of the view of the city below as I walked through Norbrook Heights. A few vehicles slowed down as they passed me in either direction but I held my head straight. I was angry. Not stupid. The last thing I needed was to get into a stranger's car. I would not be a news headline.

"Stupid phone!"

I shook the offending instrument as I walked, ignoring the soreness that was starting to make my feet tingle. I had no idea what time it was now, but by the height of the sun in the sky and the shades of orange it was beginning to cast, I knew it was getting late.

I continued my journey down the hill. When I got to the main road to take me back to the city, I was just in time to see a cab leaving one of the houses after making a drop-off. I flagged it down as it left the house and hopped inside. My feet felt instant relief. I gave the driver directions to get back to the office. Almost everyone was gone by the time I sat at my desk. I had to do something before going home. My father would have taken one look at my face and known something was wrong.

I plugged in the phone to charge, hoping for a miracle. As I rifled through the papers, I felt a sense of calm begin to sweep over me. And had it not been for my bare legs and undone hair, I would have sworn I had imagined the whole incident at Axel's house. I gritted my teeth as I thought of him.

How long had he been standing there looking at me naked? I could only imagine the view he'd had! My cheeks burned at the thought of Axel seeing me naked. I was not a virgin as I had a boyfriend in my senior year of high school and had foolishly believed that we would be married right after graduation. But he had gotten what he wanted and moved on long before we collected our diplomas. I had picked myself up and declared that no man would make a fool out of me like that ever again. But Axel was not just any man.

As I replayed the image of turning to see him standing there looking at me in shock, I cringed at the thought I'd had of him taking me into his arms. Even now as the thought returned, I fought the tide of emotions that came with it. I was having far too many fanciful notions when it came to Axel. And I could not allow my emotions to get in the way of my job. My job.

Did I still have a job? Was Axel serious about firing me? I refused to believe that he could have been so petty. And what was all that about my having a man there at his house? Why would that have been his first thought? And what had he been doing at the house in the first place. That had not been the arrangement.

I typed and printed at an alarming rate and was shocked when the cleaning services came through the office. As I packed up my desk, the phone rang. I almost squealed in relief to hear it ring.

"Hello?"

"Lisa? Are you okay?"

I smiled. "I'm fine, Dad. I got caught up in some work at the office. I'm leaving now."

"Oh. Okay."

I made a few notes on a post-it for the documents I needed to complete first thing in the morning. As I thought about coming to work the next day, I forced myself to be positive. There was no way I was going to take Axel seriously about firing me. He needed me. I was the best assistant he had ever had and everyone knew it. Tonight, he would reconsider. Tomorrow morning, I would be back at my desk and running errands for him again. I didn't even need an apology.

As I headed to the bus stop, I turned my thoughts to more pleasant things than my altercation with Axel. Valentine's Day was in a few weeks, and I already had orders coming in for jewelry. I had ordered some supplies and had started working on pieces in the evenings and on weekends. There were a few people from the office who had patronized my little side hustle as well. And they had spread the word too. This was yet another reason I was grateful my phone had sorted itself out. I could not afford to miss any calls.

When I got home, Nora had already left, and Dad was in bed watching TV. I checked on him before eating dinner then hopping into the shower. I hadn't planned to wash my hair until Saturday but didn't want to have the chlorine in my hair for that long. So, I spent a little time shampooing and conditioning.

Inevitably, my thoughts went back to Axel and how he had seen me naked. I felt a sudden warmth unfurl in the pit of my belly and my pussy began to tingle. My skin felt as if it was on fire as the image of Axel's hands on my body hit me forcefully. And just as forcefully, I pushed it aside. I scrubbed my skin brutally as if that would push aside the conundrum of emotions that were hammering at me.

I worked on my hair to get it into some semblance of order. I was due a trim soon, especially as we headed into summer. I usually kept it at waist-length, but it had gotten away from me in the last few months. It was now about mid-thigh but this was still no match for the longest I had ever allowed it to grow which was past my knee. I had cut off eighteen inches and donated it to charity.

As I worked the partially dry tresses into two braids, I knew I had at least thirty-six inches of hair. I wondered what it would feel and look like to cut it all the way to my shoulders or neck, or worse yet, a pixie-cut. I finished my braids. Those would all be considered at the appointed time. But right now, I needed to get into bed.

I checked on my father once more and went through the nightly routine of locking the windows and doors before I crept into bed with my tablet. I reviewed our monthly budget as the month end was next week. I was pleased to see the tidy little sum I'd been able to put towards the outstanding bills. I had even started a vacation account into which I was putting a little extra each pay day. This year I wanted to take my father to the mountains for a weekend. And if I continued to save at this rate, I could invite Nora to come as well.

The next morning, I was up and ready for work. I left and arrived at my usual eight-fifteen. I hailed the receptionist in the lobby who stared at me as though she was seeing a ghost. I shrugged it off and stepped into the elevator. My mind jumped ahead to the documents I needed to complete as soon as I grabbed a cup of coffee. I started to hum, my day already feeling greatly improved at the thought of all that I was going to get done before the weekend.

The doors slid open and I stepped to the security panel and punched in my code. The screen flashed red as a robotic voice stated that I had entered an invalid code. I punched the code in again, this time more carefully. The same message flashed and blared, this time with a warning that should I enter the wrong code a third time, security officers would be dispatched to escort me off the premises. A feeling of unease crept down my spine as the argument with Axel came back to mind. Had he been serious?

I raised my fingers to enter the code once more when the door swung open. There stood Rosie, a distressed look on her face. She shook her head.

"He told me to tell you to leave." She thrust an envelope into my hand and closed the door.

My mouth dropped open as she shut the door in my face. I leaned against the wall for a full minute to grasp the enormity of what happened. My fingers trembled as I opened the envelope, knowing I would find the promised severance check. I placed it into my purse and took out my phone. My heart pounded as I dialed Axel's number. I already knew what I planned to say whether or not he answered.

"You got your check. Have a good day."

"Wait! Were you the soldier at the diner ten years ago?"

I heard him go silent and I continued.

"Ten years ago, my mother was murdered, and I was being kidnapped when a soldier saved my life. Are you that soldier?"

There was an unnerving silence on the other end. I licked my lips nervously.

"I-I think it's you. I remember your eyes. And that scar you have beside your eye. It's been a long time and I never thought I would ever see you again. If it is you, I just want to say thank you and that my father and I appreciate what you did for us that night. If possible, I'd like the chance to thank you properly."

Again, there was silence. Then there was a click as he hung up. I stood looking at the phone for a long minute before I stepped back into the elevator. The ride to the ground floor felt like it took an eternity.

I felt numb as I stepped out of the building. My feet turned in the direction of the bank to immediately deposit the check to my account. Afterwards, I went to the craft store and wandered around the aisles, picking up a few items before heading to the cashier. As I dug into my purse for my bank card, I found the credit card he had given me. I would need to return it as well. But not today. I could not face the humiliation again.

When I got off the bus with my packages it was close to lunch time. I stopped at a deli and ordered a few sandwiches. Even if Nora had already made lunch, we could have something for dinner. With my current mental state, I was not in the mood to cook.

As I stepped into the apartment, I was greeted with silence and shock. Nora had been in the middle of giving my father's legs their daily massage when she looked up and saw me in the doorway. My father felt her falter and looked up as well. Out of nowhere, the tears I didn't even know I had been holding at bay came pouring out. I smiled wanly as I put the packages down and wiped my face.

"Guess who just got fired?"

"Fired!?" They both blurted out, their eyes going wide. I nodded.

In as few words as possible and leaving out being discovered nude, I told them what had happened the day before and ended with walking into the office to find that my code had been deactivated and a severance check had been issued.

"But! But! He can't do that! Is that even legal!?" Nora sputtered as she helped my father into his chair.

I nodded. "I'm afraid it's his company and he can do whatever he pleases."

"But that's not fair! You were trying to help him."

I shrugged helplessly. "He doesn't quite see it that way. Just the same, I now have the record for lasting the longest, you know. That has to count for something."

"He's a tyrant and a bully! That's what he is." Nora went to the kitchen to begin sorting out the deli items. "It's just wrong of him."

"It comes with the territory of being a soldier. Speaking of which, Dad, do you remember that night mom died?"

My father's head snapped up and his mouth drooped sadly.

"How can I ever forget? But now is not the time to talk about your mother, Lisa."

"I know. But I discovered something important. Do you remember the soldier sitting in the corner? The one who rescued me?"

He nodded slowly.

"I think it's Axel Vance."

"As in Axel Vance, your boss!?"

I nodded.

My father passed his hand over his chin. "Are you sure?"

"I'll never forget his eyes, Dad. I'm sure. I asked him but

he didn't respond. But I'm sure. I've known since the first day but I never got a chance to ask him until this morning."

My father took a few deep breaths, shaking his head in disbelief.

"That's amazing. Saved us twice in one lifetime. This job was a godsend when we needed it most. I'm sure he will reconsider and take you back."

I shook my head. "I doubt it. Axel Vance is the kind of man who sticks to his guns when his mind is made up on a matter. But you are right. He's saved us twice in one lifetime." I laughed. "Maybe the third time will be the charm."

"I'd like to meet him and shake his hand. I never got the chance to thank him that night."

I shook my head sadly. "Let's see if that third chance materializes. But as it stands right now, I'm as good as done with Axel Vance as he is with me. But I feel optimistic. And you know me: I can make lemonade out of lemons. Valentine's is around the corner and now I have the time to get a real jump start on those orders."

"I'll still give you a hand here so you can work on those orders as well." Nora placed a tray across my father's lap with his lunch.

"I'd really appreciate that, Nora."

"Anytime. Take a couple days off and give yourself some breathing room before getting into the want ads again."

I nodded. "I'll do just that."

I retreated to my room and left them to whatever it was they did in the afternoons. As I sifted through the orders I had to work on, I pushed Axel out of my head. I set up a tray with the beads and got busy.

The following week I received a few calls from former co-workers expressing their disappointment with my dismissal. I took the conversations in the spirit with which they were intended and even fielded the curious questions as to what I had done. I kept the information vague and simply said we had a disagreement on an issue. I spoke to Lola a few times as well and she came over one evening to collect the orders for those at the office. I introduced her to my father and Nora before retreating to my room. She wasted no time in getting to the meat of the conversation.

"Lisa, we miss you so much. And with Valentine's around the corner the office just seems so empty without your creative touch."

I smiled. I had indeed had plans to decorate the office for Valentine's and to make it extra special.

"I miss you guys too. Please send them my warm regards. And, if possible, can I ask you to pick up something from me some days before? I have a little treat I'd like to send as a token of my appreciation for everyone's support and the kindness you showed me while I was there."

"Vance has been a bear since you've been gone, you know. I don't know what you did when you were there, but we all knew he was a little easier to deal with when you were around. And, the fact that he hasn't replaced you has us all keeping our fingers crossed that he'll take you back."

I raised my eyebrows. "So, who's doing all my work?"

"He splits it between Cheryl and me. There's a little bit of an extra bonus for us, but we'd give it up in a heartbeat if he rehired you. You are a perfect fit for VSS and we all know it, including Axel Vance. It's that blasted pride of his that's caused this. I feel it in my bones that he's the one that was wrong in whatever your disagreement was. But, knowing Axel, it will be a cold day in hell before he admits he was wrong. We're still rooting for you though. And we'll keep your spot warm until he comes to his senses."

I laughed as I packed up the orders and bagged them for her.

"We'll see."

She left soon after and I even gave her the credit card to return to him. I mused on all that she had said and couldn't help but feel the same. I did miss my coworkers, and, in some weird way, Axel as well. Knowing that he hadn't replaced me gave me a burst of hope. Maybe, just maybe, he would come to his senses as Lola had said, and offer me back my job. But if such a thing occurred, I honestly didn't know what I would do. Things would be different because he now knew who I was. And not only that, I had the issue of my feelings about him to deal with as well. You see, I could not be a hundred percent sure, but I was positive that in the weeks I had worked for Axel Vance, I had allowed the guard around my heart to slip. And in spite of his horrible behavior towards me, I wanted to do nothing more than take care of him in every way, both at work and outside of work. When the realization had hit me, I had examined every nuance of my feelings. This was no crush a PA had on her boss. No. This ran deep. Very deep. And it scared the hell out of me.

12

AXEL

I was being very unreasonable, and I knew it. But I simply didn't care. I knew everyone was even more on edge around me than usual. Again, I didn't care. I took perverse pleasure in making everyone else as miserable as I felt. What was that adage? Misery loves company?

Ever since that Friday morning two weeks ago when I had followed through on my threat to fire Lisa, I had been in hell.

It hadn't helped that I had spent an utterly miserable night before despite Adam's presence. When I had gone to bed after dinner and drinks, my thoughts had immediately turned to Lisa. It was as though her presence hovered in my house, tormenting me. I imagined I could still smell that light powdery fragrance she seemed to like. I could still see her in the laundry room, bent over and waiting for me. And my body had ached. For the second time that evening, I had taken matters into my own hands, swearing profusely as even the temporary relief was inadequate for what I was feeling.

The next morning, as soon as I arrived, I had informed reception that she was no longer employed at VSS and therefore should be asked to leave if she showed up for work. As a precaution, I had deactivated her code. Imagine my surprise to get a notification of a failed code access attempt. I had immediately pulled up the camera on the outer door. And there she was. Without hesitation and before any emotion could cajole me to do otherwise, I had flown out of my seat and all but ran to Rosie's desk and handed her the envelope with Lisa's check, instructing her to deliver it and tell her to leave. I had felt Rosie's eyes boring into me as I headed back to my office.

I had watched the brief exchange, my heart in my mouth. When my phone rang, I was shocked to see her name on the screen. What was even more shocking was the conversation we had had.

For the rest of the day, I growled and barked at everyone. Not even spending a grueling three hours at the gym that afternoon could ease the agony that had ripped through my soul at the words that were on replay in my head.

Are you that soldier?

Each time the question repeated, all I could see was the girl I had held safely in my arms until the paramedics had arrived. I had smoothed the blonde tresses away from her face, wishing with all my heart that her life was not about to be turned upside down. I had been stunned at her words and revelation. It had taken the wind out of my sails and left me teetering on the brink of a total loss of control.

I remembered how I had wanted to protect her that night. And I felt like a bonafide jerk for withdrawing my protection now that I had the chance to do just that. Shirley had called me on Monday to do her usual check-up, especially as Lisa approached the end of her second month. In as few words as possible, I had told Shirley that it hadn't worked out for us. Her next words had stunned me and had made me wish the ground would open up and swallow my wretched soul. Lisa was the sole breadwinner in her home and taking care of a sick father. This job had been a godsend as medical bills were high.

Anyone who approached me that day got the sore end of my rage. It had not helped when one morning I got to work and found the credit card on my desk. I had all but forgotten about that. I was more brutish than ever and the staff stayed wide. But they couldn't understand that I was hurting, and that the hurt was a result of my own stupidity and pride. My fingers itched to call Lisa and tell her she had her job back. But Axel Vance did not grovel. If I did that, if at some point she did mess up and I had to legitimately fire her, it would be hard. No. I could not allow her to have such an advantage over me. And so, I continued to wallow in misery. At the very least, though, I stopped taking it out on the staff. Instead, I worked off my frustrations in the gym.

And so, one week passed. Then two.

Before I knew it, it was a week before Valentine's Day. I sat in the office that afternoon, finishing up an agreement for security at a function the following weekend. Quite a few parties were being held and we were in high demand. My phone rang and I answered it as usual.

"Vance."

There was a pause and I frowned. Then a man's voice came over the line.

"Axel Vance?"

"Yes. And you are?"

"I'm Gerald Mulligan. Lisa's father."

You could have pushed me over with a feather. I felt hot and cold at the same time. My mouth opened but no words came forth. He continued to speak.

"I just wanted to tell you thank you for what you did that night, Axel. It would have shattered me to lose them both. I couldn't save my wife. But you saved my child. I'm forever grateful for that."

"It was the thing to do, sir." The respectful title slipped from my mouth before I could give it any thought.

"I do wish I could meet you face to face and do this in person, but I'm an invalid. I don't get out much these days. I want to thank you as well for giving Lisa a job when we were really in a bind and strapped for cash. You have no idea how much this job meant to us."

"How did you get my number?"

"Lisa didn't give it to me in case you're wondering. She doesn't know I'm calling you either."

"That doesn't answer the question."

He chuckled. "I have my ways. I wanted to express my gratitude and also to ask a favor. Is there any way you could let Lisa have her job back?"

"Negative."

I heard him sigh and I felt like I could kick myself. Here was an excuse. It would not be my pride at stake to call her and ask her to come back. It would be on her shoulders as it was her father who had called to beg for her job. I had a prime opportunity to come out on top and I blew it. Shit.

"It didn't hurt to try, though. Again, thanks for everything."

Before I could utter another word, he ended the call. The rest of my afternoon was shot to hell. Thankfully the staff stayed out of my way.

Every time I looked at the camera and saw her empty

desk, emotions swirled through me. It had been two fucking weeks. Why had I not had at least two people attempting to replace her as yet? The truth slapped me in the face but I turned from it each time. At some point in those two weeks, I had convinced myself that perhaps I didn't need a new PA. I ignored the little voice that added to that dialogue by saying that I didn't need a new PA because Lisa was all that I needed.

I had split the tasks for making appointments and typing documents between Cheryl and Lola, two of the senior secretaries. When I needed special errands to be run, they decided between themselves who would get the task done. No. I didn't want a PA. I simply needed Lisa.

That evening when I got home from the gym, I walked through the empty house. The vase of flowers had dried up but I had refused to throw them out. Lisa's hands had touched them. And one evening last week as I had run a load of laundry, I had found a few strands of long blond hair on a towel in the drier. It was the first time I was doing laundry since Lisa had been there and I figured this was probably the towel she had used to dry her hair that afternoon. Suffice it to say that the strands of hair were now in a zip lock bag and the unwashed towel was tucked beneath my pillow. I rested my cheek against it each night, imagining it to be Lisa's arms. I was obsessed, and it freaked me out. I felt as though I was treading a delicate line and one step in the wrong direction would send me spiraling out of control. And Axel Vance was not a man who lost control.

I rustled up a solitary meal and took it out to the balcony. The nights were not as cold as before. Spring was approaching and the weather was warming up nicely. As I ate, I brooded. That morning, Shirley had called yet again to ask about when she should send Lisa's replacement. I had

again been non-committal in my response. Shirley was a
good recruiter and I had gotten many of my employees from
her. But the PA buck stopped with Lisa. And until I could
sort through my emotions, the vacancy would remain. If I
were to be honest, I didn't know what was stopping me from
filling the vacancy. What was I waiting on to have someone
take her place? I knew the answer: I wanted Lisa to ask me
for her job back. But I suspected that would never happen.
She had shown a bit of her backbone when she had stood
up to me and I suspected that on principle alone and her
staunch belief that she had been wrongfully dismissed
would prevent her from coming to beg me for anything.

I opened a can of beer and sat looking out over the city.
Not for the first time, I wondered where she lived and what
she would do if I turned up on her doorstep. But I would
never do that. That would be admitting weakness and
defeat. She knew where I lived. I wondered what I would do
if she turned up on my doorstep. I felt my groin tighten at
the thought. I knew exactly what I would do. I would get this
itch scratched. And then what?

I took a swig as I tried to ignore the little voice in my
head telling me that Lisa was no one night stand or casual
fling. There was something about her that told me she
would be the kind of woman one went into a relationship
with for the long haul.

I tried to push the feeling aside by reminding myself I
had met her when she was just a young girl.

"But girls grow up into beautiful women, dude. You're
not breaking the law or anything."

I sighed and went to get another beer. I wondered how I
would feel if I had viewed her as just the attractive woman
that she was, regardless of our previous meeting. It would be
a situation involving two consenting adults regardless of our

age difference. But there was still something to be said about feeling this need to protect her the way I had protected her that night.

As I drank, I thought about the phone call from her father. He had thanked me for coming to their rescue – twice. Surely, surely that was a sign I was meant to be in their lives. I wondered if there would be a third opportunity to step into their space once more, especially after I had royally fucked up this second time. All my protective instincts were on high alert. It made me want to dig a little deeper into the Mulligans and see what I could do to assist them further. Maybe there was a way I could do it without them knowing it was me as well. Shirley had mentioned Mulligan not being well and he had mentioned it himself.

My brain started to work overtime as I thought about any contacts I had in the medical field who could look into their case. Then there was also the issue of the bills to be paid. That was the least I could do. But I would have to tread carefully so that they had no idea I was behind their sudden good fortune. Now that I had some semblance of a plan, I had to give it a little more thought. There were some phone calls I could make tomorrow.

I went to bed after checking a few emails and responding to those I deemed as needing an urgent response. That night, my dreams were vivid.

I was walking in a field of sunflowers. It was a beautiful day. As I walked, I picked flowers until my arms were laden. When I got to the end of the field I looked down and found that the field had given way to grass. When I looked up once more, there was Lisa standing a few feet away from me. She was wearing a summer dress with sunflowers all over it. Her hair was loose behind her and the sun seemed to turn her into a golden goddess. When she saw me, her eyes came alive. She smiled and the sun seemed to radiate from her. She raised her arms and I started to walk towards her. With every step, I felt lighter and happier. When I stood before her, I went down on my knees and raised the sunflowers in my arms to her. As she reached down to take them, I saw the mound of her belly. I pressed my cheek to her tummy and felt our baby kicking. I looked up at her in awe and wonder, feeling a tug in my chest as my heart seemed to expand and burst with love for her and our child. Then she lowered her lips to mine...

I sat up, awash in sweat. My heart pounded as I blinked rapidly in the darkness. It took a few minutes for my heartbeat to regulate. I got out of bed and went downstairs to get a drink of water. My eyes fell on the vase of dried flowers once more and the dream came rushing back. I felt a strange emotion overtake me instantly. It was something that had been hovering on the periphery of my subconscious for weeks now, long before I had fired Lisa. But it was never acknowledged – until now. That dream had betrayed me. That dream had stripped away my facade and revealed my true feelings. My tongue felt heavy even as my heart felt light. There was no denying it anymore. I was falling in love with Lisa, and my subconscious clearly approved.

I took a deep swallow of water as a new emotion followed on the heels of my admission – fear.

Love exposes people. It strips them of their protection. It leaves them open to being hurt. But even as I struggled with my newly revealed vulnerability, I knew deep down that Lisa would never hurt me. Pride had flown out the window now. And in its place was a determination to get Lisa back, not as my PA, but as my woman.

I shook my head as nervousness swamped me. My

woman. I took a few deep breaths. This was going to take some getting used to with this new term of reference.

I rinsed out the glass and went back upstairs. As I placed my cheek against the towel once more, I sighed. One day, hopefully not long from now, I would find a way to bring her back to me.

13

LISA

The weekend before Valentine's Day I was kept busy working on orders. Lola would be coming by on Sunday evening to pick up the ones for the office. Then I planned to spend Monday making other deliveries for those who were in the vicinity.

My fingers literally flew across the bead tray. According to Nora, I had the kind of skills that could take lumps of coal and turn them into diamonds. I didn't doubt her. I had often caught myself daydreaming about what it would be like to have a jewelry business. I would be an entrepreneur, working from home on my own time at my own pace. But even as I dreamed about such endeavors, I knew it was something that would require much more on my part. The jewelry business was a finicky one. What would happen in between those major celebrations? And what about those who were not inclined to the sort of beadwork I did? No. This would have to remain as the side hustle for a little bit longer.

Lola stayed for dinner when she came by on Sunday evening and we made a pretty good team for a round of

Pictionary against my father and Nora. After Lola left, Nora helped me to clean things up before she went to tell my father she was leaving. I watched out of the corner of my eye as she ran a familiar hand along the back of his head and he smiled up at her. He had an aura about him that seemed to radiate happiness, and I couldn't deny this was Nora's doing.

Nora, too, looked younger than when I had first met her. To my surprise, she was just fifty. But I noticed she now took a little more pride in her appearance than before. I now noticed her hair was a thick and healthy auburn mane and her deep-set blue eyes twinkled whenever she was around 'Gerald'. Her clothing which used to be baggy was now her size, and she was not as frumpy as I had once perceived.

I smiled and kept packing the deliveries for tomorrow as they said their goodbyes. My father even got up and walked her to the door, leaning heavily on his cane. They conversed in whispers for a few moments before she closed the door behind her. He leaned against the door and looked off into space.

"Are you ready for bed, Dad?"

He looked over at me as though he had just remembered that I was there. He smiled and shook his head.

"I think I can stay up a bit longer."

"I think you're doing much better these days."

"I wish I was even further along. This damned cane makes me feel like I'm eighty. And the trembling fingers don't help that feeling either."

I smiled and went to help him to the sofa. "Nevertheless, I'm grateful for small mercies. We got you back on your feet. Now we just need to figure out what's going on with your nerves and fix it so that you'll be as good as new."

I handed him the remote and went back to the dining table to continue packing. I listened to him changing the channels for about ten minutes before I looked over at him. His eyes were fixed on the television but his stare was vacant as though he was deep in thought. I went over and sat beside him. I reached across and ran my hand over his head.

"A penny for them?"

He looked at me and smiled. Then he looked down and sighed. He folded and unfolded his fingers a few times before speaking.

"I loved your mother very much, Lisa."

"I know."

"And I know you loved her too."

"I did."

"And I would never ask you to replace her. She was your mother."

"No one can replace a person, Dad. That would be unfair to all the parties involved. Each person has to be treated on their own merit and judged by their unique qualities."

He sighed once more. "I am loyal to her memory."

"And I'm sure she would be loyal to yours if it were the other way around. But life goes on for those who remain." By now, I had a fair idea of the direction in which the conversation was going. But I remained silent, allowing him to broach the topic in his own way.

"I can't help but feel as though she would have wanted me to be happy, even if that meant being with someone else."

I smiled. "I am positive she would, Dad. And whatever makes you happy, makes me happy."

He looked at me sharply, hope shining in his eyes. I felt as though I had given him the opening he had been seeking. He swallowed a few times before speaking.

"Nora makes me happy."

"I know."

His eyes widened. "You do?"

I stroked his hair once more. "Dad, I'm not blind. Nora is a beautiful woman, not just physically but internally. I don't doubt that the majority of your improvement is because of what she has done for you, not just physically, but emotionally. I love the changes and the improvements. And I am forever grateful to her."

"She's older than I am, you know."

"Just two years. It's not like she's robbing the cradle or in cougar territory."

He threw his head back and laughed.

"You sound as though you're trying to convince me to take a chance while I'm throwing up roadblocks."

I chuckled. "Dad, you have my blessing to view Nora as a woman and not just a caregiver."

"That's a relief. I didn't want you to think I didn't love your mother or anything."

"I know that. But we are still alive. You deserve a second chance at love. It doesn't mean you've forgotten your first love. It just means you're coming to the table with the experience of knowing how to treat someone you love. And if Nora is it, I don't mind. How does she feel about it though?"

"She's struggling with her memory of Charles. But you make a valid point about second chances not meaning you've forgotten your first love. I'm going to point that out to her when she comes tomorrow."

He reached across and patted my hand. I squeezed his fingers between mine.

"Thanks for approving, my dear."

"I feel honored to know my approval was needed. Make sure you don't lose her."

He tossed his head and smoothed his hair with a cheeky

grin. "She can't resist Gerald Mulligan. I've got her hook, line and sinker. Now all I have to do is reel her in."

I laughed and hugged him.

"You reel away. I'm going to finish these packages. Let me know when you're ready for bed.

We sat in the living room for another hour or so before I helped him to bed. Afterwards, I completed the packing and labeling, separating the deliveries from those to be picked up in the evening.

Tuesday morning, I sat at the dining table working on a few last-minute orders. But my thoughts were far away. I had to restring some beads a few times as I had lost my place in the pattern. Nora had settled my father in for a nap before lunch. He was usually worn out after a morning of the physical therapy regime she put him through. She sat at the other end of the table typing as I worked.

"Earth to Lisa."

I looked up, dazed. "Huh?"

"I've been trying to get your attention for the longest while. How long are those earrings supposed to be? Floor length?"

I looked down in dismay to find that I had been stringing beads onto the line and it had spilled over to the table as it grew. I sighed.

"What are you thinking about so hard, dear?"

I placed my face in my hands and groaned in frustration before looking at her. I took a deep breath.

"Axel."

Her eyebrows shot up into her hairline.

"Axel?"

I nodded and put my head on my forearms. "Axel." Just saying his name felt good. My emotions had been going haywire for weeks now and I felt as though I was going to explode.

I looked up at Nora. She had closed her laptop and was staring at me as though waiting for me to speak.

"Do you remember that story about the night my mother was killed?"

She nodded.

"He was the soldier who saved me and I can't help but think that he's like my savior or something. The night you found me on the stoop crying, I had begged him to come and save me again. Then boom, I got the job and he's my boss."

"He came rushing in on his white horse to save the damsel in distress once more." Nora smiled and put her chin in her hand. "He's your knight in shining armor. Just like a fairytale."

"Don't fairytales always have happy endings?"

"The story isn't over yet, dear. There's still time."

"It's been almost three weeks. If he were going to call me, wouldn't he have done it by now?"

"He hasn't filled your spot. That has to count for something."

I shrugged. "I guess."

"Lisa. He's a soldier. They're trained to keep their emotions in check. Give him time. From what I remember you telling me, it took him years to get the company back on its feet. Clearly, he's not the kind of man who does things in a rush. But when it is done it is done thoroughly."

She opened her laptop and started typing again. She looked at me.

"Take a look at this."

I took a seat beside Nora and peered over her shoulder. Axel's picture filled the screen.

"This is some fellow. Look at this list! And all in that short space of time."

I read the list of accolades and awards he had received as a mere recruit. Then when he had entered active service, the list expanded. Understandably, he had opted for special assignments after turning twenty-three as his attention was now geared at resurrecting the family business. And there, yet again, were accolades and merits.

As I read, I felt as though I was looking into Axel's heart. Nora was right. This was not a man who acted on impulse. Every venture was undertaken with precision. And he had not failed at any of them. My heart raced at the thought that I felt a strange connection to him as not only my rescuer, but as a man.

Nora patted my hand comfortingly. "Give him time. If he wants to be in your life, he will be. Just give him time."

"I guess all I can do is wait then."

"That's all any of us can do."

I went back to work on my beads, Nora's words replaying in my head.

Nora left after dinner as usual, and I got Dad into bed. I showered and went through my nightly routine before climbing into bed. I browsed on my tablet for a few minutes before I found my fingers typing in his name. Once more, his face filled the screen.

There was no disputing his physical appearance. The short beard he had offset the military buzz cut he still wore. His tall, muscular body was one that turned heads. The few times I had allowed myself to look at him, I had to admit that he was a man any woman would be proud to have.

My thoughts went back to the afternoon he had found me in his house. As usual, whenever that particular memory surfaced, I felt my body grow warm. I used my fingers to trace his face, wondering what it would feel like to run my fingers along the bristles of his beard. What would those full lips feel like pressed against mine? What would those huge hands of his feel like as they cupped my breasts?

Usually, I was very good at pushing these thoughts away. But tonight, arousal fought back and won.

I lay looking up at the dark ceiling as my hand crept beneath my sleep shirt and into my panties. My clit stirred as my fingers brushed against it. I closed my eyes and swallowed hard, imagining that it was Axel's hand exploring my body. I had no term of reference for how a man made love to a woman as the one experience I had was over in a flash of pain before it had even started. But I just knew that Axel was the kind of man who knew how to please a woman.

I stroked myself slowly, licking my lips as I felt pleasure build. I swallowed as I envisioned Axel, naked and aroused, his body poised over mine as he lay between my legs. He would be a gentle lover, plying me with sweet kisses as his body entered mine slowly. I would wrap my arms around his neck, clinging to him as he pressed deeper.

My fingers were moving faster now, slick with the juices of my arousal. I used my other hand to stroke my nipples, imagining Axel sucking them into his hot mouth. I pushed my hips up to meet my hand, the way I would push up to meet his thrusts. My body tightened as I felt my climax approaching. With a muffled cry, I stroked myself hard and fast, pinching my nipples as my body shuddered through the climax.

Sweat washed over my body as I blinked rapidly. I tried to regain control of my breathing, feeling my chest rise and fall with the effort. When at last, I felt almost back to normal, I rolled over. But sleep was far from me. I lay gazing into the darkness long into the night, longing to hear his voice. I allowed my imagination to run away with me, envisioning myself lying in his arms after making sweet love, planning our lives together. He would hold me in his arms and we would talk long into the night. Then, as the first fingers of dawn streaked across the sky, he would pull me close and we would again be joined in body. But my heart knew that our joining would be more than physical. My heart knew that even as our bodies joined, our souls would be knit together as one as well.

I didn't know how I knew. But I was convinced that Axel Vance was *the* one. He was *my* one. I could only hope that he felt the same.

I thumped the pillow and rolled onto my other side, sighing deeply. I squeezed my eyes closed, willing sleep to come as I exhaled.

"Will you make the third time be the charm, Axel? Will you come and rescue my heart this time?"

The question went unanswered in the dark room.

14

AXEL

The dreams about Lisa had become intense. And I felt powerless against their strength.

Wednesday morning as I found myself jerking off in the shower at the thought of burying myself inside her just like the dream I had that night, I felt trapped. I felt as though I was going crazy with need. I missed her. I couldn't walk by her desk without something akin to pain striking me. Outwardly I had my shit together, but inside I was a wreck.

I stood under the stream of water, staring into space for a few minutes before I snapped out of it. Those few minutes cost me and I arrived at the office a few minutes past eight rather than my usual seven thirty. And this had been happening all week.

I grunted a good morning to those I passed on the way into my office. As I slammed the door and threw myself into the chair, I stifled a groan. I felt like a man obsessed and possessed. I rubbed my hands over my beard, forcing myself to think straight. But the dream was wreaking havoc on me.

We had been at some sort of function at a hotel. But one minute we were in the ballroom, and the next we were in my bedroom, locked in each other's arms and ripping away our clothing. Our mating had been intense and repetitive and had resulted in my waking up to a massive, pulsing erection. Just thinking about it now made my groin tingle and feel as though I hadn't eased the tension this morning. Lisa was not getting under my skin. She was in every sinew and tissue of my body and entwined in my soul. But each time I tried to think about how to get her back, I drew a blank.

My phone rang, jolting me out of my reverie. From the ring tone, I knew who it was.

"Good morning, Mother."

"Good morning, dear. I haven't caught you at a bad time have I?"

I glanced at my watch. "I have a few minutes before I begin working."

"Great. All I need is a few minutes. I just wanted to remind you about this weekend."

I frowned. "What about this weekend?"

"Axel! Don't tell me you've forgotten! I've been telling you about this since December. I thought you had written it down. We're going to the beach house with the Chambers. Remember?"

Deep in the recesses of my brain, I remembered her bringing up a Valentine weekend getaway.

"I don't remember agreeing to be there, Mother."

"But you can't disappoint Bethany, dear. It's been ages since you two have seen each other and she has been asking for you."

"Or have you been talking her ear off about me."

"Whatever. You two have a lot to catch up on this weekend. We're going down on Thursday. I'm sure you can take Friday off and join us."

"Let me check with my girlfriend first. I would be bringing her with me if I come, you know." The words slipped from my tongue before I had the chance to even process what I'd said. I heard my mother pause on the other end.

"Girlfriend? I didn't know you had a girlfriend."

"We're being discreet with our relationship."

"Well okay then. By all means bring her so I can meet her."

And chase her away more likely.

"Sure. But as I said, if she's unavailable, I won't be there."

"With or without this girlfriend, you will be there, Axel Vance. This is not just about socializing. There's business involved as well. Chambers asked specifically for you to come this weekend. So come with or without her."

"We'll see." I already knew what Chambers wanted and my answer remained no.

"Well, even if she isn't available and you don't turn up, I'd love to meet her when I come back."

I balked at the suggestion. "Sure. Gotta go, Mother. Duty calls. Have a great day."

I waited for her to hang up before I disconnected the call. What the hell had I gotten myself into by telling such a blatant lie? Girlfriend? I even shocked myself. I knew I was bluffing as well when I said I might not show up. And so did she, which was why she hadn't pushed my attendance. I was going to be there. Loyalty was a strong point for me. Chambers Senior had sent a lot of business my way in the early days, and I was in his debt for giving me that traction to get moving. He still wanted to buy me out and I suspected a relationship with Bethany could seal a merger, but I was not biting. I had tried business with the Chambers before when I had appointed Bethany's brother, Brian, as the interim CEO. It didn't help that while his father had sought to assist me, Brian Chambers had almost sunk the company that first year. I was still bitter on that point. But for the sake of old times, I would turn up and count the hours to freedom, if even for my mother's sake. My mother was a shrewd woman and I shuddered to think that she had seen through my lie about a girlfriend. And she had backed me into a corner with this imaginary girlfriend. I wracked my brain. Where was I going to find a woman who was free to drop whatever she was doing to go to a beach house for the weekend with me and my mother? Lisa's face came up before me. And for the second time that morning, I acted on impulse. Before I could think twice, I dialed Lisa's number.

It rang twice before she picked up the call.

"Hello?"

My heart skipped a beat at the sound of her voice. I cleared my throat, trying to sound as businesslike as possible.

"Hello, Lisa. How are you?"

"I'm fine, thanks. You?"

"I'm good. But I have a little situation and wonder if you could do me a favor. I'll make it worth your while. Are you free for a few days?"

"I'm not working. I'm free for months. Years even."

Her words were like a fist to my stomach as I remembered why she didn't have a job. I cleared my throat once more.

"I need a girlfriend."

"I beg your pardon? You need a *what*?"

"A girlfriend. I have a function to attend and I told my

mother that I would only come if I could take my girlfriend, thinking that she would let me off the hook. She didn't. Now I need a girlfriend and you came to mind. It would be just for this weekend. We leave Friday morning and come back on Monday morning. All expenses paid and, like I said, I'll make it worth your while."

"You don't have to pay me, Axel. I'll do it for free."

"But-"

"I'll do it."

I was thrown for a loop. What woman turned down money just to pretend for a few days?

"Ummm. Okay."

"You can call me with the details later."

"It's a beach house so take a swimsuit."

"Okay."

"Later then."

I ended the call and sat staring into space. What the hell had I just done?

Friday morning at eight, I pulled up in front of the modest apartment building where Lisa lived. I balked when I realized she had to travel almost an hour one way to get to work. It made me realize the extent of the sacrifices she had made to be at work on time and even that morning when she had arrived at six to decorate the office for Christmas. Before I could step out of the truck, the front door leading into the building opened and she stepped out carrying a small suitcase. I almost tripped over my own feet to meet her on the steps. I felt as though my heart stopped beating when I laid eyes on her.

She was dressed in tight jeans and a turtleneck sweater. Her hair was in a single braid which was draped over her shoulder. Her eyes were shielded by sunglasses.

"Hi, Lisa. Thank you so much for doing this for me."

"The pleasure is all mine. I'm glad I get to do something for you for a change."

I placed her bag in the back before opening the passenger door for her. As I hurried around to my side, a slight movement at a downstairs window caught my attention. There were two pairs of eyes staring at me. I waved and they withdrew.

"The send-off party?"

"Pardon?"

"The two people at the window."

"Oh! That would be my dad and Nora."

"Oh. Okay."

I had no idea who Nora was but at this moment it didn't matter. I had Lisa near me. Strangely enough, all the agitation I'd been feeling for the past weeks disappeared in her presence. It was as though balance had been restored to my world. I felt at peace and I felt at rest. I glanced at her profile for the first few minutes as we drove. We didn't speak until we were on the highway.

"You must be wondering what these shenanigans will entail and why I'm going to these lengths."

She laughed. "I am curious."

"Picture a mother with an only child who feels the need to try to dictate the path of said child's life. That dictation includes matchmaking with the daughter of a longtime family friend."

"And I surmise that this family friend's daughter will be there this weekend?"

"Affirmative."

"You could have decided to skip it."

"I suggested that as well on the premise that my girl-friend might be unavailable. But I had to change that course as this family friend is also a longtime business associate so I do need to be there. And my mother still wants to meet my 'girlfriend' even if 'she' couldn't make it this weekend."

"So even without my coming along this weekend you would still have needed to present someone. Why me though?"

The question came out of left field and I paused. I didn't dare tell her the truth.

"I thought of you as someone who I knew would have the maturity to handle the role as well as the authenticity to convince my mother. You're a genuine person and that will shine through."

"Oh. Okay."

Did I hear a hint of disappointment in her voice? I reached across and took her hand. I smiled at her shocked face.

"You're my girlfriend, remember? We're going to be expected to at least hold hands."

But the joke was on me as her fingers curled into mine. The shards of electricity that seemed to shoot between us from the simple touch sent my senses reeling. A few miles down the road, I placed her hand on my thigh. That was an even bigger mistake as I felt my cock get excited. It took every ounce of concentration in me to keep him under control. Abruptly she moved her hand as she dug into her handbag and I felt a sense of abandonment.

"So, how have things been at the office?"

"As usual. How have things been with you?"

"I'm taking care of my father and making ends meet."

I almost jumped out of my skin when she placed her fingers against my lips. I opened them and found a stick of gum shoved into my mouth. When she had taken a stick for herself, she rested her hand on my thigh once more as if it were the most natural thing in the world.

The first three hours of the journey passed in a flash as we shared a little bit more about ourselves. I told her about my childhood with my father and what had sparked my desire to get into the security business. I touched a little on my military career and some of the places I had been before coming back home. As for her, I learned that she had once dyed her hair jet black in high school and had shaved it off completely to allow her blonde tresses to grow back.

"Don't ever do that again."

She laughed. "Dye my hair or shave it off?"

"Both. You have beautiful hair and I love the length of it."

"It's funny you should say that. I am thinking of cutting it for the summer."

"Don't."

"But it's for a good cause. I'm donating it for wigs for cancer patients."

I looked at her then back at the road. I covered her hand and squeezed it gently.

"Okay. It will grow back, right?"

"It usually does."

"Well, I guess I can make an exception this time. But don't make a habit of it."

"You're a fine one to talk about hair. Have you allowed yours to grow out at all?"

"Never."

"It would be nice to see you with a full head of hair, though."

Instantly I made a mental note to see how I felt about growing my hair out for a few months.

"What about the beard, though? Is that okay with you?"

"I love the beard."

I grinned. "Good. It stays."

It was nearly noon when I turned off the highway. A few miles later I pulled into a diner. The instant I brought the truck to a halt I turned to face her.

"Lunch time. We're about another hour away but I'm starving!"

"That makes two of us. And I need a restroom."

We both took care of nature first then found a booth. Automatically, I slid into the seat which put my back against the wall and gave me a view of the diner. She looked at me queerly for a few seconds then dropped her eyes to the menu. I saw her swallow convulsively.

"That's how you sat that night."

I went rigid. I didn't have to ask what night she was talking about as there was only one night that it could be.

She kept her eyes on the menu as she spoke.

"I was sharing a joke with dad and I looked up and there you were, just sitting in a corner by yourself."

I smiled. "You saluted me."

She laughed softly. "I was shocked when you did it too."

I looked around the diner. It was nothing like it had been that night. This afternoon was teeming with customers. I reached across and covered her hand with mine.

"Have you ever been back there?"

She shook her head. "No."

"I noticed your family that night, you know. I was just looking around and observing. There was an older couple, a newly engaged couple, and you guys. I was the only single person and I remember thinking that the only thing missing from the relationship cycle was a single woman." I laughed. "I had even joked about meeting my soul mate there and telling our kids later on that I had met their mom in a diner off the highway."

She smiled and squeezed my fingers. "You're mistaken, you know. There was a single woman in the diner."

"Who? The waitress?"

She shook her head. "Nope. She was there. With her parents. It's just that she wasn't yet a woman."

The waitress chose that moment to take our orders. The enormity of her words hit me. And with it came a curious sensation in the pit of my belly.

We finished eating and were soon back on the road.

"You said earlier that you take care of your father?" I tried to sound as casual as possible and not give away the fact that I already knew her father was ill.

"Yes."

"If you don't mind my asking, what's wrong with him?"

"I don't mind. The truth is, we don't know. A few years ago he developed mobility issues. We've been trying a number of treatments but nothing seems to be working. Admittedly, he is doing better these days. A few months ago he could barely get out of bed or feed himself. Now he's at least back to his cane and can hold a spoon."

"What specialists have you seen?"

"The ones the insurance pays for." She smiled ruefully and shrugged.

I didn't need any more information. As soon as I got back on Monday, I was going to make some calls.

The rest of the journey passed with more casual conversation and we soon saw the sign welcoming us to Coral Springs. It was another fifteen minutes before I turned into the massive gate of the beachfront property. I saw Lisa's eyes go wide and she turned to look at me.

"I thought you said we were going to a beach house."

"I did."

"This isn't a beach house. This is a beach mansion."

I shrugged. I didn't want to shock her further by telling her this was the one we had downsized to after dad died.

Without another word, I parked and switched off the engine.

15

LISA

From the moment Axel had called me two days ago to now as I sat gaping at the beach 'house', it all felt like a fairytale.

When the phone had rung, I'd been speechless for a few seconds to see his name on the screen. I had turned the screen to Nora and she had stifled a squeal.

"Answer it!"

The conversation had been a shock. And now as I struggled to come to grips with the one eighty degree turn things had taken with Axel, I forced myself to be calm. But no sooner had Axel opened the door and I'd given him my hand to exit the truck, than a woman descended upon us. She was the spitting image of Axel. This had to be his mother.

She was tall and slender and had just a few hints of gray in her thick black hair. Her eyes were the same brilliant blue and twinkled as she looked at her son. But when they turned on me, the twinkle faded and they became almost piercing.

"Axel! You're finally here with your *girlfriend*."

I was instantly on my guard. I smiled and stepped forward.

"Hi! I'm Lisa Mulligan. It's nice to finally meet you Mrs. Vance."

I could see that my approach had caught her off-guard. But she soon regained her composure. She extended her hand and I took it in a firm handshake.

"Nice to meet you, Lisa," she murmured. Then she surprisingly drew my hand through the crook of her elbow.

"Call me Elizabeth. Do forgive my beast of a son, dear. Imagine! To have you driving on those dangerous highways for *hours* when I could have just sent the jet to pick you up. The flight is half an hour tops."

I looked back at Axel who had unloaded our luggage and was wheeling them behind us.

"I didn't mind the drive. We do enjoy each other's company. I would take another five-hour drive right now."

"Just the same. You must be exhausted. Let me show you to your room. I've put you in the orchid suite. I hope that's fine with you. Axel, do stop by the lounge and greet the Chambers. Max will see to the bags and I'll see to it that Lisa gets refreshed and settled. Surely you can do without her for a few minutes."

Before Axel could respond, I felt myself being pulled into the house. We walked past some open double doors through which I could hear peals of laughter. I was half-dragged up a massive staircase and hustled down a hallway. She stopped at a door at the end of the hallway and I took advantage of the reprieve to catch my breath. She threw the door open and we stepped inside.

My eyes were immediately drawn to the picture window and my feet followed suit. The ocean lay beyond, crashing against the shoreline. The beach was dotted with umbrellas and lounge chairs and I immediately felt the urge to change into my swimsuit and take advantage of the daylight hours. I stepped onto the balcony and looked down just in time to see Axel appear beside the pool, a brunette hanging off his arm. I turned to find Elizabeth at my elbow looking at the couple below. She smiled.

"Don't mind Bethany. She's an old family friend."

I plastered a smile on my face. "Oh! *That's* Bethany. Axel did say she would be here as well." I couldn't help but be smug at her shock at my response. She pulled me inside and I went with her.

"I do hope this suite will be to your taste, dear. It's where Axel always stays when he's here. And I guess as his girlfriend you'll be sleeping in the same room?"

"Of course. Isn't that what couples do?" I responded with a bright smile even as my heart ricocheted in my chest.

We both looked up as the servant brought in the bags. Elizabeth took a seat on the couch as we waited for him to leave. No sooner had the door closed behind him than she turned to me once more.

"I must say that you are a bit of a shock. Axel never told me he was seeing someone."

"We wanted to keep things a bit private."

"You seem rather young as well. You're not in the same decades are you?"

"I'll be twenty-three this year. Our birthdays are just a month apart actually." I thanked the heavens for that little snippet of information I had stored when I'd been making plans to set up the birthday club in the office. I'd found it coincidental that Axel's birthday was the fifth of June while mine was the sixth of May. Fifth of the sixth and sixth of the fifth.

"Twenty-three! You're merely a child!"

I laughed. "Axel never lets me forget that I was just a child when we met. I've never let him forget that he was a man." From the look on her face, I could tell she was unsure whether or not to believe me.

"Where did you meet?"

"In a diner late one night, actually. Let's just say, we couldn't take our eyes off each other."

"So, you're a waitress?"

"No. I was on my way back from vacation and stopped for a bite to eat. He chased me and swept me off my feet." I stifled the laughter that was bubbling within me. The truth sounded like a movie script even to my ears. She was asking all the right questions. But only I knew the real truth behind the answers.

"So how long have you been together?"

"That's enough, Mother."

We both looked up to find Axel in the doorway. For a big man he moved like a cat. His eyes locked with mine as he walked over to me. He pulled me to stand in front of him as we faced his mother. As he wrapped his arms around me, I leaned into his warm embrace. His chin rested comfortably on top of my head and I giggled. He looked down at me and smiled then looked back at his mother.

"Bethany needs some help picking out her outfit for dinner. You might want to give her a hand. As I told her, I don't have the eye for that sort of thing. I can take care of Lisa."

"A diner, Axel? Of all the places you could come up with for a cover story, a diner? It would have been more plausible if you told me you got one of the secretaries at work to put on an act."

"Believe what you will, Mother. We did meet in a diner."

"Don't forget how you chased after me." I stroked his

beard as I looked into his eyes. He smiled and I felt my heart melt.

"Oh. I will never forget that. Knocked a fellow out cold to get you too. And I'm glad I did." He leaned down and brushed his lips against mine as if it were the most natural thing in the world. I heard his mother gasp as he kissed me. My lips melted beneath his, opening under the gentle pressure he used. I turned in his arms, my arms going up around his neck as he held me by the waist. My eyes closed as the onslaught continued. Then slowly, he raised his head. I opened my eyes and looked up at him. His eyes bored into mine as his large hands stroked my back.

"She's gone," he whispered.

The words were like being doused with ice-cold water. My arms slipped from around his neck but his hands remained on my waist.

"I'm sorry about that."

"That's okay. I'm sure the kiss made it more believable."

"I'm sorry about my mother interrogating you. I have no regrets about the kiss."

"Ohhhh. Thanks for coming to the rescue yet again. I was sure she was going to ask me for my blood type and a DNA sample next."

"I don't doubt that she would if given the chance."

"How much did you hear by the way?"

"Just the last question. I got here in the nick of time it seems."

Finally, he let his hands slip away, caressing my hips gently as they did. He turned to his backpack and rummaged through until he found a shirt and pants.

"I'm going to get these ironed for dinner. What are you wearing?"

"I wasn't sure what kind of affair dinner would be so I brought a few options."

"Let's have a look."

I pulled out the skirt and blouse along with the dress and a short jacket. I saw his eyes go wide as he looked at the dress. It was one of my favorite dresses. It was covered in sunflowers and always made me feel as though I was walking through a meadow. He cleared his throat.

"As much as I love the dress, for tonight I think the skirt and blouse will do. Footwear?"

"I brought flats and heels."

"The flats will do."

I pinched his arm gently and he turned to look at me. I smiled.

"What?"

"You lied."

"I lied?"

"You do have an eye for picking out women's outfits."

He threw his head back and laughed, and I thought it was the most magical sound I had ever heard. This was a side of Axel I'd never seen. And I liked it.

He left me to get our outfits ironed. I went to sit on a lounge chair on the balcony, and before I knew it, the gentle breeze had lulled me to sleep.

I wrinkled my nose as something tickled it, scrunching up my face. I boxed at whatever it was but it refused to budge and became more persistent. It was accompanied by a chuckle and my eyes flew open to find Axel sitting in the chair beside me. He was using the end of my braid to tickle my nose.

"Have a good nap?"

I covered my mouth as I yawned.

"I sure did. I don't usually sleep during the day. But this ocean breeze!"

He smiled and nodded. "It usually has that effect on me too. This is my second favorite place to be."

"What's your first?"

"My cabin in the mountains. I've got a few acres with a river running through it."

"That must be a sweet spot."

"It is." He held my gaze as he continued to play with my hair. "I don't think I've told you thanks for doing this for me."

"It's the least I could do for what you've done for me."

He checked his watch. "Dinner is in another hour. I wanted to make sure you were awake. Your outfit is in the closet by the way."

"Okay. Thanks."

He brushed my nose with my braid once more and smiled before getting up and going inside. I watched as he left the suite. I turned to look at the view once more.

The sky was being painted in shades of orange as the sun began to set. For a split second, I wish I was an artist and had the ability to capture this moment in time. But alas! I had to secure it in my heart.

I went in and showered and changed. When Axel returned to the room, I was standing on the balcony, allowing the breeze to tease my loose hair. I watched as he gathered his things and headed to the bathroom. I sat on the balcony, giving him the privacy he needed. I twisted my hair back into a loose braid and secured it with a hair tie. I took one last look at the view before going inside.

We went down to dinner and I was immediately introduced to the rest of the group.

There were the Chambers: Bethany, Brian, their father

Byron and their mother Bethune. They were an odd set and it was clear that dollar signs spoke loudly between the parents. Brian spent half the night chatting up to me while Bethany tried her best to keep Axel in conversation. There were about three other families. But the Chambers were the only ones staying with the Vances.

Throughout the night there was much talk about upgrading private jets and taking vacations in other parts of the world. I realized quickly that these people spoke in units of millions. There was talk of stocks and bonds and fancy cars. At intervals, questions were directed at me which I deflected. It was clear that they considered me to be out of their league. But my self-esteem was not so fragile to allow the snobbery to matter. Instead, I focused my attention on Axel.

Out of everyone, he seemed the most uncomfortable with all the talk of wealth. As a matter of fact, he acted as though he didn't have a trust fund that could buy a small nation and that the very mention of money annoyed him. Just the same, I wondered if I would feel the way he did had I grown up around wealth such as this. At the very least, I would hope that I would not be like Bethany Chambers. I immediately knew I didn't like her.

Bethany was a beautiful woman. I had to give her that. Her thick black hair and long lashes were the perfect foil for her emerald green eyes. Her skin was like cream and flawless. She was tall and slender but with curves in the right places. I was skeptical about how natural those were, though. With her kind of money, body parts could be bought. But her personality was acidic and snobbish. She spoke down to whoever she felt was beneath her and even her own brother was on the receiving end of her acid tongue. It was only on Axel that she turned the sweetest of smiles. But thank heavens he wasn't taken in by her act.

After dinner, there was talk of a round of games. The group split up and people wandered to various parts of the house. Axel used the opportunity to give me a quick tour. We were in the downstairs library and I was admiring the collection of mystery novels when I saw a picture on the wall. It was Axel and his parents. I pointed at it.

"You were a handsome little fellow."

"Were? Are you saying I'm not handsome now?" he grinned and lifted his eyebrows.

I laughed and pushed him playfully. "You're even more handsome now." I turned to look at him. "I don't get it, though."

"What don't you get?"

"You grew up with all this money. Yet it seems to irritate you."

"It doesn't seem to irritate me. It does irritate me."

"You're a rare one. You have jets and homes and exotic vacations at the touch of a button. Yet you've chosen to live below your means. There's nothing wrong with what you're doing, you know. It's just a rare thing. And on top of that, I'm sure there are many more Bethany Chambers around, yet you're single. Why is that?"

I felt his eyes bore into me, as though he was processing the question carefully.

"I believe in love. And I won't settle for less. When I marry, it will be to the woman I love. It will be the woman who is my missing rib. But what about you? You're a beautiful woman. I'm sure your father has had to be beating them off with a stick."

I laughed. "Ummm. Nope. I beat them off myself so they

don't get very far. And no one quite meets my main criterion."

"And what is that?"

I tilted my head and looked up at him. "You're looking for your rib. I'm looking for my savior."

The instant the words left my lips my eyes widened. I saw him intake a sharp breath and I knew our thoughts had gone back to the night he had saved me. Instantly I changed the subject.

We soon found ourselves in the games room with the others and I enjoyed a few light card games. Axel was never far from my side and even made it a point to tug on my braid now and then. The little gestures didn't go unnoticed by at least three people. Elizabeth and Bethany could barely contain their fury. But Brian's leering looks made me extremely uncomfortable.

It was nearly eleven when the group split up. Those who had other villas drove out of the compound while the Chambers and Vances settled in for the night. Axel and I walked up to our suite, holding hands as we were conscious of the audience we had. My heart raced as I remembered there was only one bed in the room. The kiss that afternoon came back to haunt me instantly. What was going to happen now?

As soon as the door closed behind us, he turned to me.

"Relax. I'll take the sofa."

"Okay." I didn't know if I was more disappointed or relieved.

Quietly I took out my night clothes and slipped into the bathroom to change. When I came out, he was already in a pair of shorts and shirtless. He had a pillow and blanket on the sofa. I averted my eyes and slipped beneath the covers of the king-sized bed. He turned out the lights and I could hear him settling into the sofa. I closed my eyes, but sleep wouldn't come. By the tossing and turning I heard on the sofa, neither could he.

Ten to fifteen minutes later, sleep was still far from me. I sighed softly. Suddenly, I heard Axel swear and toss the covers aside. There was a rush of breeze in the room as he opened the door and went to stand on the balcony.

16

AXEL

The pressure in my shorts was unbearable. And not even the chill of the ocean breeze could lessen the intensity. Thinking Lisa was only a few feet away from me and I had to keep my hands off her was torture. What had I been thinking to bring her into my space like this, especially with the issues I'd been having to keep my mind off her lately? Everything about her from the moment I'd picked her up at her apartment to watching her slip between the sheets had been wreaking havoc on my nerves. And that kiss this afternoon! As fleeting as it had been, it had only given me a hint of what it would be like to take her into my arms.

I took a few deep breaths, allowing the salty air to fill my lungs. My fingers gripped the banister tightly as I looked out over the ocean. The pounding of the waves matched the pounding of my heart and the pulsing of my cock. I focused on trying to regain control. I almost jumped out of my skin when I felt a soft hand touch my bare back. I turned to find Lisa standing beside me. How the hell has she snuck up on me like that?

"Can't sleep?"

My throat worked convulsively as I looked down at her. Then, out of the corner of my eye, I caught a movement below. Short, dark hair. Bethany. Without a second thought, I pulled Lisa to me, sandwiching her between the banister and my arms.

"We have an audience," I whispered, before I lowered my head. Her arms came up around my shoulders and I didn't have to pretend to groan when our lips met.

The fire was instantaneous and I knew I had lost the battle the moment she pressed her body to mine. There was no doubt she could feel my rock hard cock pressing into her abdomen.

I ground into her, parting her legs with a strong thigh. My hands slipped beneath the hem of her sleep shirt to caress her bare legs. As I crushed my lips to hers, I felt her tremble. But she didn't back down.

Our tongues met and merged, suckling and licking with an urgency that needed to be addressed. I no longer cared who was watching or not watching.

I swung Lisa up into my arms and marched back inside, our lips still fused. Gently I lowered her to the bed as the ocean breeze from the still open door washed over us. I pressed my body into hers, circling my hips as I trembled with the force of my need. I had to stop. I needed to stop. But when her legs came up around my waist, I was a goner.

I pulled her shirt up and off and retreated just enough to take off her panties and my shorts. I buried my face in her neck as my trembling hand reached down to test her readiness. I almost sobbed as I found her hot and wet. When her tiny hand reached down and gripped me, I was helpless. Together, we positioned ourselves for joining. I felt sweat bead on my forehead the second my pulsing cock head entered her steaming pussy.

"Fuck!"

I fused my lips to hers once more as I pressed forward, feeling her grip me as I entered her fully. She cried out against me as I slid into her, and I felt her tremble.

Our bodies moved with an urgency that told me this was not going to be a marathon session. I knew I was close to losing it but I held back just long enough to feel her tighten around me as she climaxed with soft whimpers and murmurs. Seconds later, I convulsed as I poured myself into her.

I held her for a few moments, pulsing deep inside her as the edge wore off. I was still rock hard and flexed my cock. I heard her gasp. Now I was ready to rock her world.

I withdrew slowly, leaving just the head in before I thrust back in forcefully. I was pleased to hear her cry out in pleasure as I repeated the motion. I captured her hands in mine as I fused my mouth to hers once again. Her sweet breath and soft cries of pleasure sent my senses whirling. My tongue mimicked the thrusting of my cock and I soon felt her pressing urgently up into my body. I allowed her to meet me, skin slapping against skin in the darkness. I pulled her knees up to give her a different experience and was rewarded with her cries of pleasure as I knew I was touching something special. She fell apart around me then, and I reveled in the pulsing of her body and the velvety folds of her pussy that fluttered around me. But I wasn't finished.

Every fantasy I'd ever had since the day I'd found her in the laundry room came rushing back. I waited for her breathing to regulate as she came down from another climax. I slowly pulled away from her until I was standing over her. I rolled her over gently, pulling her onto her knees.

In the dimness I felt her stretch her torso out, lying flat as she stuck her ass in the air. I nudged her knees apart and knelt between them. Then slowly I reentered her. Her head went back as she gasped softly. I stroked her hair and found the end of her braid. As I began to thrust slowly, I undid the strands and fanned her hair out. I gripped her waist as her ass danced against my groin as she pushed back. One hand slipped lower to find her clit. She squealed as I pinched it, trembling deep within.

"Axel!"

Just hearing my name rolling off her tongue in this moment sent shivers down my spine. I picked up the pace as I felt my balls tingling. I bent over her until my chest was flat against her back, thrusting with all my might and never letting up on stroking her clit. When I felt her pussy grip me like a vice and explode around me, I held her tightly as I thrust one more time. I felt my body shatter into a million pieces as I gushed and spewed deep into her womb. We were like a bowl of Jello as we trembled in each other's arms. We lay crouched like that for long moments. I was loath to let her go. But finally, we had to part. Wordlessly, I picked her up and carried her into the shower.

A couple minutes later we were cleaned up and back in bed. As I held her close, my eyes felt heavy. Her soft breathing told me that she had already fallen asleep. I knew we had crossed a line but I would deal with that tomorrow. For tonight, I wanted to spend the rest of the night holding her. And I did just that.

When I woke up at first I was puzzled. For one, I had had the best night's sleep in weeks. But suddenly, when I remembered why, I bolted upright. I looked at the pillow next to me. All that remained of Lisa was the indentation of her head. I ran my hand over my beard and looked around the room. Where was she? Then I heard the sink in the bathroom running. I exhaled the breath I hadn't realized I was holding. But now I had another problem. How would we handle what had happened between us last night?

I was ecstatic. But she hadn't signed up for this when she had agreed to help me this weekend. How would she feel? I didn't have long to wonder as the bathroom door opened. Her shining eyes met mine. I searched them and saw nothing but sincerity and joy. She had no regrets. And neither did I.

"Good morning." I smiled and was met with a radiant smile.

"Good morning. Did I wake you? I tried to be quiet."

"You were quiet. It was just time for me to get up." I threw the covers aside and saw her eyes slide downward and her cheeks turned red. I held her eyes as I stood and stretched, grinning as I watched her fight the temptation to ogle me. I walked over to her slowly, bending to kiss her cheek as I passed her in the doorway.

When I came out, she was dressed in a modest one-piece swimsuit and pulling on a pair of cut-offs over it. I pulled on shorts and a t-shirt before pushing my feet into slippers.

"What strength do you use?"

I looked at her and found her holding two tubes of sunblock lotion.

"What do you have?"

"Fifteen and forty."

"Take the forty. We can't be too careful. Shall we?"

I took the towel and tube from her hand and intertwined my fingers with hers. It felt like the most natural thing in the world. And had it not been for the fact that we needed to eat, I would have stayed in the room all day and made love to her again and again.

We were the last ones down to breakfast and I watched as everyone eyed us with speculating glances and glares. Clearly Bethany had been running her mouth about what she had seen on the balcony last night. Good. Maybe now they would get off my case. My mission had been accomplished. But as I watched Lisa butter my toast, I knew deep in my heart that I wanted to switch the charade for the real thing. I didn't want her to pretend to be my girlfriend until Monday morning when we drove back to the city and reality. I wanted her to *be* my girlfriend, then fiancé, then wife. I was stunned at the path down which my thoughts had gone. It was as though I had fallen into a hole, and I couldn't regain my footing and kept falling. And the most shocking of all was that I didn't mind.

I smiled at Lisa and brushed the back of my hand along her cheek, watching her smile widen in return. She was perfect. I decided then and there that there would be no pretending. After last night, there was no turning back or going back to life as usual. At some point before we left on Monday morning, Lisa would know that she was my girlfriend – for real.

17

LISA

I felt as if I was walking in a dream for the entire morning. Even now as I laid on the lounge chair by the pool watching Axel swim laps, I found it incredible that mere hours before we had made love. And the reality had surpassed my fantasy.

That morning when I had woken up, I had lain looking at him as he slept. His lashes lay along his cheek, the crescent scar silver on his face. My fingers itched to run through his beard and trace his full lips. I had been so tempted to lean over and brush my lips against his. But what would that have signaled?

I had gotten out of the bed as quietly as I could, picked up my shirt, and headed to the bathroom to gather my thoughts. The doubts had attacked me then as I was reminded that this was supposed to be an act. Sleeping with Axel had not been on the agenda. But it felt amazing!

I looked at him as he climbed out of the pool and walked over to me, smiling broadly. The sun glistened on his wet skin. Surprisingly, he had no tattoos which I found odd for a military man. He leaned over me and shook a few drops of water onto my leg. I laughed and kicked at him playfully. He grabbed my foot and I soon dissolved into squeals and giggles as he tickled me. Then suddenly he swooped me into his arms and before I could think twice, he made a running leap into the deep end of the pool. Moments before the water closed over us, he kissed me. I clung to him under-water, wrapping my legs around his waist as his tongue delved into my mouth. I felt us break the surface of the water and I closed my eyes against the glare of the sun. My arms went around his neck as he held me close, keeping us afloat with his powerful legs as he treaded lightly. I felt him grow hard against me and tightened my legs. He pulled his mouth from mine but pressed his forehead to mine.

"If we were all alone here, I would strip this swimsuit off you in a heartbeat."

I laughed softly. "That's a promise I look forward to you keeping any time we find ourselves alone with an empty pool."

"I have a pool at both my places, you know. Pick one. City or mountain?"

"Why pick? And didn't you say you had a river too?"

He laughed. "You're insatiable."

"You're the one creating a monster."

He leaned in to kiss me once more and I closed my eyes, losing myself in his tenderness. We heard some discreet coughing and pulled apart to find his mother staring daggers at us from the side of the pool.

"If you can tear yourselves off each other for a moment, Mr. Sanders is asking for you, Axel."

"We're just making use of the season for lovers. Isn't that what this weekend is about, Mother? Or is it only a weekend for the lover you would want me to have?"

"Business is important. And you've practically ignored

Bethany all morning, Axel. You do know she's next in line to take over from Byron. You need to be nice. And you've known her all your life."

I felt my cheeks burn as Elizabeth didn't care that I was there. The kid gloves were clearly off now. I looked beyond her to see Bethany peering through the French doors that led to the pool. She swirled a drink in her hand as she watched the three of us. I smiled and waved and was rewarded with a toss of her head as she turned her back.

I allowed my legs to slip from around Axel's waist. He turned me in his arms so that my back was flush against his torso the way it had been last night. A strong forearm held me by the waist as he walked us to the steps at the shallow end. Only when my feet touched the steps did he release me. I turned to him.

"Go see Mr. Sanders, honey. Your mother is right. You don't need to be neglecting business. And we do have the rest of our lives for pleasure."

I used my thumb to trace his lips and he laughed.

"Sensible as always. Is it any wonder I love you?"

I heard his mother make a choking sound and looked over to see her looking as white as a sheet. She turned on her heel and walked quickly into the house. Axel laughed softly.

"We've really gotten under their skin, you know. Bethany is livid! I'm sure she sent my mother out here. But I'm going to take your advice and go have a quick chat with Sanders. Don't go too far, I want us to go to the beach."

"Okay."

He pulled me close and kissed me once more before walking out of the pool. I watched as he grabbed a towel and dried his legs before heading into the house. I went back to my lounge chair and began wringing water out of my braid.

I would have to wash it the first chance I got. I adjusted my umbrella and leaned back in the chair with a book from the library. I was so buried in the story that I didn't hear anyone approach.

"Axel always had the luck of the draw. I don't know where he found you, but do you have a twin sister?"

I looked up to find Brian Chambers looking down at me. I was instantly conscious of his vantage point and him possibly having a bird's eye view of my cleavage. Without hesitation, I drew a towel across my chest, spreading it down to cover my upper thighs as well. He raised his eyebrows at the gesture.

"I guess the goods are for Axel's eyes only huh."

"How can I help you, Brian?"

"How about we help each other, sweetie?"

"I beg your pardon?"

"When whatever this thing is between you and Axel comes to an end and he does as Mommy says and gets it on with my sis, we can have some fun." He wiggled his eyebrows suggestively and my skin began to crawl.

"I'll pass, thanks." I turned back to my book.

"I can make it worth your while." He shocked me by reaching down for the end of my braid. Without hesitation, I yanked my hair out of his hands.

"No thank you."

He laughed softly. "You'll come to your senses soon. My offer remains open – for now."

I watched as he walked away. I felt anger bubbling inside at the insinuation that my affections could be bought. I recalled what Axel had said in the pool about loving me. How I wished it was true! But I knew it had been for his mother's sake.

As soon as I felt the way was clear, I gathered my things

and headed inside to the library to return the book. I was halfway down the corridor when I ran into Bethany. I received a withering stare and returned it with a smile.

"Done horsing around?"

"Pardon?" I smiled innocently.

"Oh please! Can we stop with the little miss prissy behavior you little gold digger? Listen, Axel may be taken in by you right now. But believe me he's only in it for the sex and that can get really old really fast."

"I don't think-"

"That's right, you didn't think. But let me make things a little easier for you. Name your price. We can tell Axel you had a family emergency. The jet can get you back to the city before you know it. You can cash the check first thing Monday morning and stay out of Axel's life and we continue our lives as though you never crawled out from underneath your rock."

I held my hand up and shook my head.

"Bethany, I don't know what your problem is. But I can assure you that I am not for sale. Maybe you've been able to chase away other girls before, but I'm not like other girls. I love Axel and he loves me. Get over it and move on with your pathetic excuse of a life. Excuse me."

I brushed past her, tempted to push her as I did. But the last thing I wanted was to tangle with her physically. But she clearly didn't feel the same way.

I had taken only a few steps away from her when I felt a sharp tug on my hair. I turned reflexively and caught her hand as she raised it to slap me. I twisted her wrist and she cried out in pain. I held on, digging my fingers into her wrist until she began to scream.

"I asked you to excuse me."

"You bitch!"

"Bethany! What on earth is going on here?"

I dropped her hand and spun around to find Elizabeth racing down the corridor, Axel and others on her heels.

To my surprise, Bethany burst into tears and raised her injured wrist which was beginning to turn red.

"This little gold digger that Axel brought attacked me! Look what she did to me!"

My mouth dropped open. "You attacked me and I was defending myself!"

"You almost broke my hand!"

"I did nothing of the sort!"

She turned tear filled eyes on Axel. "Are you going to let your little girlfriend get away with this?"

I turned to face Axel and found him with a huge grin on his face. "I am."

"What!?"

"Knock off the act, Bethany. I just happened to be with Mr. Sanders in the camera room showing him our latest equipment. Guess what we happened to pick up on the corridor surveillance?"

I looked back at Bethany and she was as white as a sheet. I looked at Axel. He held his hand out to me and I went to him. He raised my hand to his lips and kissed the back. He turned to his mother.

"If you can't control your guests and prevent them from deliberately stalking, lying in wait and attacking my guests, I'll be leaving. Lisa, you have every right to press charges against Bethany if you choose. You do know that her putting her hand on your person and attempting to assault you is grounds for charges, right? And while we're at it, let's throw in Brian's harassment at the pool. Let's make it a sibling affair."

I heard a choke and looked around to see Brian slinking against the wall.

Elizabeth turned to Bethany. "Is it true? Did you attack her?"

Bethany's response was to rush past the group and disappear down the corridor. Her brother followed in her wake. Soon everyone went back to whatever they were doing leaving Axel, Elizabeth and me. She turned to me with her lips pursed.

"I'm sure Bethany was just upset about something and took it out on you. I apologize on her behalf."

"Oh. I'm sure I was her target. She's a grown woman and can apologize for herself. Not that I want one."

"Never mind, Mother. We're leaving after breakfast tomorrow morning."

"Axel!"

"I'm sick and tired of the excuses you make for these people. She could have hurt Lisa. And for what? Some demented fairytale you've both concocted all her life about us getting married? Bethany is a spoiled selfish brat who has grown into an insufferable woman. I can't understand why you would want to call her children your grandchildren. We leave tomorrow and you can finish the weekend with your guests on your own. Excuse us. We won't be dining with the rest of you for lunch."

With that, Axel stormed down the corridor, pulling me with him. He headed up the staircase to our suite. He looked at me carefully, concern creasing his brow. Then he pulled me into his arms and hugged me tightly.

"I'm sorry about what Bethany did."

"Were you really watching on the camera?"

"I was. And I saw Brian at the pool as well. He didn't

touch you, but your body language said it all. You covered yourself."

"Are we really leaving tomorrow?"

"Yes. I've done my due diligence here."

"Okay. What are we doing for lunch?"

"I was thinking we could drive around the town and find a restaurant."

"I'd love that."

We changed quickly and headed downstairs and out to the truck. Lunch was an adventurous affair as Axel found a spot that was a five-minute boat ride to a restaurant on a little cay. We spent the afternoon swimming in the warm turquoise waters and snoozing on the sand. By the time we headed back to the house it was nearly five. Dinner was not until eight. We rinsed off the worst of the sand before curling up in bed for a nap. When I woke up Axel was gone and my ironed dress was hanging on the closet door. By the time I dressed and brushed out my hair, he returned. In ten minutes, he was ready and we headed down to dinner on the beach.

There was a lot of awkwardness on the part of the Chambers as they made excuses for Bethany and Brian's behavior towards me earlier. They also thanked me for not doing my due diligence of getting the police involved as Axel had threatened. I brushed it aside and settled in to enjoy the night.

There was a full moon tonight and its reflection on the water coupled with the torches lighting the dining area which had been set up gave the atmosphere a magical feel. After dinner, the group broke into smaller groups. I found that two other families had joined us: the Rileys and the rest of the Sanders. The Rileys had a fourteen-year-old daughter named Lucy who had stuck by me all evening. A few of us were sitting in a cabana with after dinner drinks when Lucy cried out.

"Oh no! It broke again!"

I looked over to find her clutching her wrist and scrunching her legs together. I reached over and rescued the beads which had already fallen off her bracelet.

"Give it to me."

I took the remains of the bracelet from her and stooped to lay the beads out on the small table. It was an easy fix and I had it repaired in no time. I handed it back to her.

"There you are. As good as new."

"Are you sure it won't come undone again?"

"It won't. I used the right knot this time. You've got to use a flat knot or a surgical knot when you do these things."

I took my seat and picked up my drink. I lifted my eyes and saw Axel staring at me as he sat with the group of men. I held his eyes and slowly raised my hand to my temple. I saluted and watched a grin spread across his face. Warmth burst inside me as he returned the salute.

It was nearly midnight before people decided to call it a night. I stood looking at the beach longingly as I waited for Axel to finish his goodbyes. When he came over and took my hand in his, I leaned into his warmth. He squeezed my fingers slightly before stooping down to remove his shoes and roll up the legs of his pants. I followed suit and eased off my slippers. We left them there by the cabana as we walked along the beach hand in hand. The light breeze whipped my hair around us.

"I have no idea how I'm going to get all this sand out tonight."

He laughed. "You'll be finding sand for days."

I smiled. "Axel? If I haven't said it before, thanks for this weekend." Even as I spoke, I felt a sense of dread creep over me. This time tomorrow, we would be back in reality. The pretense would be over. I swallowed convulsively as I remembered how our bodies had been joined the night before. My heart raced at the prospect of being with him tonight again. But would he want that?

We enjoyed the feeling of the water and sand between our toes as we walked in silence. Soon our steps turned to the house. We found our shoes and headed inside, leaving a trail of sand and damp prints in our wake. The silence stretched out between us and I was filled with trepidation at our last night together. Out of nowhere, I felt a hunger to be with Axel. I looked at him from beneath my lashes as he opened the door. Nothing. My heart ached.

As soon as we were inside, I dashed into the bathroom with the excuse of needing to wash the day's sediments out of my hair. I stripped and stood beneath the spray, ignoring the sting of tears in my eyes as I lathered my hair the first time. I took a few deep breaths to calm myself as I raised my arms to scrub my scalp. I gasped when I felt a warm body behind me and another pair of hands on my scalp.

"Let me," he whispered huskily.

I trembled as I leaned back and found his hard length pressed into the small of my back. One of his hands slipped down to my shoulder and pressed me forward. Obediently I bent over spreading my legs. My stomach clenched with desire as I felt him caress my ass. I braced my hands against the smooth tile of the wall as I waited for him. I groaned as he entered me slowly, circling his hips as he slipped deeper and deeper.

"Mmmmmmm," I moaned softly. I began to push back to meet his slow thrusts. He reached around to caress my breasts and tease my nipples. Then his hand slipped down and I was sent on a deliciously delirious journey as he massaged my clit. I felt my body grip him and was rewarded with a long low groan as he thrust harder and faster.

"Come for me, baby."

He flicked my clit faster and I cried out as I felt my toes begin to tingle. I pushed back to meet each urgent thrust, scrabbling to grip the tiles as I lost my rhythm. I felt my body begin to shake uncontrollably as I was caught in the grip of my climax. I bit my lips, stifling my cries of pleasure. He held my waist as he pressed forward and stayed there. I felt heat explode deep inside me as he poured himself into me.

He pulled out and spun me around to face him. Abruptly, he turned the shower off as he hauled my body up to meet him. He hoisted me into his arms and braced me against the wall, plunging his body into mine as I wrapped my legs around him.

The warm bathroom grew even steamier with the heat from our bodies as our lovemaking continued. I came apart in his arms clutching and trembling as I climaxed over and over. He took me to the peak, satisfying me just like I knew he would. I was spent as he sat on the marble bench in the shower. He draped my thighs over his as he remained buried inside me. He stroked my hair as he circled my hips slowly. Soon I found my own rhythm and held his shoulders as I bounced on his cock. He laughed huskily.

"You're a fast learner."

I leaned forward and kissed him hard, nibbling on his lips before pulling back.

"I have a good teacher."

Our eyes met and held as I continued to press down on him hard. He reached between us and found my throbbing clit once more. I cried out as he stroked it, grinding into him as hard as I could.

"Axel! I'm gonna come!"

"I'm right behind you, baby."

He pressed his lips to mine. I screamed into his mouth as I shuddered through yet another climax. I felt faint as my body slumped. He buried his groans in my hair as he held me tightly.

Hours later after we had finally gotten around to washing my hair and getting it partially dried and braided, we fell into bed in a tangle of arms and legs, our appetites insatiable. I had this one night. And I was not going to allow one second to go to waste.

18

AXEL

I used my forefinger to trace the line of her brow as I watched her sleep. Last night had been phenomenal. And now as I watched her resting in my arms, I felt my heart expand.

I allowed my hand to slide down her cheek and across her collarbone. Slowly I moved the sheet downward so that I could cup the full mounds of her breasts. I leaned over her and took a nipple into my mouth, sucking gently. I felt my cock stir as I heard her sigh above me. My hand went lower still. Skimming over her belly until I brushed the soft hairs at the apex of her thighs. I let my finger glide between her labia, teasing her clit which was already beginning to respond to my touch. I raised my head to find her looking down at me through hooded eyes. I brought my head up to the pillow we shared and kissed her softly while I still played with her clit.

"Good morning." I nuzzled her nose with mine.

She yawned and stretched. I cupped her pussy as I slid a thigh between her legs. I raised myself up on one elbow. I brought my other hand up and caressed her cheek.

"Did you sleep well?"

She smiled. "As well as one can sleep in just a few hours. What time is it?"

"Almost six."

"What time are we leaving?"

"I was thinking around midday since I don't see us getting up any time soon for breakfast. We'll still get back before dark."

"Okay."

I reached for her braid which I realized had become a favorite gesture of mine.

"Tell me some more about your father's issues. When did you say this all started?"

"Ummm. Almost three years ago. He had been complaining about feeling tired and lethargic all the time. Then one day he collapsed. Not passed out. Collapsed and was conscious. He couldn't walk. It wasn't a stroke or anything like that."

"And what have the doctors been saying?"

"They're puzzled. We've been getting whatever treatment insurance will cover."

"Which cannot be a lot."

"It isn't."

"Did he have a pension or anything?"

"He does. But it can only do so much."

"If you don't mind my asking, how have you been surviving since he got sick?"

"We've had some savings and I do some craft work on the side."

"And that pays the bills and puts food on the table?"

"It pays the important bills. What doesn't get paid this month, gets paid the following month."

The matter-of-fact way she said it made me feel like a world class heel for firing her.

She stroked my beard as I looked into her eyes. I swallowed and brushed my lips against hers as I reached down to cup her pussy once more. I felt her push into my hand and was amazed at her responsiveness to my touch. I nuzzled her nose.

"Come back to work tomorrow."

"Why? Because you feel sorry for me? No."

"I don't feel sorry for you. I saw how you handled Bethany. You can take care of yourself. But I do need a PA and you're the best I've ever had. And you need to have an income to take care of those bills. So, it's a win-win. What do you say?"

I stroked her clit as I spoke, loving the way her pupils dilated when she became aroused. I felt her grow wet as her legs moved restlessly. I took her hand and placed it on my already stiff cock before sliding my finger into her pussy. I leaned down and nibbled her neck. She moaned and I smiled.

"Is that a yes?"

"Hmmm."

"So, I'll see you bright and early at eight-thirty tomorrow morning?" I knew I was playing dirty as I finger-fucked her while I spoke.

She had closed her eyes and was stroking me as she bit her lips. I withdrew my hand and her eyes flew open.

"I'll see you tomorrow morning?" I allowed my finger to barely brush her clit.

She nodded and I smiled. As I rolled on top of her, her legs parted to welcome me as we sealed our new agreement.

The drive back to the city was filled with conversation and laughter and seemed to end far too quickly. I kissed her discreetly before escorting her to the door. I waited for her to come to the window and wave before driving home.

My rest that night was peaceful and my dreams blissful. Monday I arrived at seven-thirty. I placed the appointment diary in the center of her desk. I watched the cameras like a hawk. My heart dropping each time a new arrival was not Lisa. I saw Lola and Cheryl look at the desk in surprise and a little disappointment. Discreet looks from others told me that the word had spread that the PA vacancy had been filled. But the joke was on them. At eight-fifteen, Lisa walked into the office. There was a collective pause as she walked to her desk. I saw her look across at Lola and smile and nod. The office seemed to erupt in activity as one after the other, the employees came to welcome her back. At exactly eight-thirty I got up and opened my door, schooling my expression. She looked up and I felt my heart twist.

"Welcome back, Lisa."

"Good to be back, sir."

"Shall we go over today's tasks?"

Obediently she took up the appointment book along with her pen and notepad. As soon as the door closed behind us, I pulled her into my arms and kissed her deeply. And thus began the pattern of our days.

We were extremely discreet and professional. But I never allowed her to forget that we had something going on between us. As to what it was, was clear in my mind. She was my girlfriend – officially. The only problem was I hadn't given her that memo. For all intents and purposes, she might be of the opinion that we were simply having an affair. At some point, when the time was right and I was sure of her feelings for me, I would set her straight and make it official. I had no doubt that she had some regard for me. I could see it in her eyes each time she looked at me. But nothing happened before its time.

There was a noticeable lightness in the office with Lisa's return. And though I tried to remain neutral, I knew that even my change in demeanor was noticeable. It was so obvious that one morning after a senior meeting, Candace told me that she was happy I had finally found my match. Before my shock at being found out could register, she continued by saying that Lisa was the best PA I had ever had and that she was good for business. I had breathed a sigh of relief. She had meant as it pertains to the business. Our secret was intact.

Over the next week or two, I took Lisa with me to all my business meetings. I watched as she wowed my clients and had even had a few of them ask if they could hire her away from me. I shut them down so fast I know I got some weird looks. But I didn't care.

Another thing I realized having Lisa back was that the gnawing sexual desire, though still there, was somewhat under control. I enjoyed the time I spent with her, the little stolen kisses and secret gestures. It felt almost like we were married. I was so comfortable around her. One afternoon as she had sat in my office with her foot bouncing on mine, I had shocked myself by inviting her to spend a weekend in my cabin when the weather was warm enough. She shocked me even further by accepting. I immediately began to plan the perfect time.

I had not forgotten about my intention to seek medical assistance for her father either. I was waiting on a friend of mine to get some details on his case and make some recommendations. When I had everything in place, then I would let Lisa know what I had been up to on that front. Hopefully, by then we would have grown even closer so she would accept my help without any reservation.

Lisa was a part of me. And my regard for her grew stronger with each passing day. And that weekend in Coral Springs was never far from my thoughts.

One Friday evening a few weeks after she had returned, I sat in my office watching her as she worked. The memories of how she had bent over for me in the shower hammered at me. I had kept my hands off her. But there were times when the need became almost overpowering. I pushed the feeling aside and turned back to the file on my desk. I buried myself so far in work that I didn't realize how time had passed. When next I looked up, the office was empty. The clock read a quarter to six. I decided to do some more work until around six-thirty and hit the gym later. I picked up another file and had barely turned the first page and made some notations when there was a knock on the door.

"Come in!" I barked.

Lisa pushed her head inside and smiled. I smiled back.

"I thought you were gone."'

"I went to freshen up. I have the Stevens contract for you to sign." She stepped into the office and closed the door behind her. I watched as she approached me. And just like that, I was at half-mast once more. I reached out to take the file from her and captured her hand at the same time. I intertwined my fingers with hers and pulled her onto my lap as I set the file aside. I spread my legs slightly so that she could nestle in the space created. I saw her eyebrows go up and color stain her cheeks as she felt me stirring beneath her. Her eyes met mine shyly. I held her gaze as I stroked the exposed skin of her calf. My hand moved up until it found the soft skin at the back of her knee. I stroked it gently and saw her take a deep breath. I leaned forward and buried my face in her cleavage, inhaling her scent. I kissed the exposed skin of her neck and felt her hands tug on my hair as she pulled me closer. I had taken her suggestion of growing my hair out and I had to admit that I liked the feeling of her fingers in my hair.

My hand worked its way up until I was caressing her thigh. But it wasn't enough. I pushed my chair back and made her stand. I pulled her to stand between my legs and pulled her skirt up until it bunched around her waist. I hooked my fingers into her panties and pulled them down. She stepped out of them. I cleared the desk behind her and leaned her against it. My hand cupped her pussy, forcing her thighs apart. As I stroked between her labia and felt her dampness begin to grow, I heard her sigh above me. I dipped the tip of my finger into her pussy and it came away with her white cream. She made a strangled gasp as I raised it to my lips. I stood.

I eased her back onto the desk until she was lying flat and her legs hung over the edges. I pulled my chair up and sat as I parted her legs. I leaned forward and flicked my tongue against her clit.

"Shit!"

I smiled at the expression. Then I dove in and feasted.

I draped one leg over my shoulder as I lapped at her pussy. My tongue flicked at her clit in between nibbles while I finger fucked her. I licked her from top to bottom, tickling and nibbling every sensitive spot I discovered. She writhed beneath me. I felt her body tremble and I was rewarded with her hot sweet cream as I brought her to a climax. She cried out in agony as I continued to tease her sensitive clit, finally releasing her when she twisted her body away from me. I gave her time to recover.

I stood and undid my pants, pushing them and my

boxers down to my knees as I freed my cock. I pulled her closer to the edge and lined up myself with her entrance. She lifted her hips to meet me and I threw my head back as I sank into her. Her steaming pussy wrapped around me like a warm blanket. I was home.

I looked down to where our bodies joined and I was mesmerized by the sight of her swollen lips around my cock. With each thrust, I heard the slurping of her juices. With each withdrawal, my cock was coated in her cream. Sweat beaded on my forehead as I concentrated on pleasing her, circling my hips to find the right angle.

Her head was thrown back and her hands balled into fists as she bit her lips to stifle her moans. I grunted softly as I felt her ripple around me. Her hips jerked in spasms as she climaxed. I buried myself in her and leaned down to cover her torso with mine. I kissed her neck, stifling my groans in her hair as I ejaculated.

My eyes were open but I was seeing nothing but stars before my eyes. All that could be heard in the empty office was the sound of our mingled ragged breathing. Her fingers played in my hair restlessly as we came back to some sort of normalcy.

Slowly I raised my body off hers and looked down at her. I kissed her softly before reaching for a handful of tissues. I took my time to clean our bodies as best as I could before stepping back.

We rearranged our clothes and I kissed her lightly as I pocketed her panties. I laughed as she blushed.

"These are mine now."

"No fair. Where's my souvenir?"

"I promise you one the next time you come to my house."

"Your house?"

"Yes. My house. There's a little laundry room fantasy that has been haunting me for weeks now."

I hugged her tightly, rubbing my hands over her ass. "When I saw you bent over it drove me crazy. And I've been wanting to do naughty things with you ever since."

She laughed. "That makes two of us."

I cocked my eyebrow. "You've been having fantasies about me?"

She smiled and nodded. "Granted, I don't have that much experience to go by to feed them. You're my second. And Coral Springs was my second time as well. But this was the first time I've ever been eaten." She laughed. "My first time was over before it had even begun. It sucked. But somehow, I knew you would rock my world."

I grinned. "Oh yeah?"

She kissed me softly. "Yeah."

"I need to correct you on a point though. I'm not your second. I'm your last."

My eyes pierced into hers as the enormity of my words hit her. I kissed her softly then pulled back.

"Give me a few minutes to pack up my desk. I'll take you home."

"Okay."

The drive to her apartment was over all too quickly. Before I knew it, I had kissed her goodbye and was heading home. As I ate my dinner in solitude, my heart ached for Lisa. I wanted her here with me. And the graver reality was that I wanted it to be permanent. I had meant what I said. I would be her last if I had to annihilate every man on the planet and be the only one remaining. Now all I had to do was convince her to get on the same page with me.

19

LISA

Ever since the weekend at Coral Springs, I was a changed woman. There was no doubt in my mind that I loved Axel. Now all that remained to be seen was whether he felt the same. But until such time when we got to that bridge, I would keep my feelings to myself.

My father and Nora had been waiting on me when I came home earlier than expected and I told them as much as I dared regarding the reception from Elizabeth and Bethany. But they had been shocked to hear that I was to return to work the following day. My life felt like a fairytale and Axel was my knight in shining armor.

At first, I had wondered how it would work for us in the office. But we soon settled into a norm of discretion. Needless to say, I had wondered if he would ever touch me again. I didn't have to wonder any longer after that Friday evening. Each time I thought about how he had pleasured me orally I felt my cheeks stain and my pussy grow wet. I had also developed an insatiable curiosity to know what it would be like to do the same to him. Again, only time would tell. I anticipated the weekend in the mountains as well as going back to his house.

March came in with warmer weather and everything was in bloom everywhere. Axel had given me back the credit card and I used it to get some posies for each desk on the first official day of spring. After that, I ensured that there was always a fresh bouquet of flowers in the entryway. I had also suggested to Axel that he rearrange the cubicles to utilize the space more economically. The space on the floor above where we ate lunch was retrofitted to accommodate a boardroom which could also serve as a meeting area for larger groups. I was working hard and I loved every minute of it.

It had become the norm to greet each other with a kiss and to separate in the same manner. It felt like we were an old married couple working the family business together. And it felt right.

Axel had changed for the better and everyone noticed. Lola had asked me more than once what I had done to tame him, and in the same breath had begged me to maintain it. The staff loved the new and improved Axel, from his ready smiles down to the thick wavy hair he now sported. I took immense pleasure in running my fingers through it whenever we were alone, and it pleased me whenever he leaned into my touch.

I was doing just that as we embraced in his office one morning when he dropped a bombshell on me.

"I have a specialist that I want your father to see, Lisa. I've been doing some digging and checking around and finally found someone who is willing to take his case."

My fingers stopped mid-stroke.

"A specialist?"

"Yes. He has an excellent track record of dealing with unusual cases of sudden immobility like your father's."

"Will our insurance cover it?"

"Definitely not. But don't worry about the cost."

"But I have to think about the cost, Axel. We are on a budget."

"Don't worry about the cost. Like I said, he's willing to take your father's case."

"But it's not for free, is it?"

"No. But that's not your concern."

"It is, Axel. I can't take money from you."

"Why not?"

"It's just the principle. I can't."

"What if I gave you a loan? We could arrange for the payback to be deducted from your salary a little at a time. Would you take it then?"

I looked up at him, my hands resting against his chest. His eyes pierced into me. I rolled my eyes and smiled.

"I guess it could work that way."

"Great. I want to talk to your father and see if he would be willing to undergo an examination and treatment. There's one other thing, though. This specialist is two hours away. And he wants your father in house so that he can monitor him around the clock."

My eyes widened. "So that means-?"

"Your father would be in a healthcare facility."

I chewed my lip as I thought about what Axel was saying. It had been months since that depressing conversation about admitting him. And with Nora's help, he was almost like his old self. But if this treatment could fix his mobility and the trembling he experienced constantly, maybe he would be willing to try.

"So, when can I talk to him?"

"I guess there's no time like the present. Would you like to come over for dinner this evening?"

He grinned and my heart melted.

"I'd love that. Shall we seal the deal?"

I giggled. "I thought you would never ask."

I sighed softly as his lips met mine. By the press of his body, I knew he hungered for me as much as I did him. It was long moments later that he raised his head, his eyes searching mine.

"If I didn't have all these meetings today, I'd take you home and take you to bed right now."

The bluntness of his words made me blush. He chuckled and nuzzled my nose.

"I love it when you blush." He kissed me once more before releasing me. "Let's get back to work before I have you cancel those appointments and we leave for the rest of the day."

I took my usual seat and flipped open my notepad while he went to his seat.

"Who do we have lined up for this afternoon's round?"

I flipped to a page on the notepad.

"Henry, James and his wife, Leonie and her sister Fiona, and we also have Sheldon, Raheim and Theodine Spencer.'"

"The triplets?"

"The triplets."

"Awesome! I'm glad to hear they're interested in what we have to offer. Have you begun working on potential assignments?"

I flipped to another page in the notepad and went to stand over him.

"I was thinking that Theodine could be placed with

Global. She lives closer to that area and has a more intimate knowledge of that part of the city. I also got a call from the recruitment officer at Seprod. They need five people. We have more than enough people to fill those spaces. Have you given any further thought to the potential of merging with Shirley and feeding our recruits through her and having her expand her offerings to include our ex-military officers and their families in job placements?"

"We have another meeting on Monday. Trina will be present to work out the legal aspects of any merger of this nature."

He rubbed his hand through his beard as he looked up at me.

"The way things have been going, I feel as though I need to buy a building."

I smiled down at him. "That wouldn't be a bad idea. I do feel as though we've outgrown these two floors. And if we get Shirley on board, it would make sense to have central-ized operations."

He pulled me onto his lap and I draped my arm around his shoulder. He intertwined his fingers with mine as he looked up at me.

"Ten years ago when I came back, I'm sure no one would have thought that VSS could have moved beyond the two-room office my father had for years. When we moved onto this floor, everyone thought we were nuts. And now here I am, contemplating buying an entire building and expanding our operations. And, it helps to know that our competitors are taking notice."

"Chambers still wants to buy you out?"

"I think at this point he wants a merger rather than a buy-out. I know he plans to retire soon and hand the reins to Bethany."

"Why not Brian?"

"He's not CEO material. As much as I'm not fond of her, Bethany has a sharper mind and more interest and knowledge of the business. She will make an excellent CEO. Quite frankly, they aren't hurting for money. I guess it's just the principle of wanting somewhat of a monopoly in the industry. But VSS is not for sale. I would prefer to downsize or liquidate before I sell to the highest bidder."

"And that will never happen." I kissed him quickly, picked up my notepad and stood. "I need to finish preparing the board room. Michelle Green should be here in another ten minutes for an interview for the vacancy in accounts. I'll remind Rodney as well."

"Call Adrian while you're at it. Put him on the alert that we're looking for vacant buildings for lease with a future purchase potential."

"Aye aye, captain." I saluted and smiled before walking out of the office.

I made the calls and got through the tasks I had for the day. At some point I remembered to call Nora and tell her about our dinner guest. I asked her to stay as well. With her nursing background, she could add to the conversation.

The day flew by and before I knew it, I was buckling myself into Axel's car as we left the parking garage. Dinner was ready and I had just enough time to show Axel to the bathroom to wash his hands before we sat at the table. My father extended his hand slowly to Axel who was sitting on his right.

"I finally get the chance to say thanks for all that you've done for us."

Axel bowed his head slightly. "I just wish I could have done more that night, sir."

My father nodded. "We all do. But we have picked up the

pieces and moved on with our lives as best as we can. I also want to thank you for giving Lisa this job. It has helped tremendously."

"And since I'm in the season of helping the Mulligans, I'm actually here on a mission. There is something-"

I kicked Axel underneath the table and he sputtered out the rest of the sentence.

"-but we can discuss that after we've eaten."

Dinner was a simple affair of chicken with potatoes and steamed vegetables. Afterwards, Nora helped my father into his chair. I watched Axel and the shrewd way he watched my father. We sat on the sofa while Nora took the other armchair.

"Mr. Mulligan, I'm going to get straight to the point. Lisa has told me about your illness and I'd like to help. I've taken the liberty of talking with a few medical acquaintances and there is a specialist who comes highly recommended for issues such as yours. With your permission, I'd like to set up an appointment for you to see him. And if he deems your case to be worth taking, I'd like you to undergo treatment."

"Will insurance-"

Axel shook his head, cutting him off mid-sentence. "It is not covered by insurance. But as I told Lisa, I will pay whatever costs are necessary up-front. I would treat it as a personal loan and have it deducted from her salary each month."

My father looked at me. "What's your take on this?"

"I think it's worth a try." I looked at Axel. "Tell him the rest."

"It would require you entering a treatment facility about two hours away where you can be monitored around the clock."

"Nora does that. I can stay home."

"Or, I could come with you and stay close by where I can still assist each day. Gerald, I think you should give it a try. My skills have gotten you back to this point. But we know there's further to go. I think it's worth seeing someone who may be able to help us complete this journey. Nothing ventured, nothing gained."

She rested her hand on the arm of his chair and looked at Axel.

"I'm sure there are apartments I could look into renting in the area. I'm a retired nurse so you could maybe tell your friend that he's coming with his caregiver? Would that be possible?"

"Even if it isn't, I'll make it possible. So, Mr. Mulligan, are you on board? You do have the final say."

My father looked at me. "What do you think?"

I looked at Axel. "I trust Axel's judgment. I think we should give it a try."

"You'll be alone here when I go, you know."

I smiled. "I can take care of myself and keep everything running. I'll check on your plants as well, Nora."

My father looked at Axel and nodded. "I guess I'll give it a shot then."

Axel grinned broadly. "Great. I'll set the wheels in motion and keep in touch. In the meantime, start packing.

Axel stayed for a round of Pictionary. It was after ten before we finally called it a night and I walked him to the car. I kept my arms folded to resist the temptation to hug him. He did the same.

"That went easier than I expected."

"I think he sees how much Nora wants him to be better."

"There's something going on between them?"

I nodded and Axel chuckled. "Good for you, Gerald!"

"I'm happy for them."

"I'll email my friend and get things in motion like I promised. I'll let you know when he needs to get there. I'll also sort out accommodation for Nora. She may be able to stay on site."

He opened the door and got into the seat. As he closed the door, he looked at me.

"It's going to be pretty lonely for you when they leave, you know. You might have to get someone to stay with you."

"I could ask Lola."

He made a strangled sound. "Over my dead body. The only companion you'll have is sitting right in front of you."

I felt my cheeks burn at the raw possessiveness in his tone. "I didn't think you'd want to sleep over here. I mean, I could come to you as well."

"Either way, there will be no Lola sleeping over. We'll figure it out when the time comes." He glanced behind me and sighed. "I want to kiss you so damn badly right now, but I know Gerald and Nora are somewhere behind those curtains wondering what the hell is taking you so long."

"I'll give you double tomorrow."

"I'm going to hold you to that, you know." He started the engine and pulled away from the curb.

Sure enough, the following morning, I kept my word.

It was the first week of April when my father and Nora made the trip. Axel came for us on Saturday morning and loaded us into his truck. I saw to it that he was settled in comfortably. And I had no idea what strings Axel had pulled to get an adjoining room converted to a flat for Nora. All that separated them was a door. I had no doubt that it would never be closed for long. As I said my goodbyes to my father, Axel pulled Nora aside.

"Be good. Don't give the nurses any trouble." I told him.

"I have my personal nurse to bother so there's no need to

worry about that. You take care of yourself and that soldier." He winked and I felt color flood my face. Thankfully, Nora chose that moment to come over and hug me.

"Nora, words cannot express my gratitude for you doing this."

"The pleasure is all mine. Besides, I feel as though I'm on vacation. Axel says every need will be tended to while I'm here. You take care of yourself. Before you know it, we'll be back, and Gerald will be as good as new. Call us when you get home."

I kissed her cheek and kissed my father once more before yielding to the pressure of Axel's hand beneath my elbow. Once we were inside the truck, he pulled me into his arms for a long, toe-curling kiss. I felt every nerve ending in my body pool in my groin as my pussy began to throb with need.

The two-hour drive felt like an eternity as we raced back to the city. As soon as the door closed behind us, I was in his arms. I pointed to my room and he crossed the space with a few steps.

We spent the rest of the weekend in each other's arms. When he left Sunday night and I faced the empty bed, I felt as if a part of me was missing. Even when he called when he got home an hour later and we spoke until past two, I felt as if I couldn't get enough of him. I sat staring into the darkness as my mind was going at light speed. This was dangerous. I was becoming dependent on Axel. Too dependent. And at any point that things took a turn for the worst between us, I knew I would be devastated. But it was too late to turn back. I had no choice but to get what I could while it lasted. And if my heart were to be broken, I would cross that bridge when I got there.

In the third week of April, Axel and I found ourselves on

a three-day business trip. It was an annual conference and expo for anyone in the security field. The week before I had worked overtime on updating Axel's business cards as well as brochures and the company website. When we arrived at the airport, my mouth fell open at the sleek silver jet with the name 'VANCE' emblazoned on the side. The inside was luxurious and I sank into the plush seat for the one-hour flight. I now got the chance to experience the wealth which was commonplace for Axel.

From the airport we were shuttled in a limousine to the Palladium, the premium five-star hotel where the conference and expo were being held. Axel spared no expense on our accommodation and I found myself with a keycard for one of the five penthouse suites on the top floor. Axel's suite was next to mine. But then he showed me the connected balcony and innocently suggested that if I heard a knock on the French door in the middle of the night, I should not be afraid to answer it.

The next morning, he slipped across to his suite to shower and change before waiting for me by the elevator to go down to breakfast.

The day went by in a whirl of activities and I found that I was genuinely interested in the displays of the most recent security gadgets on the market. Axel was caught up in meetings and discussions while I made the rounds at various booths, handing out business cards as I did. I had just finished talking to a proprietor about the merits of night-vision cameras when I turned and bumped into someone standing right behind me. My skin crawled when I found Brian Chambers standing there.

"Well, well, well. Fancy running into you here, Lisa." He looked around. "I'm sure Axel is somewhere around."

"He is. Excuse me." I walked as quickly as I could into

another part of the room. But now that I knew Brian was there, I kept a sharp eye out for Bethany as well. Thankfully, I saw neither before I slipped out of the dining room and headed upstairs to my suite. I had messaged Axel to let him know I had left and he had said he would be up in a few minutes as well.

I had just unpinned my hair and had slipped off my shoes when I heard a knock. I ran to the door and pulled it open smiling. The smile slipped when Brian stepped into the room.

"What are you doing here?"

"I'm just stopping by to say hi. You ran off so quickly I barely got the chance to catch up just now."

I watched as he walked further into the room and took a seat on the couch, crossing an ankle over a knee as he did. He looked me up and down and I felt as though I needed to wrap myself in a blanket, in spite of being fully clothed.

"I'd like you to leave please."

"Quite uppity for a common PA aren't you?"

The color drained from my face and he laughed. He walked over to me and I stepped back.

"Yes, Lisa my dear. I asked the right people the right questions just now. I know you're just his PA. I have to say though, you were quite convincing that weekend. All that hugging and kissing. More than likely he's fucking you then."

I swallowed hard and took another step back as I became acutely aware how alone we were. I had handled Bethany. But Brian was taller and heavier. My eyes darted around for anything I could use to defend myself. He took another step towards me and I stepped back.

"I wonder what Elizabeth would think if she knew that

she had been right about you all along and that it was all an act."

He reached out a finger to trace my forearm and I forced myself not to flinch.

"You've got to have some pussy though. Axel looked absolutely enamored with you. How about you let uncle Brian get a little piece of that ass, huh?"

I gasped as he grabbed my wrist and pulled me towards him. I cried out as he wrenched my hand and forced it behind me while grabbing my other hand and holding it in a vice-like grip. I kicked at him. My bare feet hit his shin and he swore softly. Suddenly my face twisted and began to burn as he slapped me. The force of the slap echoed in the room and caused me to stumble back. He used the opportunity to lunge at me and I fell. He straddled me and pressed his hand into my neck as I struggled to unseat him. In horror, I felt his hardness against my thigh and the gravity of the situation dawned on me. I doubled my efforts to be free as he began to grind against me. He pressed my neck even more and I felt as if my air was being cut off. I kicked and clawed at him.

"You're a little spitfire aren't you? I love a good fight. It makes the fucking so much sweeter. Are you wet yet, baby?"

He maneuvered his free hand into the waist of my skirt and beneath the elastic of my panties. I felt as though I was going to throw up when felt his finger touch my clit. But I also began to feel as though I was going to black out. He began to swim in and out of my vision as I fought to breathe. Then suddenly I could breathe again. The weight of his body was gone and I started to cough.

"You bastard!"

Axel!

I heard the sound of fist meeting flesh. There was a thud

and then I felt someone over me. I began to kick and scream with all my might.

"Lisa! Lisa! It's me, baby. Calm down. It's me. I've got you." Axel pulled me into his arms and I slumped against him in relief. I tilted my head back to look into his eyes. Then this time I passed out for real.

20

___

AXEL

When I got to Lisa's suite, nothing could have prepared me for the sight of Brian on top of her. I saw red. And even as I placed her in the bed before going back outside to call security to deal with Brian, I knew I could easily discharge my weapon and put a few holes in his head. But I restrained myself.

As I stood over him, he shifted as he came around, shaking his head. I kicked him in his nuts and was pleased to hear him howl in pain.

"You son of a bitch! I'm going to lock you away and throw away the key!"

I stooped and grabbed him by the collar. "Not if I have Lisa press charges first. You're going to make someone an awesome wife in jail."

I was pleased to see him go pale. Just then, security came barging into the room. They escorted him away for further questioning while one remained behind with me to take my statement. He needed Lisa's statement as well but I told him I would call him to come for it when she was feeling better.

As soon as he left, I called the hotel doctor for him to

examine Lisa. I didn't like the looks of the bruises on her throat and face. She stirred and I rubbed her hand. Her eyes fluttered open. Then they filled with tears. I pulled her into my arms. As I embraced her, she started to shake.

"It's okay sweetheart. You're safe."

"H-He tried to... he was going to... he touched m-m-meeeeee!" she broke down crying.

I held her until her tears subsided. I caressed her bruised cheek as I looked into her eyes. Instantly I was transported back to that night in the diner as I held a twelve-year-old Lisa in my arms.

"You're safe, my love."

"You saved me!"

"That's my job, isn't it?"

Just then, there was a knock on the main door.

"That will be the doctor. Give me a second. Don't get out of this bed."

I went to answer the door and found the doctor as predicted. I stood to the side as he examined her bruises. He said they were superficial and would fade in a few days. While he examined her, security called asking for a time to get Lisa's statement. She had them come immediately and that was another half hour. As I listened to her recount the series of events, I thanked the heavens that I had not been a moment later. When they finally left, I went to turn on the jacuzzi tub. I undressed her and took her to the bathroom. I stripped and joined her, pulling her into my arms. I caressed every inch of her body as the water bubbled around us. I was determined to erase any memory of Brian's touch. Lisa's fingers rested on my thigh, clenching and unclenching.

"H-He said he knows I'm just your PA and that we were pretending in Coral Springs. He threatened to tell your mother. Then he started to touch me-"

Her voice trailed off as she swallowed.

"If you hadn't come, he would have-"

"I came. And he won't be a bother to us anymore. I promise."

I turned her face to me and kissed her, running my tongue along the seam of her lips until her full lips parted beneath mine. My hand slid over her stomach until it nestled between her legs. Even amid the bubbles, I found the hard nub of her clit and teased it lightly. She moaned as her legs moved restlessly. She tore her mouth from mine.

"Make love to me, Axel. Please make me forget."

I didn't need to be told twice. Without hesitation I got us out of the tub and dried our bodies with the plush towels. Then I took her to bed and fulfilled her request. It was way in the night that we called room service and had them send up whatever they could rustle up for us from the kitchen. I even tipped the waiter extra for a bottle of wine.

As we sat on the balcony wrapped in robes and devouring our late dinner, I looked at Lisa. And the longer I looked at her the faster my heart pounded. The words were on the tip of my tongue. But I bit them back. I needed a much better set-up to profess my love. But I could do the next best thing.

"Lisa?"

"Hmmm?"

"I want you to be my girlfriend – for real."

Her head snapped up at my words, her eyes boring into me. I reached for her hand across the table.

"What happened this evening with Brian was a wake-up call. If he thinks he can make a pass at you because technically you're not really my girlfriend, I don't want others to believe they can do the same thing. I want to drop the pretense and make it real."

"Axel, this evening was an unfortunate turn of events. But I can take care of myself."

"That's just it. I don't want you to take care of yourself. I want to do that. I want you to know, though, that I'm still special ops and can be called away at any moment. These assignments are high risk and there is always the possibility that I may never return. But if such a bridge comes, I want you to have a title and a place in my life that no one can dispute. I want you to be taken care of in every way."

"I don't want your money-"

"This isn't about my money. It's about me wanting to protect you for as long or short as you'll let me." My eyes searched hers. "Be my girlfriend. Please." I rubbed my fingers along her knuckles, holding her gaze. She dropped her eyes and bowed her head.

"I've never been anyone's official girlfriend before."

I smiled. "That's okay. I've never been anyone's official boyfriend either. So I guess we can learn together."

"Okay."

"Is that a yes?"

She nodded. "Yes, that's a yes."

I grinned and stood, pulling her into my arms. "Shall we seal it with a kiss?"

I didn't wait for her to answer as I captured her lips.

My life as I knew it was forever altered with Lisa as my girlfriend. We still maintained a very professional distance in the office. But there was no end to the time we spent together. With her father still away, we slept at her apartment most weekends. But for the weekend of her birthday in May, I went all out and had a catered dinner at my house. I got the chance to live out my laundry room fantasies and created a few more memories. But being with Lisa was not just about sex. Every time I thought about her and felt my emotions surge, I knew what we had was a relationship. And with a relationship came a more permanent status than girlfriend. But that would come in due time if I had my way. And I wasn't the only one who thought of her in that way.

I couldn't forget one afternoon as I sat in the meeting room upstairs. I had been about to head back to my office when I heard my name being spoken.

"He's really turned over a new leaf. I like it a lot."

"And so say all of us. Have you seen his hair?"

"Gorgeous isn't it? Who would have thought he was hiding that mane all this time?"

"And doesn't he seem more relaxed to you?"

"He does! And everyone is noticing too. What a difference a good PA makes huh."

"I knew she was good news when I saw what she did at Christmas. I was so distressed when I heard she had gotten fired."

"We all were. I don't know what happened. But she's back and that's good enough for me."

"I'm just glad Axel has come to his senses and knows a good PA when he sees one. With all the lumps of coal he went through last year you would have thought he would have hung on to the diamond. Lisa is the kind of woman that would make him a good wife."

"She would make anyone a good wife. I wonder if she's seeing anyone. I'm in the market for a decent sister-in-law."

"But I thought your brother was already married."

"He is. But there is such a thing as divorce, especially if I can swing Lisa his way. She's a sweetheart."

"Let's hope Axel doesn't become a fool again, though. I don't think I could bear it. And I think VSS would crumble as well. I think Lisa is behind a lot of changes we've been seeing. With her by his side, Axel can't go wrong. And I hope he knows that too."

"Shit! Look at the time. I've got a ton of work on my desk to finish before I call it a day."

"Me too. Lunch break always goes by in a flash on a Friday."

I listened as the two girls left the break room. I sat for a while, musing on the conversation. They were right about Lisa and the positive changes she had effected of course. And I was elated that the discussion had not been reduced to gossip and rumors about Lisa and me being in a relationship. Our discretion was working.

I kept up-to-date on her father's progress and was pleased to hear that he was responding positively to the treatment. At the beginning, we had made trips at least once a week. But after a month, Gerald had asked Lisa not to come for a while. They communicated daily via video chat but she respected his wishes. I had thought it strange until Nora had called me to let me in on a secret Gerald was keeping from Lisa.

I turned thirty-three with Lisa in my arms as we made love in my swimming pool. Afterwards as we floated along in each other's arms she surprised me by tugging me to the shallow end of the pool. She pulled me up to the steps.

"Sit."

I did as I was told and sat on the top step, leaving my feet in ankle deep water on the third step. She knelt before me and leaned forward to kiss me. I met her half way. I felt my cock begin to twitch once more as I hardened. I jerked as her hand wrapped around me, stroking me familiarly. She pulled back and smiled at me.

"I'd like to give you a special gift."

"I already have you. I couldn't ask for anything more."

"I know you have me. But you've never had this."

Without another word, she knelt between my knees and bent her head to taste my cock. The second her lips encircled me, I felt as though I was going to explode. She raised her head and smiled.

"I've never done this before. Will you teach me how to please you?"

I took a deep, shuddering breath as the enormity of her words touched my core. I nodded and leaned back on my elbows. She bent to taste me once more and I groaned.

With gentle touches and soft words I told her how to please me. With every stroke of her tongue along the engorged vein I felt my balls tingle. But I held it together. She found the sensitive ridge beneath the helmet head and I almost swallowed my tongue when she lapped at the oozing slit. I felt my balls begin to draw up into my groin.

"Slow down a bit, baby. I'm getting close."

Instead, she licked me harder. Lights exploded behind my eyes as I felt the blood rushing through my veins.

"Lisa, please-" I tried to urge her head up. Instead she captured my hands, intertwining her finger with mine. I gripped her hands as my hips thrust up reflexively. I could free myself if I chose, but I was powerless.

"Lisa, you've gotta stop, baby. Please. I want to come so badly. Please."

The last came out on a groan as she gripped my shaft and stroked it hard and fast. She lifted her head briefly.

"I want to taste you." She stuck her tongue in my slit and I lost it.

"Oh fuck!"

She took me into her mouth once more as the first rope shot out. I jerked and twitched, watching as she continued to stroke me as I ejaculated. She allowed my juices to run all over her tongue and lips. I almost passed out as she allowed the last few drops to pool between her breasts. My chest heaved with the effort to breathe as I lay back on the steps, staring at the sky but seeing nothing. I felt her move up to straddle me as she lay her body on top of me. My arms came up around her as I pulled her in for a steamy kiss. It felt like we had crossed into brand new territory tonight. And I loved it.

That night as she slept, I lay looking at her for a long time. What would it really take to admit that I loved her and wanted her in my life forever? The thought of marrying Lisa no longer scared me. As a matter of fact, I now looked forward to the day I would get on my knees and ask her to be my wife. I had long decided that it would happen. It was just a matter of time. I would, of course, do the honorable thing and ask Gerald and Nora for their blessings. But I wanted to time that conversation with his being released from treatment. In the meantime, I needed to begin looking at rings. I was sure I could enlist Nora's help when the time came to choose as well.

I smoothed a lock of hair away from her forehead and kissed her softly before placing my head next to hers. I was soon asleep, our breaths mingling as we breathed.

The next morning, I was treated to breakfast fit for a king. We were going to see her father today as he had asked her to visit finally. I hopped into the shower while she did her hair. I was washing my hair when she came into the bathroom holding my phone.

"Your mom's calling."

"Answer it."

Her eyebrows shot up into her hairline. She answered the call and put the phone on speaker. I continued to rinse my hair.

"Hello?"

"Who's this?"

"Hi, Elizabeth. It's Lisa."

"Lisa who?"

"Lisa, my girlfriend, Mother. Don't be difficult." I began to lather my body.

"I would never be difficult, Axel. I just thought you would have moved on by now."

"How can I help you Mother?"

"Can't a mother call to wish her only child a happy birthday. What are you doing? I hear water-"

"I'm in the shower, Mother."

"And she's in there *with* you!?"

"Well, I can't wash my hair and hold the phone at the same time."

"You *still* haven't been to the barber?"

"I have. But I find myself liking hair these days. Did you call to fuss over my hair or to wish me a happy birthday?"

"Happy birthday, dear. And I called to invite you to dinner as well. Byron will be here as well and asked me to let you know he needs to speak with you urgently. This is it, Axel. I feel it in my bones. He's going to ask you to merge."

"I'm not interested in merging, Mother. You know this."

"Just hear him out. He and Bethany have some fantastic ideas-"

"No thanks, Mother."

"You can bring Luisa with you."

"You know damn well it's Lisa. But I'll pass. Lisa and I are going to see her father so we won't be available anyway."

"Prison visitations aren't long. You can still make it for dinner."

"He's in the hospital actually."

There was a deafening silence. I turned off the shower, stepped out and took the phone.

"Thank you for the birthday wishes, Mother. Get off your high horse and get used to Lisa. She's going to be the mother of your grandchildren, you know."

"She's *preg-*"

I ended the call in the middle of her scream and turned to Lisa.

"I'm sorry about that."

She shrugged. "That's okay. She doesn't like me. I get it. It doesn't bother me."

I looked at her in amazement. "Any other woman would be throwing a hissy fit, telling me to choose between her and my mother."

"I would never ask you to choose me over your mother." She reached up with a towel and began to dry my hair. As I looked down at her, my jest about children began to take on a serious edge. I struggled to organize my thoughts. I had barely gotten used to wanting her to be in my life permanently and now I was imagining little blonde tykes running around calling me 'Daddy'. I took a deep breath. I leaned down and kissed her gently. I wanted to say the words. But I held them back. Not yet.

The drive to the facility was an easygoing one as we conversed. We had made only one stop to get a few of Gerald's favorite treats. I was excited for the surprise in store for her. I had spoken to both Gerald and Nora a few times this week, and they too could not contain themselves with the news they had for Lisa.

"I can't believe it's been so long since I've seen my dad. There's just something about touching someone in the flesh that a phone call or text can't replace."

"I'm sure he can't wait to see you either."

I reached over and took her hand, playing with her fingers which had become a favorite thing of mine.

"Thank you for a great birthday."

She smiled and shrugged. "I just made breakfast."

"You're with me. That's the only gift I need." I kissed her hand quickly and turned my attention back to the road.

We soon pulled into the parking lot. I could tell she was anxious as she bounded ahead of me to her father's room. She knocked and entered quickly.

Nora and her father were standing by the window and turned as we approached.

"Dad!"

"Lisa!" Gerald's face lit up as he walked towards his daughter – without his cane.

21

LISA

I couldn't believe my eyes as I watched my father take faltering steps towards me. He stood straight as an arrow, his smile a mile wide. He looked ten years younger. Nora beamed proudly as she watched his progress. When he got to me and embraced me, I couldn't hold back the tears.

"You're walking! You're walking!"

"I wanted to surprise you! I had to keep you away."

"You got me good."

"Come. Let's sit. I still get a bit winded."

I held his arm as we went to sit on the couch in his room. Nora and Axel had slipped out of the room leaving us alone. I curled into his side and rested my head on his shoulder. He hugged me and kissed my brow.

"So how have you been, sweetheart?"

"I just miss you. But I know you're getting better so I'll grin and bear it."

"Aww. I don't think you miss me that much with Axel around."

I looked at him and he winked and smiled.

"That man loves you."

"I wouldn't go that far. He only asked me to be his girl-friend to keep me safe after the attack."

"What attack?"

I told him about what Brian Chambers had done. He was livid.

"Axel should have had him arrested."

I shook my head. "We had to trade off. Axel beat him up afterwards. If we had pressed charges, he would have pressed charges as well. But it's okay now. Axel says he went overseas shortly afterwards so I don't have to worry about running into the likes of him again."

"Good. So, you're now his girlfriend for real? No more pretending?"

"No more pretending."

He smiled. "That is the best news I've heard for a while. And I'm happy for you both. Axel is a great man. Did you know he calls me every week to check on my progress?"

"I didn't know that."

"He does. He knew I was walking as well but we had to keep it from you. I wanted to surprise you. I'm really happy for you two. You deserve to have someone to love and to have someone who loves you."

"Well, I know how I feel."

"And that is?"

"I do love him. But I'm not sure he feels the same way. He may like me a lot. But love is a bit of a stretch."

"Trust me. He loves you. A man in love knows when a man is in love."

I looked at him curiously and he smiled. I laughed.

"So how have things been here with Nora twenty-four seven?"

"It's like living in paradise with a wonderful woman by my side. I feel as though I've been on vacation for months."

"How has Nora been working?"

"Just the same. She has her laptop and everything. Axel has seen to it that we don't need anything except for me to go through my treatment. I sometimes forget why I'm here. Then they come prodding and poking me with all kinds of instruments. I don't mind, though. It's working."

"What have they been doing, though? How did they get you to lose the cane?"

We spoke at length about the cutting-edge robot technology that was used in his physical therapy sessions as well as one of the surgeries he had had to remove a cyst which had attached itself to a nerve.

"There's still a little more to go and I have a major surgery scheduled for September. After that, the projection is that I'll be home for Christmas. By their estimation, I will be as good as new."

"That sounds like music to my ears."

He held my hand. "Last year this time, I felt so desolate. But now, I feel like I've been given a new lease on life. And it's all thanks to Nora and Axel. We've got some good people in our lives, honey. You've got your man."

"The jury is still out on that."

"Trust me. You have his heart. And I've got my woman. Nora is phenomenal."

As if on cue, there was a knock on the door and Nora opened the door and pushed her head inside.

"Knock knock? Lunch is ready."

"We're coming."

I stood and automatically reached down to help my father to his feet. He laughed and waved my hands away.

"I've got this."

He did indeed have it as he stood on his own. We walked slowly to the lounge next door where lunch was waiting. It was just after sunset when we left. My thoughts kept going back to snippets of my conversation with my father, especially when he said Axel loved me. As he drove, I looked at him now and then. Was my father right? Did this man love me?

Axel kept his promise to take me to his mountain house during the summer. We took advantage of a long weekend holiday and so, after a three-hour drive with just one stop at the grocery store, we arrived.

I looked at the security set-up that he had from the moment he turned off the main road. I almost jumped out of my skin when the trees parted to reveal the continuation of the drive-way. I laughed nervously.

"Why do I feel as though I'm about to enter an alternate universe? Moving trees, Axel?"

He chuckled and shrugged. "What can I say? I like my privacy."

As we unpacked the truck, I was mesmerized by the silence. I helped him get the bags inside and the colder items into the refrigerator.

"How long has it been since you've been here?"

"December."

"But it's so clean!"

"I have little woodland elves who come in each week."

"Axel!"

He laughed and pulled me into his embrace. "My neighbor rides his ATV through the woods and checks now and then. I had some cleaners from the nearby town come in a few days ago. I changed the security codes after they left." He rubbed his hands along my side. "Ready for a tour?"

"Sure."

He took me around the house, ending at the pool in the back. I took off my shoes and sat on the steps. I looked up as he stripped off his t-shirt and shorts and dove in, splashing me as he did. He surfaced and held out his hand.

"Coming?"

I stood and took off my shorts and t-shirt, leaving only my bra and panties. We splashed around for about an hour before hunger kicked in and we went in search of a late lunch. I rustled up some sandwiches with cold cuts while Axel rummaged through the freezer to find something to thaw for dinner. We had a relaxing evening by the pool and turned in early as we were going fishing in the morning. I had never fished in my life and found the experience quite enjoyable. Even more enjoyable was when Axel undressed me and laid me out on a flat boulder in the middle of the river. It was an experience to make love in the middle of a river with the heat of the sun beating down on us.

On our last night in the mountains, Axel built a campfire in the backyard and brought out the sleeping bags. I laughed as I ate my dinner out of a tin plate.

"I feel like a regular girl scout this weekend. Thanks for inviting me."

"You're welcome. Thanks for accepting."

"I hope I'll be invited back?"

He gave me an odd look. "You don't have to ask. That's a given."

"I don't like to take things for granted."

"With me you can." He leaned across and kissed me lightly on the lips.

After dinner, we had s'mores for dessert. As I lay on my back with my head on his shoulder, I looked up at the stars. I looked up at him to find him looking down on me. The full moon hit his face at just the right angle to make his scar visible. I reached up to trace it with my forefinger.

"This is what I remembered most about that night. looking up and seeing your eyes. How did you get this?"

"Shrapnel in basic training. If I hadn't been wearing my goggles it would have blinded me for sure."

"I'm glad it happened, though."

He raised his eyebrows in surprise. "How come?"

"How else would I have known it was you?"

He chuckled. "So, it's my ID?"

"Something like that. It helped me to find my true knight in shining armor."

He leaned down and kissed me gently. "I'm glad you found me. And I'm glad I came to my senses. I'm never letting you go." He kissed me again, this time more intensely.

Slowly he undressed me then undressed himself. I gave myself over to him, crying out as he lapped at my pussy. I soon returned the favor, teasing him by taking him to the edge and back. When at last he slipped his body into mine, my legs wrapped around him, holding him to me.

His powerful thrusts sent my senses reeling over and over. I cried out in ecstasy, shocking myself as I screamed into the night sky. When I felt him throb deep within me as he released himself, I clung to him, trembling.

Long moments later as we lay covered in blankets, he caressed my breasts as I ran my hand along his hip. I ran my finger along his cock and he chuckled.

"I've created a little monster. Insatiable little thing."

"It's your fault, you know."

"I guess I'm too good of a teacher in the ways of the bedroom. But I love having you as my student." He nibbled my lips and I smiled.

"I wouldn't have it any other way."

"It seems I'll have to take you to the mountains more often."

"How so?"

"I'm sure they heard you down in the valley, baby."

I felt my cheeks burn as he laughed.

"I finally got you screaming my name and I love it." He kissed my forehead. "I love the way your body responds to me when I touch you here." His hand slipped down to cup my pussy. I twitched and he chuckled. "See?"

He ran his finger along my wet slit and I moaned. "Just like that," he whispered huskily. "I love how your body was made for me. I love how you hold me as if you'll never let me go."

"I don't ever want to let you go."

"And I will never let you go. I'm serious, Lisa. I-"

He stopped and stared down at me. My heart began to race as I saw his eyes shine with emotion. I stroked his beard and pulled him down into a steaming kiss.

Our lovemaking was filled with an urgency and an energy that pushed us to the limit. Hours later we went inside when the night air became too cold. In the warmth of his bed, I followed through on my promise of never letting him go.

22

AXEL

I caught myself whistling while I flipped pancakes on the griddle. The smell of cinnamon and vanilla was in the air and my stomach growled in anticipation. I felt a soft touch on my shoulder and turned, smiling. I leaned down to brush a gentle kiss on Lisa's forehead.

"Morning. Why didn't you wake me? I could have helped."

"You crawled into bed at close to five, babe. You needed some rest. Did you get them all done?"

She yawned as she nodded and reached for a mug to pour some coffee. "All I need to do now is package and deliver."

"Awesome. Are you going to use the new labels?"

She smiled as she took a sip, nodding vigorously. "I think people are going to be pleasantly surprised. Thanks for giving me the idea to name my business and put it together a little more professionally."

"*Beadies* is going to take off. Mark my words. You're a good business woman and you're good at what you do."

She laughed. "Maybe it will take off to the point where I

can quit my job. I work for an absolute beast of a boss, you know."

I stared at her with narrowed eyes. "Over my dead body."

She stared back, mischief twinkling in her hazel pools. "The pancakes are burning."

I jumped and turned my attention back to the stove, listening as her laughter echoed as she left the kitchen. A glance into my living room showed the coffee table and the sofas covered in sparkling beads of all sizes and shapes. I watched as she knelt on the floor wearing one of my t-shirts and short cutoff jeans. She flipped a lock of hair behind her ear. I was still trying to get used to her new haircut.

When we had returned from the mountains, she'd gone to the hairdresser and followed through on her plan to do a big chop. Whenever she laid her head on my shoulder, I missed the weight of the braid. But I had the added bonus of now being able to run my fingers through her loose hair.

"Where do you want to eat? Pool?"

She nodded. I plated up the pancakes, scrambled eggs, and bacon and headed outside. I returned for the juice and coffee while she carried a platter of fruits I had sliced.

I looked at her, my brow furrowing in a frown. "You aren't really going to resign, are you?"

She looked at me. "I was just joking, honey. Relax."

She stretched out her foot and ran it along my bare calf. I pouted slightly.

"One man's joke is another man's crisis. I think I have PA PTSD."

She laughed. "I'll be your PA until the day you tell me to go."

"That day will never come. I'm not crazy."

We finished breakfast and I did the dishes while she got

started on packaging her orders. We showered quickly and I loaded the truck with the dainty packages.

Every night this week I had kept her company on the phone as she worked on the orders on her overflowing dining table. Yesterday evening when I dropped her home, I'd told her to load everything into the truck so that she could work in the comfort of my spacious living room. I had volunteered to shuttle her around to make all her deliveries today so that she wouldn't have to figure it out. But I had my ulterior motives as well. I knew that with all the deliveries made, I would have her undivided attention. She had gotten a massive order from a hotel that was hosting a conference and wanted to gift bracelets as souvenirs for the attendees. That was the last delivery we made.

When we got back to my house it was close to five. A few minutes after we got home, I opened the gate for a visitor and called her downstairs and out to the pool just as the masseuse set up her table. Her mouth dropped open and I was rewarded with a kiss before she followed the instructions to undress and get on the table. I lounged in the pool while I watched her being pampered, leaving only long enough to admit another visitor in the form of a caterer.

That night as I held her naked body to mine, I listened to her deep breathing as she slept. Not for the first time, I wondered how to broach the subject of us moving in together. I knew that things were still a bit cautious and discreet for us both in the office, but it was getting to a point where I didn't care who knew that we were in a relationship. The nights that she was not with me were sheer torture. And it wasn't just about sex. I wanted Lisa with me – period. And once I had her with me, it would only be a matter of time before I made it a permanent arrangement.

I ran my hand along her hip and pulled her closer as I

closed my eyes, her warm breath fanning my cheek as I slipped into slumber.

August soon became September and with it came Lisa's preoccupation with her father's last procedure. I knew both Gerald and Nora were also anxious as this could be a game changer in either direction. I slept over at Lisa's the night before and we left first thing in the morning. It was a workday so I still had to take some calls while Lisa and Nora waited patiently in Nora's suite. It was almost evening when the doctors came with a good report that the surgery had been successful, and that Gerald was in recovery. Lisa went in first while Nora and I waited.

As soon as the door closed behind Lisa's retreating figure, Nora turned to me.

"Thank you is insufficient to express our gratitude for everything you've done for us, Axel. I believe this is yours."

She handed me the credit card I had given her the first day when we had dropped them off at the hospital. While Lisa had said her goodbyes to her father, I had slipped it into Nora's hand with a whispered, "In case you both need anything."

I smiled and handed it back. "Let's wait until you're all packed and heading for home. You have a week or two to go."

"I don't know how we will ever repay you financially."

"Love has no repayment plan." The words slipped out before I could think and I saw Nora's eyebrows go up.

"I knew it. But I always err on the side of caution. But your admission makes it official. Have you told her yet?"

I shook my head. She reached across and patted my arm.

"Don't worry. Your secret's safe with me."

"And Gerald?"

She laughed. "And Gerald."

The door opened and we looked up as Lisa entered.

"Next visitor."

"That will be me. Excuse me, you two."

She slipped out of the room and I held out my hand to Lisa. She came and sat on my knee. I pushed a hand through her hair.

"How is he?"

"He's hooked up to all kinds of tubes and sleeping off the local. But he looks good. If all went well, I have my father back." Her voice cracked on the last phrase and I kissed her gently. She clung to my neck with a soft sob.

"I don't know how we can ever repay you, Axel. It's more than the money. It's the peace of mind in knowing that my father is back on his feet and has a new lease on life. It's priceless! Thank you!"

She kissed me gently then pulled back and held my face between her hands. "Thank you."

My throat clogged at her shining eyes and I hugged her tightly. We remained locked in that embrace until Nora returned. Then it was my turn to visit.

On the drive home, Lisa leaned against my shoulder, her hand resting on my thigh. I rested my hand on hers at intervals.

"Babe?"

"Hmmm?" she murmured.

"I have a proposition for your father that I want to run by you."

"Okay."

"I've been thinking about it for a few weeks actually. How do you think he would feel about working with me in the IT department? I know that's his area of expertise. And the good thing is that he can work remotely. It would give us a chance to see the extent to which the virtual office works as well. Do you think he would give it a try?"

"I know he would. And especially with being better, it will be a new lease on life for him."

"Great. I'll make the pitch as soon as he's recovered enough."

We had a quiet dinner before sitting in the living room watching a movie. As she laughed at the comedy, I ran my fingers through her hair. I sighed and she looked up at me. Her brow creased with concern. She reached up to trace my scar as she always did.

"What's wrong?"

I looked down at her, struggling to find the words to verbalize the emotions screaming in my head. I swallowed hard. I was a hard-nosed, no-nonsense businessman who was never at a loss nor ever lost my cool – until now. She frowned and sat up, the television forgotten. She turned to kneel beside me, taking my hand between hers.

"Axel? What's wrong?"

I stared at her and gave a wan smile. "Nothing's wrong. Everything's right. And because everything is right, I'm going to miss you."

"What!? Miss me!? What are you talking about, Axel? Are you going away on a mission or something?"

"Oh! No, no, no. Nothing like that."

"So what do you mean you're going to miss me?"

I leaned back against the couch and reached out for her to curl into my side as usual.

"Your father will soon be home. When he comes home, you and I will have to go back to sleeping in our own beds."

"Maybe."

"There's no, maybe, Lisa. I can't ask you to leave your father and move in with me for my own selfish reasons."

"You want me to move in with you?"

I looked her straight in the eyes. "I do."

"Okay. I will."

"You didn't hear me, did you? You can't leave your father-"

"I'm pretty sure it's my father who will be leaving me. While you went to visit him, Nora and I had a little chat. She wants to move him in with her, or she with him. Either way, they want to be together and I'm not going to stand in their way. She suggested moving him up to make it easier for me not having to move my things. But I guess I'll have to move them now. So, if you want me to move in with you, I will."

"As easy as that?"

"As easy as that. All you had to do was ask."

Her smile made my heart flutter with excitement. Lisa was going to be living with me. And if I had my way, I would soon thereafter bind her to me permanently with the ultimate question. It was merely a matter of time.

A few days later, I was still walking on cloud nine as I sat in the office going over a few files for new clients. Since we had merged operations with Shirley, there was no shortage of recruits nor shortage of clients. I had also been looking at a few buildings and had narrowed down the list considerably. But if things continued on their current trajectory, we would be expanding our office early in the new year.

I checked my watch. Lisa was still at lunch. I sent her a text to come see me as soon as she got back as I wanted these contracts sent off with the courier before the end of the work day.

My head was buried in the files when the door opened.

"You're back early, sweet – Mother! What are you doing here?"

She turned up her nose and sniffed. "If the mountain won't come to Mohammed. Is that how it goes?"

I shrugged and closed the file. "I've been busy. Business is booming."

"Too busy to see your own mother?" she shrugged off her coat and sat on the couch. She ran her hands along the arm. "This is nice."

"Thank you. My PA picked it out."

"If I saw you often enough I would have known you had redecorated the office. I barely recognized it."

"You can come to the office anytime you wish Mother. You are still a shareholder."

"But I want to see you at my house."

"We had dinner two weeks ago."

"And then you rushed off."

"I call you at least twice a week."

"And you don't talk for more than five minutes."

"Now you're exaggerating."

"I'm a lonely, old woman. Leave me be."

"There is nothing either lonely or old about you. I don't know who you're trying to fool. But seriously. What has brought you out of your loft to come and mix with mere mortals like me?"

"I wanted to remind you about the banquet for Byron's retirement. He's going to name Bethany as his successor, you know."

"I have it written down and recorded in every possible place, Mother. I won't forget."

"You wanted to see me?" the door opened and Lisa walked into the office, smiling brightly.

My mother gasped. "*You* work *here!*?"

Lisa smiled wider still. "Hello, Elizabeth! I'm Axel's PA. How are you? Would you like a drink?"

Lisa walked over to the refrigerator and extracted a bottle. My mother sniffed.

"I drink only-"

"Vervet sparkling water. I believe you prefer strawberry flavored." Lisa's smile didn't slip as she twisted off the cap and handed the bottle to my mother. I watched as my mother eyed her up and down as she took the bottle. She took a sip then pursed her lips.

"You've cut your hair. It makes you look older."

"I think 'mature' is the word you want to use. It was a bit hot during the summer, plus I'd met my length quota."

"Length quota?"

"Yes. I donated it to *Kids Wigs*."

I saw my mother's eyebrows go up. I smirked.

"The company that makes wigs for-"

"Children with cancer," Lisa finished.

"I know who they are. I sit on the damn board." She took another sip of water before handing the half-finished bottle to Lisa. "How come I've never seen you at the donor's banquet?"

"That makes two of us." Lisa turned to her after resting the bottle on top of the refrigerator.

I chuckled when my mother gasped. She turned on me furiously.

"Are you going to allow her to be rude to me?"

"In all fairness, Elizabeth, you started it."

"You have no right to speak to me in that manner. You're just a PA. So, Brian was right after all."

My eyes sparked fire. "Brian told you that?"

"Well not in so many words. He told Bethany before he flew out-"

"And she told you."

She turned to Lisa. "So, you can drop the act about being Axel's girlfriend."

Lisa and I burst out laughing. I went to stand beside Lisa and slipped my arm around her.

"It's not an act Mother. We are seeing each other. And since secrets are being revealed, did Bethany tell you why Brian left?"

"He had business to tend to overseas."

"Well, if that business is related to avoiding assault charges, he is right."

"Assault charges?"

In as few words as possible, I recounted Brian's assault of Lisa. My mother's face went white. She looked at Lisa.

"I don't know what to say. In spite of how I feel about you, that is something no woman should have to go through. Are you okay?" she spoke in a gentle tone.

Lisa and I looked at each other then, at my mother.

"Yes. I'm fine. Axel was there to rescue me."

My mother got up and came to stand before Lisa. She looked at her and I thought I saw the glimmer of tears in her eyes. She spoke quietly.

"You should have pressed charges, my dear."

"Axel beat him up. I dropped the charges against him so he would drop the charges against Axel."

The room was silent for a while as my mother stared at Lisa. Finally, she spoke.

"I have an excellent hairdresser who won't use a chopper on your hair."

Lisa looked at me, puzzled. But I recognized Elizabeth Vance's somewhat acidic version of an olive branch and smiled.

"I'm sure something can be arranged the next time Lisa wants a trim. Right babe?"

"I-I guess."

I kissed her forehead and walked quickly to the desk for the files. I handed them to her.

"I need these to be dropped off by four today."

She took them without a word and left the office. I turned to my mother who had gone back to the couch.

"What was that all about?"

"What was what all about?"

"Why should she have pressed charges?"

I saw her throat work and she looked away. "Because I know what happens when you don't. Assault becomes a habit."

I felt as if someone had dropped a rock in my stomach. "Mother? What are you saying? Did dad-"

"Oh! No! Never. Your father would never do such a thing. But I have, well had a friend who was with someone."

"Had?"

She looked at me. "He ended up strangling her a year after the first incident. I wished I had been firmer with her the first time I noticed the bruises." She shook her head. "I can't believe Brian would do such a thing. He's such a sweet boy."

"And that's the problem, Mother. You keep seeing him as a sweet boy and Bethany as a sweet girl. But they are two grown and spoiled adults. Brian nearly sank the business that year he ran it while I was overseas. I practically had to rebuild it from the ground up, you know."

"And I'm very proud of all the hard work you put into it. Is Brian the reason why you don't want to merge with Chambers?"

"One of the reasons. I suspect it was at his father's instructions as well. Sometimes I wonder if dad's failure was as a result of his 'friend's' advice. I think he is jealous of what we have accomplished to date with very little input from him."

"I never knew that."

"I didn't want to insert any bias in your relationship with them. They are your friends, not mine. I'm not interested in a merger as well because I think VSS can do quite well on its own. This year alone I've seen a forty percent increase in client intake. Plus, we're expanding our operation to include recruiting. We should be moving to a bigger location in the new year as well. I have Lisa to thank for a lot of that too. She's a very good PA. And an excellent girlfriend."

I smirked as my mother pursed her lips but not before I saw a faint smile. She tilted her head and rolled her eyes.

"She gets a pass – for now."

"Forever."

Her eyes widened as she looked at me. I smiled and brushed her cheek lightly with my fingers.

"Blame yourself. I get my views on the permanence of love and relationships from you."

"Well, I guess I have no choice but to wish you all the best. At least you chose someone sensible."

"Yup."

"So will you be at the banquet? You said you remembered, right?"

"Remembered is not equivalent to attendance. I will not be there. I have other plans for that evening. Lisa's father is coming home."

"From the hospital?"

"No. From prison."

She had the grace to blush at the recollection of her scathing remarks about Lisa's father a few months ago.

"And I guess even if you didn't have an excuse, you'd still be a no-show?"

"Affirmative."

"Bethany is going to be disappointed. I know she was looking forward to having serious discussions on the merger with you."

"There is no merger."

"Well, I know that now. She'll just have to grin and bear it."

"Yup. By the way, Lisa and I are still private about our relationship, so don't go ordering a billboard or banner."

"Okay."

She picked up her coat and I helped her to put it on before walking her to the door and opening it. She looked up at me.

"My birthday is coming up. Now that you have a better *PA*," she raised her voice at that point "I trust I'll get a better gift and you'll be appropriately attired?"

The slight lift to her mouth belied the innocence in her tone as we both recalled last year's fiasco.

"Your birthday is months away." I smiled and kissed her cheek. "Drive safely."

I watched as she paused to tap Lisa' desk and give her a small wave goodbye. Lisa returned the gesture with a small smile.

As I sat at my desk, I felt as though an invisible weight was lifted from my shoulders. I hadn't known how my mother's resentment of Lisa had worn on me until it had been removed. I turned back to work.

It was nearly six when my business phone rang.

"Hello?"

"What's this I hear about you missing the banquet, Axel?"

"Hello to you too, Bethany."

"Elizabeth was joking, right?"

"Nope. I won't be there. But congratulations. You've worked all your life for this moment."

"Axel. You must reconsider. There will be many corporate giants there in our industry. It would be a good look for Chambers Guardianship and VSS to have an alliance."

I frowned. "An alliance?"

"Yes. I know you've been a bit sulky lately. But you can't deny that our companies merging would be an unbeatable combination. We would be a force to be reckoned with in the security industry. And it would be even better when we make it public that we are seeing each other-"

"Hold on a second. Bethany. In what delusional world are you living? How many times do I have to tell you that there is no us?"

"But Axel, this is what has been expected of us since we were children."

"Expected by who exactly? Let me try and break it to you once and for all *again*. I am in a relationship. I am happy with my *steady* girlfriend."

"You aren't still masquerading with Linda are you? Brian told me she was only your PA."

"It's Lisa. And there's no masquerade."

"Axel. The game has gone on long enough. We all know she's just a fling. And it's time to come to your senses. You must realize that if you're not an ally you're the enemy."

"What exactly are you saying Bethany?"

She laughed. "How do I put this succinctly? If you don't attend this banquet and insist on refusing to merge our operations and eventually have a personal merger if you know what I mean, I'll have no choice but to ruin VSS."

I was silent for a moment as angry thoughts swirled in my head. I chose my words carefully.

"So, what you're telling me is that you'll finish what Brian started when I took over the company?"

She laughed again and it made my skin crawl. "Brian is a dimwit. But I think you know I'm a woman of my word. I can and will ruin you Axel. Mark my words."

"Take your best shot, Bethany. Goodbye."

I disconnected the call and sat staring into space. What the fuck!? I ensured that the recording for this conversation was renamed specifically and saved. I had a feeling I would need it for evidence.

The following week, I realized that Bethany had not been joking. We lost three potential clients who were getting ready to sign on the dotted line. Investigations revealed they had signed with Chambers instead. This was only the beginning. Week by week, all the progress we had seen all year now seemed to be going in reverse. In our executive meetings, the concerns were tabled. I knew Bethany was behind it. But I was not going to play her game. Instead, I pushed forward on the expanded offerings, tapping into fields where Chambers had no clout. So where we were losing traditional clients, we were gaining in new and innovative areas. Then the sabotages began.

At first, when a client reported that their entire camera system was malfunctioning, we thought nothing of it. But when other reports began coming in of attacks on businesses specifically secured by VSS as well as threats to some of the employees, I sat up and took notice. The adage about hell having no fury like a woman scorned was playing out in front of me. But I wasn't worried.

Ever since the conversation with Bethany, I had engaged my lawyer. Now, every occurrence was documented and filed. The evidence was mounting. I was sure Bethany would make a fatal move and that would be her undoing. But with her taking the attack to my staff, I acted quickly by assigning some of our own bodyguards to certain key staff members. As my PA, Lisa was one of those who now had a security detail on her tail whenever I wasn't with her.

We often arrived at the office together due to our new living arrangements. But if she had to run errands, she had two guards with her at all times. At first, she was resentful of the bodyguards. But when I outlined the gravity of the situation, she reluctantly complied. This simply became a way of life.

As we headed into fall, we settled into a new norm. We still intended to move our operations to a bigger building. Losing some clients had hit us hard, but we were still in a position to be viable for expansion.

I heard through the industry grapevine that Bethany was a hard taskmaster and ran Chambers Guardianship with an iron fist. I smiled in anticipation of her chickens coming home to roost in the next few months. I simply had to ride out her fury and let her play all her cards and rack up my evidence. Then it would be time to launch my counter-attack.

23

LISA

I swiped the credit card and waited for the register to ring up my purchase. Out of the corner of my eye, I saw Peter hoist the packages into his arms as though they were nothing more than feathers. Ahead of me, Tim was already waiting at the door. I sighed silently at my incognito security detail. To the untrained eye it might have been any other woman out on a shopping spree with her significant other. Except, that Peter had a full head of gray hair and was older than my father and Tim was actually Timothine.

I completed the transaction and headed out of the store.

"We have one more stop to make and then we can head back to the office."

Peter grunted and nodded before stowing the packages in the truck. Timothine took the steering wheel while I sat in the back with Peter.

As the mid-morning traffic went by, I reflected on the past year. Last year this time, I'd been sitting at home hoping for another two-week stint or for a few orders to come in for some extra cash flow. Last year no one could

have told me that this year my father would
walking, but that he would be running. He ₂
taken up jogging and the last I heard he was ₍
training for a marathon. He had also taken A.... ...
job offer. Life was good for us. I had a great boyfriend; my
father was as good as new, and I had an awesome soon to be
stepmother. Dad had confided in me that he wanted to
propose to Nora at Christmas. He had my blessings.

I got all the other things I needed for the holiday baskets
I was making for the staff and headed back to the office.
Peter and Timothine disappeared to wherever they usually
disappeared to when they were in the office. But I knew that
at the touch of a button, they would reappear.

I popped a mint into my mouth as I slid into my chair. I
took a sip of water and sighed with relief as the queasy
feeling I had been having all morning left. I had had the flu
a few weeks before but this weakness seemed to be lingering. I hadn't even had breakfast this morning as I didn't want
a repeat of a few mornings ago when I had rushed to the
bathroom as soon as we got to the office and emptied the
contents of my stomach. Axel had wanted me to go home
and rest but I'd told him I could stay on his office couch. I
had done just that.

"Are you okay?"

I looked up at Lola's concerned face.

"Just this flu that doesn't seem to want to go away."

"Maybe you need to go to the doctor. I heard there's a
serious stomach bug going around. Gina in sales has been
out all week with it. Maybe that's what you have."

"Maybe. I don't have much of an appetite either and
everything I eat seems to want to come back up. If I don't
feel better, I'll go this weekend for sure."

I got busy with my tasks for the day. Before I knew it,

.ich had slipped by and then the afternoon. I went through my evening routine of clearing up any last-minute documents before packing up my desk. As I waited for Axel, I rested my head on my forearms on the desk. I slipped into a doze.

The next thing I felt was a hand on the back of my neck, massaging it gently. I sighed as I opened my eyes and looked up to find Axel standing over me.

"Tired?"

I nodded and yawned. "A bit."

"Let's go home."

I could barely keep my eyes open on the drive home. And as soon as I got inside I headed straight upstairs. I walked out of my clothes and straight into the shower. I closed my eyes and allowed the hot needles to soothe my body. I gasped as I felt Axel's arms come around me.

"Are you okay, babe?"

I shook my head wearily. "I can't seem to shake this flu."

"Do you want to go to the doctor tomorrow?"

I shook my head. "It will pass. I just need to get my energy levels up. That's all."

I leaned back and allowed him to lather my body and rinse me off. He dried me off and bundled me up with a robe and tucked me into bed before heading downstairs. I dozed off once more and was awakened by the scent of warm broth. My stomach rumbled as I sat up. His face was etched with concern as I took slow sips, trying not to recoil as my stomach rolled rebelliously. He smoothed my hair away from my brow as I finally pushed aside the half-eaten bowl.

"I think you should stay home for the rest of the week. And next week if necessary."

I began to shake my head. "There's too much to be done."

"It can get done when we both get back."

"You're staying home with me?"

He kissed my hand and used it to cup his cheek. "Not exactly. I got an email this evening. I'm needed overseas for a few days."

My heart skipped a beat. "An assignment?"

He nodded gravely. "Yes."

"I don't suppose you can tell me where you're going or what you're going to be doing?"

"No."

"When do you leave?"

"Saturday. It's for ten days."

"Oh. Okay."

"So you would actually have the week off since I won't be here. I'll have Tim and Peter stay with you."

"But-"

"No buts, Lisa. I'm not taking any chances with my main staff. You know every inch of what goes on at VSS including our plans to come. Plus, you're my girlfriend, a position she desires. I'm not taking any chances."

"When will it all end?"

"When she makes a mistake and crosses a line that makes it hard for her to deny her involvement in everything that has been happening."

"When will that be?"

"Hopefully soon. But in the meantime, Tim and Peter stay. I have enough rooms here and security is tight on the grounds." When everything had started to happen, Axel had employed a team for his house for twenty-four hour protection. "But I want them here in case you need to leave the house."

"I don't have a choice, do I?"

"Nope."

He brushed his lips against mine before standing.

"If this were not the kind of mission it was and if you were well, I would take you with me you know."

"I know. Bring me back a souvenir?"

He grinned and caressed my cheek.

"Definitely."

I slept in the next morning and woke up well into the morning. I felt awful and was glad that Axel had stocked the mini fridge in the bedroom with a few light snacks. I didn't have the energy to go downstairs and could barely make it to the bathroom and back. The following day I was a little better but still feeling weak from not eating regularly. By the time he left on Saturday morning, I had settled into a routine. I slept late most mornings, took a quick shower when I woke up, tried to move around to keep my body going, grazed here and there, then slept for an hour or two in the afternoon when my weakness was intensified. I had thrown up a few times but now that there was hardly anything in my stomach, it was mostly dry heaves. I had lost a little weight as well.

Axel had been gone for a week when I finally decided that I could not continue like this. I used all my energy to get dressed and headed downstairs. Tim and Peter who were sitting at the counter watching a movie on a laptop looked up at my approach.

"Could you take me to a pharmacy please?"

Tim came over and placed a motherly hand on my forehead.

"You don't feel feverish, which is a good thing. This flu is no joke. My niece has it right now and I feel so sorry for the poor little darling. I'll go bring the car around."

I waited obediently by the front door, admiring the November sunset with all its orange hues. Peter's hand underneath my elbow guided me into the car and we headed down the hill.

I stopped at the first pharmacy I could find. I pushed a cart up and down the aisles, picking up a few random things including a book of crossword puzzles, something for an upset stomach and sanitary napkins. As I examined the package to ensure it was the brand and quantity I always used, something went off in my brain. I frowned as I looked at the package, staring with unseeing eyes as I thought about the barely used pack underneath the bathroom sink. A random thought flitted into my head. Just as hastily it flew out. But as I stood in the line for the cashier, my eyes fell on a box. Without thinking, I added it to my cart. For good measure, I added a few other brands. At least I could rule *that* out as an explanation for how ill I was lately.

I nibbled a few mints as we headed back to the house. Peter took my purchases upstairs and I emptied them onto the bed. As I went to the bathroom to put away the napkins, I took the pregnancy tests with me. I sat on the toilet as I read the instructions. Within a few minutes, I had five sticks lined up on the counter. I went back into the bedroom and forgot all about them as I found a movie. It wasn't until I went to brush my teeth that I remembered they were there. I picked up a stick and everything went still. A glob of toothpaste foam dribbled down my chin and hit the counter. But it was an afterthought as my toothbrush clattered into the sink. With trembling hands I picked up one stick after the other. I checked the boxes for the instructions and the key for the results. Whether it was a word, a color, or lines, they all said the same thing. I looked at myself in the mirror for a long time, the word seared in my mind. Pregnant.

That night, my dreams were troubled. All I could see were the little sticks dancing around in a circle and singing as my stomach got bigger and bigger. The next morning, I checked my calendar and my cycle. I was as regular as clockwork. How had I not noticed that I had skipped a period? I spent the rest of the day on the internet researching signs and symptoms. With each piece of information, I felt conformation settling into my spirit. But I still needed an official word. I needed to go to a doctor.

I skimmed through the telephone book until I found someone half an hour away. I called and made an appointment for the next day. Now all I had to do was figure out how to get away from Tim and Peter.

The gods seemed to be in my favor as I went downstairs the next morning to find only Tim at the counter.

"Good morning. Feeling better?"

"A little. Where's Peter?"

"He had a family emergency and had to run out for a few hours. But if you need to go somewhere, I have instructions to pull one of the ground guards."

"I'm not going anywhere. Maybe a walk around the grounds. That's it."

"Okay. Let me know still. The car is ready and waiting."

"Sure. No problem."

As I prepared a light breakfast and forced it down, my brain was moving at the speed of light. I went upstairs and made a quick call then changed into a pair of sweats and a pullover for the cool weather. I had a fanny pack with my phone, purse and keys concealed underneath the bulky top. When I went downstairs, Tim looked up.

"Going for that walk?"

"Yes."

"I'll come with you."

I forced a laugh as panic took hold. She was not supposed to want to come with me!

"It's just to the gate and back, Tim. I'll be fine."

"But Axel said-"

"You're my guards once I'm off the compound or outside the office. Look. There are two guards at the gate and two more patrolling the grounds. I'll be very safe. Trust me."

She went silent, nibbling her lip. "Okay," she finally said reluctantly. "But remember if you need to go anywhere the car is ready and waiting."

"Sure thing."

I slipped out the front door and made a show of walking around the house at least once. I widened my circle gradually, thankful that I had a little more energy to carry out this charade. I felt my phone vibrate and casually headed to the gate. If the taxi driver had followed my instructions, he was waiting out of sight around the corner from the house. I just needed to get out the gate. The guards in the booth at the gate looked up as I approached. These two were new on the rotation and I felt hope bloom within me. Hopefully they were not aware of the tight ship Axel was running.

"Good morning. Just going for a run down the hill and back."

"Good morning. Have a good run."

My heart soared as I slipped through the gate. It had been easier than I thought. As soon as I stepped outside, the taxi came screeching to a stop at my feet. I hopped in and released the breath I hadn't even known I was holding.

Half an hour later I was ushered into the doctor's office. I had asked the taxi to wait with the meter running. Considering where he had picked me up, I knew he had calculated the massive fare he would be collecting. I had paid him a portion already as a sign of goodwill.

An hour later my heart was racing as I listened to the doctor's instructions.

"You did the right thing by taking some bed rest already. The first trimester is always the hardest. But in another five weeks you'll be heading into your second trimester and it will be smooth sailing with just a few bumps along the way. Again, congratulations!"

I smiled against the lump in my throat. "Thank you."

I paid the requisite fees and collected a few pamphlets from the receptionist. I folded them and placed them in the fanny pack. As I stepped outside, I realized it had started raining. I stepped onto the sidewalk to the taxi when I felt someone bump into me.

"Excuse me!" the tall gentleman exclaimed and reached out to steady me.

"No problem." I attempted to step around him only to find myself being grabbed from behind. He reached out again, this time with a rag in his hand and before I could respond, it was clamped over my nose and mouth. I felt my head grow light instantly and I was lifted into the air. I barely made out a sleek black car as I was hustled into the back seat. The last thing I saw before I slipped into unconsciousness was the pouring rain against the windshield.

It felt like hours later when I woke up. I was on a couch. I blinked as I looked up at the unfamiliar ceiling.

"Finally awake I see?" the cold voice of a woman made me sit up and spin around.

My heart dropped as Bethany walked towards me.

She smiled but I couldn't shake the feeling of a lion stalking its prey.

"We finally get to finish what we started in Coral Spring. And there's no Axel to come to your rescue this time."

24

AXEL

"What the fuck do you mean she just walked out the gate and jumped into a car?"

Timothine was visibly trembling, but I didn't care. When I had realized I would be home a few days earlier than planned and had wanted to surprise Lisa, the last thing I had expected to find was my security team in disarray and frantic. My presence was not helping matters either. And to make matters worse, Lisa had not been seen since. It was a full twenty-four hours and no-one had thought of calling me to report the matter let alone calling the police.

"We've questioned the taxi driver from the company. He said he dropped her off at a clinic. She paid him to wait but when she came out, she went with two other men into a black car. And that's all he remembers. He just thought she had called her friends to pick her up and he went on his way."

"I want to see him. Now."

"Yes, sir." I watched the woman sprint out of the room as I watched the gate footage once more, looking for any clues.

It was just as they had said. Lisa walked out the gate and willingly got into the taxi. My heart thudded as I watched the image of the vehicle as it turned the corner and disappeared off-screen. I felt the way I did that night almost twelve years ago when I had watched the robber hustle the young girl out of the restaurant. I had to find her.

"He's on his way, sir."

"Good."

I headed to the kitchen to get a beer from the fridge as I waited for the taxi driver. When the young man arrived I had downed three cans and was on my fourth.

I could see he was nervous as I interrogated him once more. He repeated everything that he had told my guards.

"Sir, I swear I had nothing to do with her disappearance. I was waiting as she instructed. Then she came out and she just walked on with those men."

"Are you sure she walked or was she being carried?"

"She was walking pretty close to them. One even bumped her and was holding her arm. At one point I wondered if she was feeling well because she was leaning on him."

My eyebrows shot up. "Leaning on him?"

"You know. Like when a guy and a girl can't keep their hands off each other. Real close."

I saw red as confusion now entered my mind. Did Lisa know the men the driver said she had gone with in the car?

"Where was it that you had taken her?"

"One six seven four Parchment Street."

"What's there?"

"I dunno. A bunch of offices and shops and stuff. Look, can you just pay me for my time and let me go? I've got a passenger to pick up in a few."

I handed him over to Timothine as I grabbed another

beer. Something was eluding me. I opened my laptop and found the address he had given. It was indeed a bunch of offices and shops. Who knew which one Lisa had patronized. And I didn't have the authority to go and knock on every door either. If only there was a camera-

I stared at the screen. A camera. There had to be some sort of security camera somewhere at the front of the building. And if there was a camera, had it caught the moment Lisa had left the building? It was time to get the authorities involved.

Two hours later, I sat in an interview room along with Timothine and the two guards at the gate as they recounted what had taken place. When they were through with their report, I turned to the investigator.

"I have reason to believe that Lisa was kidnapped. But to confirm that, I need to see the surveillance tape from any security cameras that may be in the area where she was last seen."

"Not a problem, Vance. We can make that happen."

And make it happen they did. An hour later we were back at the station with the tape. As they ran it, I saw Lisa enter the building. We fast forwarded, searching for the moment she exited. A few minutes after she entered, a black car drove past the taxi. I watched as it seemed to circle the block a few times during the tape until it parked two cars away from the taxi. I saw a flash of white as Lisa came into view at the entrance. She seemed to pause as she put her hand to her face as though looking for someone. My heart sank. Had the driver been right? Did she know the man?

We slowed down the tape and watched in slow motion as she stepped onto the sidewalk. One man approached from the front and I saw two others slide in behind her. My heart soared. This was a set-up! They were strangers after all!

I watched as the man in front seemed to bump her. Then there was a flash of white in his hand.

"Stop! There! What's that in his hand?"

We zoomed in and replayed the snippet. It was definitely a rag. Chloroform. She had been kidnapped!

I watched helplessly as her limp form was half carried half dragged to the car. The angle didn't show the plates.

"Do you have any enemies who would want to hurt you through her?"

"Many. But I know of one in particular right now. Bethany Chambers."

There was silence in the room for a moment. Then the lead investigator spoke.

"You can't mean *the* Bethany Chambers of Chambers Guardianship."

"One and the same. Our families have a history. It's an old ax that she's grinding. But she's crossed the line now."

Suddenly there was a loud beep from my pocket. I took out my phone and opened the app that had made the sound. I looked at the screen and my face lit up like the sun.

"Axel Vance, you are such a jackass! That's the first thing you should have checked! Yes!"

"What is it?"

"A tracker I have in one of Lisa's bracelets. Put in these coordinates."

As I punched the information in and zoomed in on the location, the Chambers' mansion came into view.

"Bingo. I've got you now, you bitch."

My jubilation soon turned to dismay as the dot on the screen began to move.

"Shit! She's moving her! We need to go!"

"We're right with you!"

I ran out of the station with Tim, the guards and half a dozen police on my trail. We hopped into my truck and I synced my phone with the truck's GPS. I took off into the afternoon traffic with police sirens on my tail. I watched the screen closely, feeling my adrenaline rush as I got closer and closer. Soon we were on the highway and I could clearly see the black vehicle a few cars ahead. I knew the instant they realized they were being followed as they picked up speed. I pressed the gas, the police sirens squealing hot on my tail.

I pulled up beside the car and immediately pulled back as a bullet whizzed over the truck. I pulled out my handgun and lined up to take a shot at the back wheel. I couldn't risk firing into the car. Lisa was in there. I took a shot, cursing as it hit the road surface. I pulled my head back as another bullet whizzed by my head. I took another shot and was pleased to see the car swerve and the tires squeal as the wheel blew out. It careened out of control and ran onto the soft shoulder. My heart leaped in fear as it flipped over and landed on its side.

The police surrounded the car as I brought my truck to a screeching halt on the soft shoulder.

"Come out with your hands up!" The bullhorn sounded like thunder in my ears.

I watched as three men wriggled out of the window, holding their hands above their heads. The officers swarmed them even as I sprinted to the car, my heart in my mouth. Lisa was wedged between the back seat and the front seat, her hands bound. There was a trickle of blood on her forehead and she was pale and unconscious. I reached inside and felt for her pulse. It was strong but erratic.

"An ambulance is on the way. Don't move her. She may have broken bones."

I crouched beside the wreckage as I continued to stroke her forehead.

"Wake up, baby. I need to know you're okay."

I waited until the paramedics arrived along with the fire department. As much as I didn't want to leave her, I stood aside to allow them to do their job. But as soon as she was free from the wreckage I was by her side. I tossed the truck keys to Tim and hopped into the ambulance.

I stood by the window overlooking the parking lot as I waited for the doctors to finish with Lisa. The paramedics had checked her over and the wound on her forehead was merely superficial.

"Mulligan?"

I turned. "Here."

"This way, please."

I followed the doctor to the room where Lisa was. I looked at the machines hooked up to her."

"Is she going to be okay?"

"Yes. Just a few scratches and bruises. She's a bit dehydrated as well and her stomach is empty. She hasn't eaten in at least twenty-four hours. If it had been four weeks or less, she might have miscarried, especially with the physical and emotional stress she has been under in the past few hours. But the baby is fine."

Baby!?

The word screamed in my head even as I pasted a smile on my lips and choked out the words, "Thank you."

"With a week or two of bed rest, she will be as good as new. I've prescribed a round of prenatal vitamins as well as she's coming up with deficiencies. You can pick it up from the nurses' station when you leave. I'll let you have a few minutes with her now."

The doctor slipped out of the room and I pulled up a

chair to sit by the bed. I shifted the hospital robe and lay a trembling hand on her stomach, feeling the warmth of her skin beneath my hand. Pregnant. Lisa was carrying my child. I felt the prick of tears and my throat clogged.

I sat like that until I had to leave.

By the next day, she was conscious. Nora and Gerald went to see her as well as several coworkers. I was also shocked to turn up one morning and find my mother at her side. I knew it was partially guilt for how she had treated her in favor of Bethany.

As for Bethany, she had been arrested the same evening. She had tried to deny any involvement in the kidnapping. But her goons had turned on her and were singing like canaries, not only about Lisa, but also about other tasks they had executed at Bethany's command. A search of the house had also yielded Lisa's fanny pack and phone. When I added all the evidence I had been collecting, her case was as good as closed. When the media got wind of it, there was a frenzy. I didn't even try to take Lisa home in the truck and used the helicopter instead.

I spent the next few days nursing Lisa back to her full capacity. But I felt empty. There was something in her eyes that made me uneasy. She had yet to bring up the pregnancy. And I decided that if she didn't bring it up, neither would I. My thoughts went to dark places as I observed her daily omission of this piece of information. And when I realized that her visit to Parchment Street was to a doctor, my heart sank. She had planned to get rid of our baby.

For the next week, I watched as she slowly distanced herself from me. We were both back at work, but gone was any comradery. She worked as efficiently as always but her smile was forced and her eyes dead.

On the day that marked one year since she had first

started working with VSS, I had a gift basket delivered to the house. She only flicked at the card in passing and headed upstairs. The next morning she asked for the day off and I allowed her to sleep as I headed to the office.

At about nine o'clock, Lola knocked on the door.

"This just came for you. I brought it right in since Lisa's not here."

"Thanks."

I slit the envelope expecting to find the usual kind of document. Instead, I withdrew a single sheet of paper. As I skimmed the few words, I saw red. I slammed my laptop shut and shoved it into the case. As I bolted out of the office, I had only enough time to tell Lola that I was out of the office for the day. My heart was racing as I headed home. The scene that met me was exactly what I had expected. But it seemed as though Lisa had not been expecting me to arrive. With a grunt, I removed her bags from the taxi, paid the driver and sent him on his way.

"Axel. I don't want to cause a scene or anything. Please. Just let me go. It's better for both of us this way."

"Are you resigning because of the baby?"

I watched as the color drained from her face.

25

LISA

I felt all the color drain from my face as Axel's blue eyes glittered angrily. And how the hell did he know about the baby?

"The baby?"

"Yes! The baby! I know you're pregnant Lisa. And you haven't said a word to me about it. Are you planning to abort our child? And don't even try the line about another man's baby. I know it's mine."

"Abort? How could you think I could do such a thing?"

"I never thought you would keep it from me either. But you did, didn't you? And now you're resigning because you're trying to run away before I find out."

I clamped my lips together and turned on my heel. He read me too well. He followed me inside and turned me to face him.

"What did you think was going to happen when I came home tonight and found you gone?"

"I didn't think anything. I just wanted to leave." I kept my voice low but inside I was screaming at the anguish I had been feeling for weeks.

When I realized Bethany had in fact planned to kill me, all I could think about in the moment was our unborn child. Then after the accident and the hospital where he had remained as stoic as ever, I had felt broken. I loved this man with all my heart. But even in a matter of life and death he hadn't flinched. He had remained as blank as a clean slate, showing no emotion. Well, scratch that. Right now he was staring at me with a level of rage I had never seen.

"Do you really think I'm going to let you literally pack your bags and walk out of my life, Lisa?"

"It's best this way."

"Best for who? Not for me and certainly not our baby. Is it best for you?"

I dropped my eyes and sank onto the couch, wrapping my arms around my torso as I felt the tears threatening to fall.

"You weren't supposed to read the letter until later."

"Well I guess it's a good thing I did."

"Why did you come?"

"I don't accept your resignation. And you're not leaving me either."

"I'm not retracting it and I am leaving."

"Why?"

"Because I have to go." My voice was hoarse with unshed tears.

"Why?"

I pressed my hands to my face as the tears began to course down my cheeks. I felt him kneel before me and his hands pulled mine down. I turned my face away, sobbing with all my heart.

"Look at me, Lisa."

"No!"

"Why do you want to break my heart?" his voice was soft

and suspiciously husky. "We can be together. We can make this work. I'm not letting you go."

"You're going to have to, Axel. I can't be with someone who doesn't love me, even if I'm carrying his baby."

"Don't love you? Lisa, do you honestly believe that I don't love you?"

"I don't know how you feel about me, Axel. I wish you would-"

The press of his lips against mine cut off whatever I was about to say. I sobbed as I realized how much I had missed his touch all these weeks. He pressed his forehead to mine as he took a shuddering breath.

"Lisa, I love you with all my heart and every fiber of my being. I almost died when I came back and found you were gone. I felt as if I was going to go out of my mind. All I wanted to do was hold you and never let you go when you were in the hospital. And then when the doctor told me you were pregnant-"

I went into shock as for the first time in my life I saw Axel break down sobbing. I pulled him to me, cradling his head on my lap as he wept.

"I love you so much, Lisa. I love you with all my heart. Please, don't leave me. Don't leave me."

I caressed his head and rained tiny kisses wherever I could reach.

"I'm so sorry. I'm so sorry. I didn't know you loved me."

He looked up at me. "How could you not know? You're living in my house. You're sleeping in my bed. You're carrying my child! How could you not know? I don't move every woman into my house or my bed. I don't go around having unprotected sex. I love *you!*"

He reached up and pulled me to him once again, searing

my mouth with his hot kisses. When at last we pulled apart, we were both breathing heavily.

"Tell me you won't leave me."

"I won't leave you."

"Tell me you'll stay with me always."

"I'll stay with you always."

With a smile a mile wide, he stood and swooped me into his arms and headed upstairs. As he undressed me, tears filled my eyes. He took his time with me, kissing every inch of my naked flesh. When he reached my belly, I felt the heat of his tears as he kissed the slight mound. He spent his time going in small circles, kissing and nipping. When he finally went lower, I arched my back as pleasure ripped through me. I cried out as he lapped at me, pressing his tongue deep and taunting me. When he finally allowed me to reach my crest, I spread my legs and pulled him up to meet me.

The first touch of his hard body made me cry out again. I didn't know how much I had missed this until this moment.

We gave ourselves to each other with an urgency I'd never felt before. It seemed as if I couldn't get enough of him. And each time I went flying with cries of ecstasy, I wanted to go higher. When he finally poured himself into me with a loud cry, we collapsed in a puddle of trembling sweaty limbs and racing hearts. I held him tightly to me. I would never let him go – ever.

It was evening before we remembered my luggage was still on the porch. Axel retrieved it and the take out he had ordered and paid extra for so that they would deliver it on the hill.

That day marked a change in Axel that I hadn't anticipated. It was as though I was dealing with a brand-new person. He had made a one eighty degree turn. This was especially evident in the office. It was not easy to stop myself from confiding in Lola when I would return from lunch to find little gifts and trinkets on my desk. And he wasn't above brushing his hand along my back whenever we walked in or out of the office. I knew tongues were wagging and I hoped it was in a good way.

Before we knew it, Christmas was here. I walked through the ballroom admiring the décor. I was pleased that they had followed my instructions to the letter, down to the gold name cards for each table. I went through the routine of placing each gift at each seat as I had done last year. I heard footsteps and turned to find Axel standing in the doorway. My heart skipped a beat as I looked at him standing there. His dark gray suit fit him like a glove. He had gotten his hair and beard trimmed. As he looked at me, the room seemed to fade. I stood transfixed as he walked toward me slowly. I smelled the musk of his cologne as he stopped within arm's reach.

"You look beautiful."

"I'm not dressed yet."

"I don't mind."

"I bet you'd say I was beautiful if I showed up in rags."

"Your beauty isn't in what you're wearing, my love. It's in your heart. And that's just another reason I love you."

I felt my heart melt every time he told me he loved me. He reached out to lift my chin.

"Go get dolled up. I can't wait for this party to get started." He kissed me softly as I slipped by him.

I headed up to the suite he had rented for us for the night as he had declared I was not going to get dressed in a hotel bathroom. I showered and quickly changed into a short black dress. It was the only thing that could work to conceal the slight rise of my tummy. I slipped my feet into low heeled pumps. As I reached for my bracelet, my eyes fell on a rectangle box that had been placed on my purse. I opened it and gasped when I found a diamond necklace with matching earrings and bracelet. I plucked out the note that was taped inside.

Wear these tonight, my love.

He didn't have to tell me twice. I slipped on the jewelry, reveling in the feel of the stones on my bare skin. I had planned to wear my hair down, but these diamonds needed to be shown off in all their glory.

I hunted down a few bobby pins and soon had my hair up in a French twist of sorts. My hair was almost at the middle of my back now and the length was perfect for that style. I spritzed on a few drops of perfume before checking myself in the mirror. There was a glow about me that could not be hidden. I placed my hand on my tummy and smiled. In a few weeks, this baby would not be hidden either. I switched off the lights and left the suite.

The banquet was an excellent one. This year, I had pitched the idea of making it an awards banquet. He had told me to run with the idea. I had drafted a small committee and together we had made it happen. Lola stood by the table with the plaques as I called out the names of the awardees. She handed them to Axel. Who better to give out the award than the CEO. Finally the last award was handed out and Axel took the mic to give his speech.

"Before I speak, there is one award that has not yet been handed out."

I looked at Lola and the table. I was shocked to see that there was indeed a plaque there.

"Lisa, could you come here please."

Lola looked at me, her face wreathed in smiles as she

handed the plaque to Axel. I walked toward him slowly. The staff stood as Axel turned to me.

"I think everyone would agree with me when I say this award is well-deserved. Lisa, you walked into this company and turned things around in a way you cannot even begin to understand. I'd like you to read what this plaque says."

He handed me the mic and stepped behind me. I cleared my throat and held up the plaque.

"Presented to Lisa Mulligan, the love of my life. Will you-"

My words faltered, my eyes misted over. The room erupted in cheers and screams. One look behind me at Axel on his knee told me why. Lola danced over to him with another mic in hand as he held up a small black box.

"Lisa, I'm a man of few words and emotions. But when it comes to you, I'd recite a dictionary if you wanted. Fate has meant for us to be together long before we even knew we would be together. Will you promise to be with me forever? Will you marry me?"

I could hear a pin drop as I took a deep breath. I lifted the mic to my mouth.

"Yes."

Pandemonium erupted as Axel slipped the ring on my finger before rising to pull me into a heated kiss. Later that night as I lay draped across his body wearing only the diamonds he had given me, now including the engagement ring, I couldn't believe how happy I was. He stroked my back gently as he nibbled my ear.

"Te amo."

I chuckled. "Je t'aime."

"I'll find out how to say it in every language if I have to, you know."

"We have our entire lives to find out." I snuggled into his shoulder as he pulled the covers over us.

Axel and I had been invited to Dad and Nora's for Christmas dinner. As soon as I stepped inside Nora embraced me.

"Let me see it!"

I looked at her. "You knew!?"

"Who do you think helped me pick it out?"

"I can't believe you two!"

"What's all the shouting in here?"

I turned to my father as Axel's hand slipped around my waist. I held out my hand.

"Axel asked me to marry him."

"Oh my! Congratulations. But I thought you were going to wait until New Years."

I gaped at my father as well. "*You knew too!?*"

"I had to get his blessing, love. Of course he knew."

"I can't believe this! Next thing you're going to tell me the entire office was in on it too."

"Well, not the entire office. Just Lola. She had to get the plaque for me."

"And here I was wondering how I was going to keep our relationship a secret from her. No wonder she never asked me about those gifts."

"Well congratulations again you two. I can't wait for us to start looking at gowns for you. Do you want to be a spring or summer bride?" Nora grabbed my hand as she looked at the ring once more.

"That's a question you'll both have to answer, Nora."

"Huh?"

I smiled as I turned Nora around to face my father. I stepped aside as he slowly went down on one knee.

"Nora, words cannot express how much I love you. And

it goes beyond what you've done for me this past year. I'm an honorable man and I want to do the honorable thing. Will you be my wife?"

Nora dropped to her knees and planted a kiss on my father that made me blush.

After dinner as we sat in the living room discussing wedding dates, I demurely slipped in that the later the date the bigger the dress would have to be. When the dime dropped it was another round of celebration for our unborn child.

As I laid in Axel's arms, I felt a lightness in my spirit that was unbelievable. Last year I asked for my miracle soldier. This year I had him. Life did not get any better than this.

EPILOGUE – LISA

I stepped aside carefully as another waiter offered me yet another treat. I didn't refuse. I took it to my little nook near the library and sat munching. From there I had some well-needed privacy but could still hear the festivities in the next room. I took a sip of juice as I moved on to another delicacy. I chuckled to myself as I gorged. In less than a month I would no longer be able to use the excuse that I was eating for two. I hiccupped and moved on to a third treat.

"Lisa! Canape *again*? I swear you're setting up this child to have an expensive appetite."

"That's why she will have a very involved grandmother who will dote on her with all the expensive treats her heart desires." I smiled as Elizabeth came to stand by me.

She laughed as she rubbed my belly. "I agree. Don't you agree my little munchkin? Grandmama can't wait to meet you and spoil you. Yes I will. Yes I will. Oh! She kicked! Did you feel that, Lisa."

I groaned as I placed my hand on the other side of my stomach. I felt the sharp nudge.

"I wish she would stop kicking sometimes. I swear she's going to be a ballerina or something."

"And as soon as she's out you're going to want to put another one back in to feel those kicks again."

"I thought putting one in was a team effort. And believe me, I put in the effort."

I looked up as Axel walked over to us. I blushed at the thought of us making another child as I looked at my husband. He leaned down to brush a quick kiss on my lips, lingering just a little.

"Just as long as you do your part. Children need siblings." Elizabeth patted his shoulder lightly.

"I didn't have any and turned out just fine, Mother." He brushed my cheek as he stood.

"Not by choice. But I am happy that you think we did a good job."

"You and Dad did a great job. I learned from two of the best parents. Thank you."

"You're welcome. Now go back to your guests. This is your party, remember? Shoo! Lisa and I have baby stuff to discuss." She waved at him dismissively.

I watched in amazement as Axel obeyed his mother and left us alone. On New Year's day when we had broken the double news to Elizabeth, the slight melting of her attitude towards me that I had experienced the last time I had seen her at the office, became a full-blown puddle. I suspected Bethany's arrest on a slew of charges including kidnapping and attempted murder had changed her tune in my favor. Whatever it was, as Axel had predicted, the news of the baby made her come around fast. I had a staunch ally in my corner and I was amazed at how resourceful she had been in helping Nora and me pull off our double wedding in March. The baby shower on my birthday in May had been another showstopper. And now here she was hosting Axel's birthday party as well. Seeing this side of her made me realize she was not all that bad after all.

"Have you decided on a name yet?" She rubbed my stomach once more.

"We were thinking of Irene or a derivative in honor of my mother. We were also thinking of the middle name – Elizabeth." I watched to see how she would respond. Axel and I had discussed it at length and we hoped she would be pleased. I wasn't disappointed.

She gasped and placed a hand to her chest in true Elizabeth Vance dramatic fashion.

"I would be honored, my dear." I detected a mistiness in her eyes as she patted my hand.

"I'm glad you like it. Axel and I thought it was best that she have – oh!"

I grabbed my stomach as I felt a sharp pain shoot through me. Elizabeth knelt by me instantly, her eyes full of concern as she looked at me clutching my stomach.

"What is it dear?" She placed her hand on my stomach and I felt the baby roll.

I scrunched my face in pain and groaned loudly as I felt a sudden gush of liquid flow from my body. I looked down in horror at the wet stain which was spreading on Elizabeth's expensive chair.

"I think my water just broke."

"*What!?* Elizabeth looked down and screamed. "It did! Axel!!!"

She took off in the direction of the main ballroom screaming for her son.

Hours later the screams were my own as I struggled to bring our child into the world. Then at approximately eleven fifty-seven pm, Irene Elizabeth Vance took her first breath and let out an angry cry. I watched through misty eyes as they placed her on my chest and Axel cut the umbilical cord. There was a flurry of activity as the medical team did their due diligence of cleaning us up and recording her vital statistics. It was another hour before I was wheeled to my private room. Axel didn't leave my side all night, watching us as we slept.

The next day I was rested enough to have visitors. Axel kept a tight rein nevertheless. A few days later I was discharged. It was a strange feeling going home with an extra person. That first night as I sat in the nursery nursing our daughter, Axel came into the room. He pulled up a chair and leaned over to look at her as she nursed, her cheeks ballooning in and out as she sucked.

"She's beautiful, isn't she?"

"She takes after her mother."

"And she has her father's eyes. It's a win-win if you ask me."

He stroked my cheek and smiled. "You're amazing, you know."

"Tell me that again when it's three in the morning and I'm covered in puke and stinky."

"Even if you're covered in shit from head to toe and haven't bathed in three days, I'll still think you're the most beautiful woman on earth. Let me burp her."

I handed him the baby, watching how he held her gently in his hands. I had an instant flashback to the night at the diner. And here he was with another little blonde girl looking up at him. His eyes were suspiciously bright as he whispered to the baby, rocking her gently.

"I'll always protect you." He looked at me, love shining in his eyes. "Both of you. Forever."

COMING SOON... SAMPLE CHAPTERS

Chapter One

Pamela

"Want to come to class with me?"

I didn't bother responding. But then as my mind turned my roommate's invitation over and over, my concentration waned from the show I was watching, and my interest began to grow.

I sat up on the couch 'd been sprawled on for the past two days and saw her leaning against the counter while scrolling through her phone and lifting a spoon of cereal to her mouth.

"Why would you invite me to your class?" I asked.

Meredith looked at me and shrugged.

"It's not the first time I've invited you. Since you're going through an existential crisis perhaps accept it, and come along? Who knows, you might get inspired by something? Plus, there's Professor Bach. I make it a point not to drool over him like everyone else, but it's our final year and for once I would like to be silly."

"'What's silly about drooling over a hot professor?" I asked.

She rolled her eyes at me.

I smiled. "Is he really that hot?"

Her attention returned to her phone. "You've asked me this question at least a hundred times and yet you've never bothered to check him out."

"I've been busy," I said and sunk back on the couch.

"Of course, with a major that you're still not sure you should pursue."

I closed my eyes. "I'm figuring it out."

"All that incurred debt..."

At this, I frowned, and she caught the dark scowl on my face. "I'm sorry," she apologized, her smile sheepish. "But I do think you should come out with me. You've been cooped up in here for too long. At least meet me after class. We can go to lunch or something."

Her suggestion sounded good, but I honestly felt too lazy to get up.

A few minutes later, I heard the clattering of her keys as she came over to the living room and began to dig through cushions of the armchair.

"What are you looking for?" I asked.

"My lipgloss," she said. "I'm sure it fell in here last night."

I returned my attention to my show. She soon found the tube and stopped to look at the TV.

"How many times have you rewatched Sex and the City?" she asked.

"A hundred," I replied groggily.

"It can't be that good," she said.

"It's not. It's just comfortable and relatable."

"Come to class with me," she groaned. "Your stench is all over the couch."

"I bought the couch," I said.

"No, you didn't. We *found* the couch. You only bought the fabric for the overhaul. Why am I even having this conversation right now? I'm already late. All the seats must have been taken by now."

"People come early to his class?"

"All the girls always want the front seats hoping he'll notice them so of course they're there way ahead of time and fighting for them. It's pathetic I tell you."

I looked at her and was reluctantly intrigued. "What exactly is the class about?"

"Data Structures and Algorithms."

"Ugh," I spat.

She laughed. "I'm leaving."

"What kind of algorithms?" I called after her. "Like the one Instagram uses to frustrate all the influencers?"

She laughed again and was soon by the door. "Come by and find out."

"I can slip in through the back door?" I asked.

She beamed. "You can. Let me know if you'll be there and I'll save you a seat. Darryl said that he was probably not going to make it but just in case he does, he'll be seated by me."

"Of course," I said.

She blushed scarlet. "Who knows? You might meet someone just like Darryl too."

I scoffed. "Someone like Darryl? You mean a nerd you've ignored all through you years in college but then found him a ridiculously good kisser during a drunken night out?"

At her silence, I looked up from the couch wondering if

she had left, but instead saw her standing at the doorway and watching me.

"Complete the story," she said with a straight face, and I couldn't hold my amusement.

"What?"

"Complete the fucking story. I'm late."

"You're aggravating," I said.

"Fine, I'll complete it then. This ridiculously good kisser now went on to be the very best possible lover to ever exist and now I think I'm in love."

The last part of that sentence made my eyes widened in surprise. "What?"

With a knowing smile, she turned around and pushed the door open.

"Meredith!" I shot up.

"Come to class," she yelled. "I'll tell you what you want to know at lunch."

She banged the door shut and I was once again left alone with my existential crisis.

Five minutes later, the episode I'd been watching came to an end and rather than switch to the next, I stopped and looked around. All the blinds had been pulled shut by me much to Meredith's complaints, but she had soon submitted to my desire for a dark and cozy apartment rather than a bright and uncomfortable one. It occurred to me then that it had been almost three days since I had last seen the sun, and a day and a half since I had taken a shower. Plus, my entire spine was beginning to ache. All of this I finally accepted was the perfect nudging to indeed get off the couch.

With a sigh, I moved my feet to the floor, my hair all over my face and eventually managed to pull myself up.

About ten minutes later, and as the warm stream

drenched my head and soothed the ache in my muscles, I couldn't help but feel somewhat relaxed.

I still didn't think I had the energy to step out of the house until my own classes the following day, so I took things by the minute until my hair was blown dry. And then I had absolutely no reason to stop myself from going to lunch with Meredith.

I pulled on a pair of light blue jeans, a clean white t-shirt, converses, and slung a tote bag over my shoulder. It wasn't the most attractive of outfits, but I was comfortable, and would be back in no time so I pushed the concern away.

In no time, I was out of the apartment and headed towards Meredith's computer science department. She hadn't been bluffing, as I soon found. The class was indeed packed to the brim even though it was a Monday morning. I was so struck that for the first few minutes all I did was peep through the door until a few students who were arriving late forced me to move away. I texted Meredith then. Thankfully she had a seat waiting for me by her side.

I wasn't ultimately glad however because although she wasn't in the front row, her row was still close enough that it would be impossible to hide that I was sneaking in after the lecture was already thirty minutes underway.

I was surprised that the professor was even letting this happen, so I kept my head down and held my breath until I was safely seated.

Excitement flashed in Meredith's eyes at my arrival, and then she leaned over and whispered in my ear.

"How's our famed hottie?" she asked, however the professor in front was the last thing on my mind.

"I need your charger," I said as I pulled my phone out of my bag.

The next minute consisted of my fumbling to plug the

charger underneath my seat, but then suddenly I heard Meredith speaking by my side.

Everything she said out loud for that matter sounded like gibberish, so I looked up, wondering what the hell was going on.

It was then that I realized that the eyes of the entire class were on us. Well, except those in the front row as their attention was solely on the professor in front who had on a pair of dark rimmed glasses.

He also had hair falling in thick effortless waves down the sides of his face, and his hands in his pockets giving off the air of reckless sophistication.

My breath caught for a moment, but then when I realized that Meredith was still talking, I leaned slightly away from her and subtly held a hand to the side of my face to hide. I was for sure going to kill her after this for not even warning me.

Soon enough she was done, and he began to respond once again. I heard the words... advanced methods of algorithm analysis... time and space complexity classes and NP-completeness... but I might as well have been hearing Persian.

Meredith however had that proud look on her face that I was so familiar with, for when she had impressed even herself and I couldn't help but jab her side.

"You sure it's Daryl you're infatuated with?" I asked.

She jabbed me right back. "Shh."

With a sigh, I slouched even further into the seat and watched the show in front of me.

The professor was indeed something to look at, I guess, especially since he was quite stylish.

He had on a white dress shirt, tucked into a pair of black straight-cut jeans with a pair of loafers on his feet. It was simple but for some reason, perhaps it was the way in which the clothes hung off his tall frame, the elegance he exuded seemed fitting for a runway.

I wondered what his name was because as I stared longer, I couldn't help but realize that he looked somewhat familiar.

Maybe I was wrong, but the longer I stared and tried to convince myself otherwise the more my scowl deepened.

I needed to take a closer look at him, I realized.

"What?" I heard Meredith ask.

I turned to see the question in her eyes, and only then did it occur to me that I must have spoken my thoughts out loud.

"I want a closer look," I told her. "Of him."

Her brows shot up. "Now you want to act like the thirsty ones up in front?"

Shaking my head, I rolled my eyes at her and returned my attention to him.

"*You* were the thirsty one just now, 'Miss I need to answer a question so that all the attention including the hot professors can be on me.' Would it have killed you to know the answer and not share it?"

"Actually, it would have," she replied. "Plus, I'm not thirsty. I have Darryl."

I rolled my eyes. "What if he had recognized that I wasn't from his class.?"

"I'm sure he already has," she said, and alarm struck me. "What?"

"He won't call you out. He is the only professor I'm certain in this entire school that never bothers with decorum, yet he gets it more than anyone else. None of the girls want to offend him so their attention on him and his work is always rapt, while the boys I guess don't want to offend the girls for being rowdy, so they keep their lips zipped."

I sighed again. "So, no one is paying attention because he knows his beans?"

"Oh, he knows more than his beans. He is the second half of a partnership that runs a unicorn company that provides cyber security protection for the biggest companies in the world."

Once again, gibberish. "What are you saying? He runs a company that sells unicorns?"

A snort of laughter escaped her, which seemed to distract the entire hall for a few seconds and truly the glares we received were quite troublesome.

My gaze was instantly on the professor, wondering if he too had been distracted, and my heart jumped as I realized that he was staring straight at me.

He was speaking, calmly, unhurriedly but for once, his gaze wasn't lazily scanning across the room. Instead, it was on me, most definitely not on Meredith. However, since it didn't make sense as to why this would be the case beyond the possibility that perhaps he had realized that I wasn't one of his students, I was tempted to look behind to see if there was someone else in particular that had caught his eye.

"You're an idiot," she said, and I couldn't help my smile. He looked away.

"If he has such a successful business, then why does he work as a professor?" I asked.

"Who knows?" she shrugged. "Perhaps he doesn't like running a business. I've heard his partner is the one at the helm of things, but he owns about 65% of it. Perhaps he brought the funding? Or he's the brains?"

"Where would a professor get that much money from?" I asked and she shrugged.

"Maybe his family is wealthy."

"Maybe," I said, and once again truly wished I could go forward to take a closer look at him.

I watched him through to the end of the class and could feel my heart lurch from time to time when he looked at me.

Eventually, the class was dismissed and just as expected all the birds flocked to the front. I sighed and turned to Meredith.

"Where are we going for lunch?"

She however was preoccupied with her phone, the widest smile spreading across her face.

"Um," she lifted her head, and I could see just how flushed she was.

"You can choose anywhere you want, I'll even pay," she said and in her tone I knew there was a catch.

I sighed again. "And in return?"

"You keep yourself busy for forty-five minutes to an hour until I join you."

"Meredith," I groaned, and she put her hands together in a plea.

"Darryl's waiting outside."

"Of course he is."

"I'll be back in no time. We'll be quick."

"Ew," I said. "Now I'll have to deal with that stupid smile you wear afterwards for the entire afternoon. You know what, forget this I'm going home."

"Oh c'mon," she complained as I grabbed my bag, and began to head up the stairs.

Suddenly however, I heard someone call her name.

"Miss Scott," the call rang out and we both turned.

At first, I wasn't sure who it was, but then he held out his hand in a gesture for her to come over and the confusion was cleared up.

"Yikes," she muttered, jumping to her feet.

"You think he's going to scold you for bringing a stranger to his class?"

"Who knows?" she said. "But I suspect more that it might have to do with my project."

"Come with?" she asked.

I shook my head firmly. "Oh no, I can't be among the thirsty ones."

"Stop," she ordered in her school headmistress voice that she employed when she was not planning to ever back down..

"Fine," I conceded and stood.

We were soon on our way, and as we approached, I couldn't really tell what had truly spurred my decision to give in so quickly. I'd thought I'd be able to just leave but there was something about him that made me almost desperately want to take a closer look at him.

My curiosity however soon waned when we were forced to wait. He had his eyes on us from time to time, but I couldn't even see clearly enough through the number of students waiting for an audience with him.

Eventually he moved away from one and began to gather his things, but the request for another conversation kept coming, causing an exhausted look to come over his face.

"Ah so he's not some immortal," I said dryly.

Meredith snickered.

However, a gnawing feeling began to hack my insides, as I was finally able to see him a bit more clearly. I stared and stared until finally he called us over. His gaze was on Meredith and my heart began racing in my chest.

"I'll be quick," she said, indicating that I was to wait for her, however I soon found that I was already moving forward, my eyes wide.

I couldn't believe it.

Or perhaps this was some kind of trick my mind was playing on me. His gaze once again met mine and perhaps at my expression, he too stopped to watch me.

"Gideon?" I called the moment I arrived.

Meredith was appalled. "Professor Bach," she quickly corrected under her breath. He turned his attention to her, and they began their conversation, however I couldn't help but stop him mid-sentence.

"You're Gideon Bach! Aren't you?" I asked in shock. Suddenly it was as though I was set ablaze from the inside out.

I couldn't believe it, and instantly bounded over till the distance was almost entirely closed between us.

"I'm Pamela," I pointed to my chest, nearly jumping with excitement.

"Do you remember? Pamela Fraser? We used to live right next door to each other."

I could tell that the entire auditorium had suddenly gone quiet, and all incessant chatter had stopped as everyone was now paying attention.

He looked at me, his expression neutral and void of emotion. And then his next words hit me like a truck.

"I'm sorry, but I don't know you. Miss Scott?" he called, and Meredith went with him leaving me with my mouth agape and doubting my sanity. I could do nothing but watch them, in particular him, as they conversed. Meredith's gaze was now full of curiosity as she had no doubt been taken aback by my seemingly insane outburst. She would look at me from time to time, however I eventually couldn't look away. Neither could I leave without making him realize that we truly knew each other. He had matured so much and left so many years ago when I was still so young. I'd kept him in my memories since then but couldn't believe just how much of it had blurred. But now, I was seeing him in the flesh once again and even if I got everything else wrong it was impossible to get his name wrong, right?"

I noted the moment Meredith began to finish up with him, so I hurriedly rushed over before another group of students took our place. They both looked at me once again somewhat startled at my sudden intrusion.

"Our house caught fire," I said to him.

"Pam!" Meredith exclaimed.

"I'm serious," I told her. "Not our apartment. My home back in Anaheim. You used to live in Anaheim, right? You rescued me? About nine years ago."

His devastatingly handsome face looked at me as though I had just announced that I crashed rockets for no reason.

"My apologies, again," he said unhurriedly. "But I don't know what you're talking about."

I had never been more confused, and for a few seconds began to wonder if the entire accident had mentally damaged him in some way. But then if it had, how was he a professor?

He had always been incredibly smart. The smartest boy I had ever known. At the time I had even believed he was the smartest in the entire world and with all he was up to so long after, I couldn't say that I had been wrong.

He was doing so incredibly well but then he couldn't recognize me. How was this possible? Tears misted my eyes.

"I've searched for you," I told him. 'For a very long time. And everywhere." My voice softened. "You really don't remember.?"

He was quiet now, and as it seemed, so was everyone else.

With an aggrieved sigh, I gave up and started to head

out. "Meredith, I'll be waiting outside," I said and there was no objection whatsoever. From anyone.

I leaned against the wall when I got out, confounded at how there was absolutely no recognition on his face whatsoever for me. He might have as well been staring at a blank wall, while I on the other hand recalled almost everything about him down to his mother, Angela.

A light bulb came on over my head then as it occurred to me that perhaps I should have brought up his mother. Maybe that would have caught his attention because there was absolutely no way he could write this off as coincidence.

I turned around then and pushed the auditorium's door open, eager to head to him, but I was stopped by the person I almost ran into.

"No," Meredith said, her hand flattening on my chest.

"Oh," I staggered backwards. "You're done."

"Yes, and so are you. We're leaving."

I panicked. "No, I need to talk to him." I tried to move her out of the way. "I know his mother."

However, she wouldn't let me.

"No Pam," she said. "I don't know what that was earlier on, but it was so embarrassing. How could you pretend to know him?"

I paused then, my gaze on her incredulous.

"What? You thought I was faking it?"

She smiled, but at the complete lack of amusement on my face it soon faltered.

"W-weren't you?"

I couldn't believe her. "Why the hell would you think that?"

"Well, it isn't uncommon. Most of the girls do everything to try and-"

"And you thought I'd be one of them?"

Her lips parted but no words escaped.

My gaze lifted once more to the door and the moment I saw that he was heading out through the opposite end of the auditorium, I felt my insides deflate but I couldn't call out to him.

Chapter Two

Gideon

I sighed on my return to my office.

Her memory was impeccable. But then I guess if your home was nearly burned to the ground while you were asleep in it, it wouldn't be too hard to recall the person that rescued you from it even years down the line.

Seeing her come into that class had brought the kind of shock to me that I hadn't experienced in so long. I was well aware of her presence in the college even though up till now, our paths had thankfully never crossed. I hadn't particularly gone out of my way to ensure this but, and as I had hoped, it had worked out as such. She wasn't someone that I particularly wanted to keep in mind, so I'd long made the decision to react the way that I did to her.

She was no doubt confused, and due to the awkwardness, I hoped that she would accept things as they were, and not attempt to reconnect with me again or try to convince me that we once knew each other.

This was exactly what I wanted, but as I settled back into my chair and thought of her, I felt anything but happy.

She'd since changed from the awkward eleven-year-old that had had the biggest crush on me.

Back then, I'd been about to turn nineteen and was endeared by the little girl next door I'd known forever but was suddenly turning red and shy every single time she saw me.

I'd loved her company in the past because she'd been outspoken and free spirited, and I couldn't help but wonder if she was still that way.

I'd caught sight of her in various scenarios around campus, and in most of them she had the brightest of smiles on her face.

But not recently.

In the past year I'd seen her about twice, once in the library and the second time by the corner of a food truck, eating and just staring off at nothing. I noticed the same gaze in most of the senior students especially as their final year loomed so there was no cause for concern. However, in that particular moment when she had looked so lost, I'd wished I could go up to her for a chat, I'd wondered if she would even be able to remember me.

And today, I got my answer.

She most definitely did, and a part of me I had to at the very least admit, was glad.

She was gorgeous.

In her earlier years she'd been adorable to me and was sort of the little sister I'd have loved to have had, but now... she took care with her appearance. Not so much that every outfit was clinging to her skin but fitting enough to show-case her striking figure.

Today, she had on a pair of blue jeans and a tucked in shirt. Simple but elegant and it had been quite the distrac-tion for me in class.

It was truly a shame I pretended not to know her, because I wished I could as the adult version of her seemed quite interesting. Suddenly, there was a knock on the door, and it instantly brought me out of my thoughts. I realized I had been flipping through a folder and was now seated behind my desk. All things I had done automatically whilst my mind had been preoccupied with her.

"Come in," I groaned as I turned my computer back on, eager to tackle my remaining work for the day.

It was Oscar, and I was glad for the reprieve.

"There's a student here to see you," he said.

I frowned because we had long discussed how these matters were to be handled in the past.

"I tried to turn her away but she's insisting. She also mentioned the two of you used to live right next door to each other and that she just saw you today after nine years for the first time and that you're expecting her."

At this I stopped.

"She said that I'm expecting her?"

"Yes, that you couldn't act too familiar with her because of all the students that were around at the time."

I understood now why he had been unable to simply send her away.

"What should I do?" he asked.

"Send her away," I replied. "I am not receiving any visitors."

He seemed relieved at my streamlined response.

"Alright sir," he said and exited the office.

Chapter Three
Pamela
Once again, I was struck.

"What?"

"Please come back another time. The professor is extremely swamped and will remain so for the rest of the day."

The door was then shut in my face, and I was left to lick my wounds alone in the corridor.

The plan after class had been to head to the deli to wait for Meredith, but then I couldn't put my encounter with him out of my mind. And so, I had found my way all the way across the campus in search of him. His office was easy to find, but then all I got was his snooty secretary's reply that every single person, especially like me that just simply showed up, had been turned away.

However, I'd managed to convince myself that he'd acted that way because there were people around, because and otherwise, how could he not recognize me? I hadn't changed that much, had I?

Once again, I glanced at the door he had shut in my face and things started to become clearer to me. Maybe I wasn't imagining things. I could recall back then that even before the fire, he had begun to severely withdraw. He hadn't changed schools and although he had gotten busier since it was his final year, I hadn't expected just how coldly he would treat me. The fire had happened, and we had to move away. And that had been the last of us.

It was obvious to me now that he too had thought the same, and now so many years later, I was the only one who had forgotten.

With a scowl at the door once again, I turned and went on my way.

My mood was dark, sourer than it had been all month and it was something that no outing could resolve so I decided to just head home.

I texted Meredith to cancel our lunch plans, giving some excuse, and despite her protest, stood my ground and made my way back to our apartment.

Once back I called my mom for some casual chit chat, but before I could come around to asking about the family that we used to live next door to, Meredith came bounding through my bedroom door. "I'll call you back."

"You canceled on me? I've been looking forward to that lunch all week."

I frowned at the intrusion. "All week? We made the plans today."

"Exactly. That's how much I really wanted to go to 'The Corner' today."

I watched as she lowered her butt onto my bed. Her expression began to soften as she took in mine.

I turned away and started idly scrolling through my computer at my desk.

"You're a hundred percent certain he's the one, aren't you?"

I didn't respond.

"And a thousand percent sure that he's pretending not to know you?"

Once again, I didn't respond. So she rose to her feet with an elaborate sigh and exited the room and soon enough and thankfully I was left alone.

She soon however returned, and before I could ask her to leave, I noted the two slices of tiramisu she had brought on two plates. I stared at the dessert and felt my sourness begin to dissipate.

So, I took it, knowing now that I couldn't kick her out.

We ate in silence, and then about halfway through, she spoke up.

"So, how are we going to get him to admit that he knows you?"

I look up, taken aback by her words. "We?"

"There's obviously a serious reason why he's acting like a stranger isn't there? I mean who acts that way?" She made a face. "It's not as though you were actually throwing yourself at him. You were childhood friends."

"Well, I wasn't exactly a child..." I corrected.

"Fine then. Teenagers?"

"He was a teen. I was eleven."

"What the fuck Pam," she cursed dryly, a forkful of tiramisu in her mouth and it was amusing to say the least.

I laughed.

She gave me a forgiving look, and then she lowered her gaze to continue eating.

"To be honest we weren't exactly friends," I said quietly. "But we knew each other."

It was a little while later before she spoke again. "You want to just forget about him too and move on?"

"I wish I could, but I just want to know, you know? Why?"

"You can't always know everything."

"In this case I want to."

"And it has nothing to do with him being extremely attractive?"

At her mention of this I scowled at her. "He was hot when he was younger too."

"And you let that slip away. I'm sensing a pattern here."

"Stop," I half-complained, albeit amused.

"You mentioned earlier that he saved you from a fire. You were serious about that weren't you?"

"Of course I was," I replied. "Why would I joke about that?"

"What happened?"

I thought back to the scenario, and the scare of my life that I had gotten from it.

"It ruined my parent's finances, that's for sure. Plus, my

dad's business started taking the strangest hits. It was the toughest time of our lives."

I went silent again, so she nudged me with her knee. "The fire?"

I shrugged. "I was asleep which made it a hundred times scarier. It was just me and Gideon's mother that were in the house."

"Gideon's mother?" she asked.

"That's the professor's first name."

"I know," she gave me a look. "My exclamation is for your mention of his mother. Why was she at your house?"

I shrugged. "I can't even remember. But it was one of those friendly neighborhood calls. Maybe she was delivering some wine over or something. My parents used to exchange wine with his parents in that way."

"And your mom?"

"She wasn't home. I think she was still at work at the time or something. It was a weekday, and she had a night shift at the hospital."

"Hmm," she said. "So, then what happened?"

Fear gripped my chest as I recalled the smoke and haze... and heat.

"I woke up coughing. I didn't even understand that anything was wrong and was too lazy to get up, so I just kept coughing until I realized that it wasn't subsiding. That's when I smelled the smoke and realized what was happening. "

"Is that why you never sleep deeply?"

"Maybe," I replied. "For about five years after that I had chronic insomnia and almost couldn't sleep at all. Anyway, I heard shattering, everything was breaking. For a while I thought I was in a dream because no one came to get me. There was no fire in my room, but I could see the glow from beneath the door and the heat seemed to be charring my skin. What's worse is that my window didn't face the front of the house so even when I screamed and tried to break the window so that I could at least put my head out to breathe, it didn't work. The glass was so hot. I think I grabbed a shoe or something and started to scream and pound on it. And that's when I saw him… or rather he saw me. His room's window was opposite mine. One moment it was dark and the next the lights had come on and he was standing in front of it."

"I don't think I'll ever forget the horrified look that came to his face when he realized I was still there. He ran out of the house but by then I think I was already collapsing on the floor. Everything after that was a blur. He carried me on his back and then found our way out. My dad was so horrified at how I could have been so easily forgotten… that even now he always checks for me whenever he leaves or returns to the house."

"Wow," she muttered, her tone barely audible but her attention rapt. "That must have been horrifying."

"It was," I said. "I was so thankful to him, especially because he sustained some burns. I wonder now if the scars ever left. I heard that the front door had been in flames when he'd run in, and his mother had nearly collapsed from screaming. He had to get me out at all costs and… I wanted to repay him back somehow. But after that he became so cold and withdrawn. I never heard from or saw him again… until today."

Meredith set her finished plate down on my desk. "I think I get it now," she said. "No wonder you were so shocked to see him and hurt when he acted as though he didn't know you."

I grew silent again. "I wonder if he hates me?"

"Why would he hate you?" She asked.

I shrugged. "Maybe the trauma of the whole situation? Maybe he hasn't recovered from it and of course since I was the cause-"

"You weren't the cause," she said, her tone stern. "Did you start the fire?"

"No," I shook my head.

"Exactly. But how did it start though?"

"No one knows. There was too little evidence by the time the fire was put out.

She nodded then and reached out to pat my shoulder.

"I think you should just forget about him," she said.

Although it took a while, I eventually nodded in agreement.

My grandma used to say, nothing good ever came from digging up the past so maybe it was for the best that I never saw him again.

Preorder the book here:
Hot Professor

ABOUT THE AUTHOR

Thank you so much for reading!
If you have enjoyed the book and would like to leave a
precious review for me, please kindly do so here:

Taming The CEO Beast

Please click on the link below to receive info about my latest
releases and giveaways.
NEVER MISS A THING

Or
come and say hello here:

ALSO BY IONA ROSE